Chastity

The Shackleford Sisters Book Seven

Beverley Watts

BaR Publishing

Cover art by Midnight Muse
Typography by Covers By Karen

Contents

Prologue

Chastity Shackleford's twin sister had accused her of being an incurable romantic. Indeed, she herself would have agreed entirely, three weeks, four days and seven hours ago, even if she was of the opinion that Charity's words had been a trifle blunt.

But, three weeks, four days and seven hours was precisely the length of time it had taken to finally knock the last vestige of romance from her soul.

And now, shivering alone in the Earl of Cottesmore's vast, cold bed, she couldn't help but reflect - mostly in disbelief, it had to be said - at the unfortunate incident that had occasioned her current unhappy position.

In truth, it could be argued that her present dilemma should be laid firmly at the door of her twin, given that it was Charity who had suggested she accept the Duke of Blackmore's offer of a Season in London.

Truly, having shared a womb, and spending practically every waking moment together since then, one would have thought Charity possessed enough common sense to realise that allowing her twin to brave the marriage mart on her own was quite simply a recipe for disaster.

Indeed, Chastity was persuaded she would not now be in

this most vexing position had Charity herself not fallen unexpectedly in love and abandoned Blackmore for the wilds of Cornwall with her new husband.

Gritting her teeth to stop them chattering, Chastity turned her head and eyed the barely visible door apprehensively. She didn't know which would be worse. The Earl of Cottesmore actually noticing her in his bed before climbing into it or discovering her presence once he was between the sheets. Definitely the latter. She sincerely hoped he was not in the habit of taking a pistol to bed.

Of course, what she should be doing was considering not how the Earl might effect her demise - or indeed what the devil he would do with her body once he'd done the effecting–but what words she could best use to persuade him that murdering her in his bed was actually *not* going to help with their current predicament. Or rather *her* current predicament. Although, to be fair, he wasn't yet *aware* of *her* current predicament.

He was a man of the world. Surely he would listen while she explained the reason for her unexpected presence in his bed. Naturally, she'd have to convince him that she wasn't there to trap him into marriage. Well, she *was*, but it was purely business. He needed to know that she'd entirely eschewed affairs of the heart, though, in all honesty, there was nothing romantic about freezing to death in a lord's bed. Which, if he didn't get a move on, was a very real possibility. But then, mayhap she'd be simply saving him the job. What on earth had possessed her that she could *ever* have believed this to be a good idea? To be hon…

Her thoughts screeched to a halt as she heard a sudden noise outside the window…

Chapter One

Two weeks earlier

The ball held at the Duke and Duchess of Blackmore's London townhouse to herald in the year of 1815 was widely regarded as the most prestigious event of the year. Whilst the lingering euphoria of Napoleon's exile to the Isle of Elba undoubtedly contributed to the festive atmosphere, the ball's success was in no small part due to the popularity and standing within the *ton* of Nicholas Sinclair and his beautiful, though unconventional, wife, Grace.

The fact that the Duchess was the daughter of a local vicar appeared to have been forgotten or, if not forgotten, certainly disregarded. Indeed, it was widely agreed that her grace was looking simply radiant, as were those of her equally unconventional sisters who were present.

And if many of the gentlemen attending sported anxious frowns concerning the economic plight of Great Britain in the aftermath of the twenty-three-year war in Europe, well, such cares and considerations were easily drowned in a few glasses of the Duke's most excellent port.

It had to be said that whilst the Duchess of Blackmore's humble origins were generally overlooked, the presence of her father at events such as these, or rather his penchant for generating unfortunate incidents such as the one involving Queen Charlotte and the duck pond, was naturally of some concern to the rest of the family.

However, exile to the small, delightful drawing room along with Malcolm, the Duke's long-standing and similarly outspoken valet, was in no way seen as a slight by the Reverend. In truth, Augustus Shackleford shouldn't really have been in London at all and was entirely delighted to be foregoing the tedious and stultifying conversation enjoyed by polite society. Especially as the table was positively groaning under the weight of a delicious array of the cook's tempting tarts and pastries, and the jug of port sitting tantalisingly on the sideboard was entirely up to his son-in-law's usual standards.

Naturally, Percy Noon, the Reverend's long-suffering curate was also present, as were the two younger Shacklefords, Prudence and Anthony. Both, much to their older sisters' relief, had absolutely no desire to take part in the festivities. Indeed, Prudence had declared that she'd rather have her toenails removed with red hot pincers.

And then of course there was the Reverend's foxhound Freddy who was perfectly content lying under the table ready to demolish any crumbs that happened to fall his way.

All three men were in a particularly jocular mood as the clock approached midnight, and Reverend Shackleford was persuaded that this was possibly the best New Year's Eve he'd ever spent. For one thing, he hadn't seen Agnes, his wife, since well before supper and was confident she would be happily discussing with all the other tabbies her latest obsession with yellow fever for hours yet.

His only daughter of marriageable age as yet unwed was Chastity, and he wasn't about to do anything that might throw a rub in the way of Grace's plans to bring the chit out.

So all in all, he was happy to make himself scarce until he was required to give his blessing to whoever was unfortunate enough to land himself with the totty-headed baggage.

∞∞∞

The totty-headed baggage in question was currently being escorted onto the dance floor by Viscount Trebworthy. Indeed, her father would have been ecstatic considering the young man was heir to a dukedom and rich as Croesus to boot. Unfortunately, he was also tall and skinny with breath like an open privy. In truth, Chastity was not entirely convinced she was actually going to survive the Cotillion. Determinedly, she fixed her gaze on his bony chest and endeavoured to breathe through her mouth. Hopefully, he would think her completely devoid of any personality and seek to be rid of her as soon as they vacated the dance floor.

Regrettably that proved not to be the case, and in desperation, pleading a sudden excessive thirst, Chastity sent the Viscount off in search of a glass of water, then promptly made herself scarce, finally collapsing onto a chair hidden in a quiet corner.

Dear Lord, but she missed her twin. Charity was the only sister who'd been unable to join the family for Christmas. The distance and the state of the roads between Falmouth and London made travelling such a distance nigh on impossible during the cold, wet winter months. Why the devil did Charity have to go and choose a man from deuced *Cornwall*? Notwithstanding the small detail that Jago Carlyon was perfect for her twin, surely she could have settled on someone equally perfect who didn't live so bloody *far away*.

Sighing, Chastity furtively watched the room from her secluded corner. According to her dance card, her next two dances were unclaimed. So it was imperative she keep her head down for the rest of the Reel and more importantly the Waltz that was to follow. The thought of being in such *close* proximity to the Viscount for a whole ten minutes was too desperate to even contemplate.

It had to be said, that so far, London was not living up to her romantic notions. In actual fact, it was failing dismally. She was reminded at every turn why exactly she and Charity had hated it so much growing up. Reading her stepmother's periodicals and gossip sheets from the security of Blackmore was one thing. Actually mixing with polite society was another matter entirely.

She'd been in London for nearly three weeks and already she realised that most members of the *ton* were vain, self-centred peacocks bearing no resemblance to her girlish imaginings.

Coming back to the present, Chastity suddenly realised that the reel had finished, and guests were busy regrouping for the waltz. To her horror, she spied Viscount Trebworthy heading determinedly her way. Damn and blast, she'd been rumbled. Wildly, she glanced about, abruptly taking note of a tall, dark-haired gentleman leaning nonchalantly against the wall to her left. He was alone and sipping on a glass of punch. From her angle, she was unable to see his face, but truthfully, as long as his breath didn't smell like the bottom of a cesspool, she could survive facing him for ten minutes.

But she only had mere seconds to convince the stranger to dance with her. Without giving herself any time to reconsider, Chastity jumped to her feet and tapped the man on his shoulder. As soon as he turned his head and directed his icy-blue eyes towards her, she entirely lost the use of her tongue. Dear God, the man was an Adonis. Albeit one with raven black hair.

Far, far too late, she wondered what a man of such exceptional looks was doing propping up a wall at the back of a ballroom. Alone. His expression gave her an immediate answer. It was one of disdainful boredom, but his eyes, oh his eyes. They were the colour of winter. And so cold that she took an involuntary step back. What the devil had she been thinking, attracting the attention of such a mysterious individual.

Out of the corner of her eye, she saw Viscount Trebworthy stumble to a stop. For a second, he remained still, then he turned and almost ran in the opposite direction. *Deuced coward*, she thought, ignoring the fact that less than thirty seconds ago she'd have been thanking the Almighty for such a reprieve.

'May I help you?' She became aware that the Adonis was speaking. And more than that. His incredible eyes were regarding her as if she were something nasty he'd found on the bottom of his shiny Hessian boot.

Which made her next words all the more preposterous. Indeed, she could scarce believe the sound of her own voice as she uttered them. 'I was wondering if you were engaged for this dance, sir.'

His expression turned incredulous.

'Am I to understand you are propositioning me Madam?' His voice was deep, husky and quite possibly the most arresting sound she'd ever heard. Her face coloured up as she stammered, 'I am uncertain as to what exactly a proposition would entail, sir. I am merely asking to take up ten minutes of your time.'

Charity was aware they were beginning to attract speculative glances and was entirely certain that if he didn't hold out his arm soon, she would die of mortification. What the deuce had she been thinking? She would never live this down. *Never*. If anybody had actually *heard* her request, she was ruined. Underneath her pale lilac dress, the sweat trickled down her back.

Her relief was short lived when a second later, he gave a lazy grin and held out his hand. If his voice had been arresting, his smile was quite simply devastating. Her heart slammed against her chest, and the voice inside her head was screaming *run*. After casting a wild glance round at the interested stares being cast their way, Chastity knew she had no choice but to brave it out. Truly, her idiocy was breathtaking.

Biting her lip, she bent her head in acknowledgement and laying her hand over his, she allowed him to lead her to the floor. At first, he did not speak but simply swept her into his arms as the first strains of the waltz began to play. Her relief that he was an accomplished dancer was almost hysterical. *Ten minutes*, she just had to get through the next ten minutes. It was nothing. She stared determinedly at his chest as they whirled round the dance floor. So insistent was the mantra in her head, she hadn't realised that she'd actually spoken the words aloud.

'If this is not to your liking, my lady, I am more than happy to forgo the rest of the dance.' Alarmed, she looked up, terrified she'd offended him, and he was about to leave her standing alone on the dance floor.

'I... I... Please accept my apologies, Sir,' she faltered. 'I am aware that my conduct has so far been less than exemplary. I don't... That is... I'm not usually in the habit of asking strangers to dance with me.'

'I'm very glad to hear it,' was his dry response. 'I take it you were seeking to escape Viscount Trebworthy.'

'Oh no, not at all,' she lied desperately.

To her surprise, he chuckled. 'I have had occasion to be within breathing distance of the individual, and you have my complete sympathy. The man is desperately in need of a good dentist.'

Reassured that he appeared to have a human side after all, Chastity gave a timorous smile. 'Do you have a name, sir?' she asked hesitantly when it appeared he'd said all he intended to. If any of her family had happened to spy her on the dance floor, they would at least expect her to know the gentleman's name. And she had little doubt that she was being observed by at least one of her sisters. 'My name is...' she continued, only to pause, fearing she was committing another faux pas in offering it.

'Miss Chastity Shackleford,' he finished. Surprised he knew her name, she was unsure what to say. For some bizarre reason, his admission made her braver, and her stare was almost challenging as she waited for him to offer his own. Instead, he gazed down at her impassively for several endless uneasy moments and she felt her bravado slip away. Somehow, in asking his name, she had stepped over some imaginary line. His beautiful eyes were guarded, but they had a slight mocking gleam that had her desperately wanting to know who he was and why he would look at her with such disdain. She did not think it due to her earlier boldness.

Despite her confusion, Chastity was almost sorry as the music finally drew to a close. 'Thank you for the rescue,' she murmured to his chest as she prepared to step out of his arms. 'It was most kind of you to take pity on me, Sir.' He gave a short laugh, and the bitterness in it had her looking up at him in surprise. She became aware that he had not released her from his grip and felt the first stirrings of alarm.

'I've been called many things, Miss Shackleford,' he commented drily, 'but to my knowledge, never kind.' To Chastity's relief, he finally loosed her hands and stepped back slightly. She took hold of her skirts in preparation for her customary curtsy.

'However, if you choose to consider my actions so,' he continued, causing her to pause and look back up at him in unease, 'then perhaps I can impose upon you to do a small kindness for me in return.' He stared down at her with the same mocking gleam in his eyes, and Chastity immediately felt the last of her boldness disappear.

'Naturally, I am happy to be of assistance if I can,' she murmured, the uncertainty in her voice a direct contrast to her polite words.

His smile became almost feral at her obvious discomfort. 'Then perhaps you would be so kind as to inform Nicholas Sinclair that Christian Stanhope has returned and will await his pleasure.'

And with that, he gave a low, perfectly executed bow and walked away.

Chapter Two

'You did *what*?' Truly Chastity had never seen her brother-in-law quite so angry. Nay, not angry, *furious*. Oh, he didn't raise his voice to her. As always, Nicholas Sinclair's outward appearance was calm and collected, but the whiteness around his mouth, his clenched jaw and flared nostrils spoke volumes. And then of course there were his eyes which were currently shooting daggers. At her.

Nervously, Chastity swallowed, glancing up at her sister who responded with an answering squeeze of her shoulder while glaring at her husband. 'Perhaps you would be kind enough to furnish us with a little more information as to why Chastity dancing with a particular gentleman should send you into such a towering rage.'

'I am *not* in a towering rage,' Nicholas responded through clenched teeth. Grace simply raised her eyebrows and waited.

'Aye, ye are that, laddy. You look as if you're ready te send the lass te the bloody locker. I dinna ken why you're taking your rage out on Miss Chastity. If Christian Stanhope has popped out of whatever cesspit he was wallowing in, it surely isn't the lass's fault.' Malcom's mild rebuke earned him an icy glare. The valet stared back unconcerned, and at length, Nicholas slumped back in his chair. 'My apologies, ladies,' he muttered. 'It is some years since I've heard that name. To be honest I've tried very hard not to think of it.'

'If you hold such animosity to this ... Mr. Stanhope,' Grace commented carefully, 'then what on earth was he doing in our house? Did someone invite him?'

'I have no idea,' Nicholas sighed, the last vestiges of his anger disappearing. 'He has clearly not been in London for long. I would have heard of it otherwise.'

'I dinna ken why ye'd think so,' Malcolm countered. 'It's not as if he moves in the same circles. Stanhope could quite easily have been hanging around like a bad bloody smell for a year or more. Avoiding dukes is not that much of a feat to us common folk.'

The Duke gave an inelegant snort and shook his head. 'If he's back in London, then he has good reason. I doubt he would have been able to keep away for any length of time. Recklessness is only one of his many less than desirable qualities.'

'Who is he?' Chastity finally mustered up the courage to ask. 'I mean, he *seemed* like a gentleman.' Even as she spoke, she thought back to the mockery in Christian Stanhope's eyes, the sense of mystery he exuded and realised that despite the fine clothes, he'd looked anything but.

Sighing, Nicholas ran his fingers through his hair, suddenly looking every one of his two and forty years. Giving Chastity's shoulder one last squeeze, Grace went over to the sideboard and poured two brandies. After giving the first to Malcolm, she walked over and handed the second to her husband, bending down to give him a quick fierce kiss at the same time. 'Whatever this man is to you, my love, I'm entirely certain he's not worth risking an apoplexy for.'

'Do you think me so in my dotage that you need to ply me with strong drink?' Nicholas commented drily. 'You'll be bringing me a blanket next.' Nonetheless, he took the proffered brandy and returned her kiss before turning towards Chastity.

'According to eyewitnesses, Christian Stanhope murdered one of my ship's company,' he offered tersely in answer to her question. 'But before he could be court martialled, he jumped ship. I haven't seen or heard of him since.' He took a swallow of his brandy and added, 'Until now.'

'Well, he certainly isn't lacking in nerve,' Grace observed.

'Aye, well, I can't deny he was a bloody reckless fool,' Malcolm agreed, shaking his head and favouring the Duke with an explicably hard stare.

Chastity longed to ask exactly what had happened, but looking at Nicholas's closed face, she knew he was unlikely to indulge her curiosity.

'Did he give you any indication as to under which rock I might find him?' her brother-in-law probed. Chastity shook her head and frowned.

'As you say, he definitely had an aura of danger around him, but I … I did sense a sadness too. Mayhap he regrets what happened to that man.' From the corner of her eye, she saw Grace look over at her sharply and couldn't prevent the sudden surge of colour in her cheeks.

'Well, if he wishes to speak with me, he clearly knows where I am,' Nicholas growled. 'He has an inflated sense of his importance if he thinks me likely to jump to his deuced bidding.'

'Do you want to speak with him?' Grace questioned with a frown. 'I mean, if he was about to be court-martialled before he disappeared, then surely he has still to answer for his crimes.'

'I doubt very much the Royal Navy will be interested in coming for him after all this time.' Malcolm shrugged. He was still eying his employer inscrutably.

'How long ago did this all happen?' Grace asked curiously.

'It was seven full years before Trafalgar,' Nicholas answered reluctantly. 'So that's, what ... seventeen years ago?' He shrugged. 'Difficult to believe so many years have passed.' He was clearly directing his last remark to Malcolm, and the Scot nodded but offered no further clarification of the incident.

'So, is he likely to call?' Grace queried. 'And if he does, should I allow him admittance?'

'I can't imagine even Kit Stanhope being so barefaced as to call on a peer of the realm without invitation,' Malcolm declared. 'He'll most likely send a note.'

Nicholas shook his head and frowned. 'The man certainly has enough presumption. But his words indicated that he expected me to be aware of his address.' He turned towards his valet. 'Malcolm, make some discreet enquiries. We have not been long in town and are likely not acquainted with the latest gossip.'

'Chastity and I are taking afternoon tea with Tempy and Hope,' Grace declared. 'I believe the Viscountess Morehaven will also be attending.' She gave a slight chuckle. 'Lady Morehaven is the biggest windbag in all England. If there is any gossip to be revealed about Christian Stanhope, she is certain to divulge it.' She rose to her feet and looked over at Chastity, her expression promising a few astute questions.

'Will Miss Beaumont be joining ye in London at all?'

Malcom's casual words stopped Grace in her tracks. Surprised, she looked over at the Scot whose face was carefully blank. 'I believe she will be coming at the end of the month,' she responded, equally nonchalantly. The valet nodded, then without further comment, climbed to his feet, nodded to those present and ambled from the room, leaving the other three occupants looking at each other with open mouths.

∞ ∞ ∞

Christian Stanhope, the unexpected sixth Earl of Cottesmore, gazed into the depths of his brandy and reflected on the fickle nature of fate.

Two years ago, he'd been contemplating the purchase of a gentleman's residence in New York. But two things happened that changed everything. Almost overnight.

The first was the damned letter. A mere third-or was it fourth?-cousin to the former Earl of Cottesmore, Christian Stanhope could never have imagined in his wildest dreams that a fire would wipe out the entire line. Except for him. He shook his head. He would have told the solicitors exactly what they could do with their bloody title, except for the second thing.

Another letter, this time attached to the cloak of a seven-year-old child left on his doorstep with nothing more than the clothes she was standing up in.

A girl the note claimed was his.

She couldn't have arrived at a more inconvenient time, since he'd been in the middle of entertaining a few acquaintances and the unexpected knock on the door had dragged him away from a very agreeable flirtation with a young widow.

If the child hadn't looked so malnourished, he'd have immediately sent her on her way, believing someone was playing him for a fool. But New York was in the midst of the coldest March in decades, and the child's threadbare cloak and small solemn face, white with exhaustion and fear touched something deep inside him he'd had no idea was there.

Tucking the letter in his pocket, he'd ordered his maid of all work to see the girl fed and given a room to sleep in overnight. He would see what was to be done in the morning.

But on returning to his dinner party, he found his enthusiasm for revelry had inexplicably vanished. After an hour, he'd pleaded a sudden onset of megrims, and left his guests to see themselves out. Ignoring the plaintive looks from the young widow, he retired upstairs to his bedchamber. After shutting the door, he seated himself by the fire and took the letter out of his pocket. Rereading its contents, his outrage at having a waif and stray foisted on him out of the blue began to dissipate.

He remembered the child's mother. It had been a night much like this one. A small intimate dinner party in Boston. Frowning, Christian searched his memories for the woman's name. Mercedes. That was it. She was Mexican. She told him to call her Mercy. Olive skinned with the softest brown eyes and the wickedest laugh. It hadn't taken much. A smile, a touch, a kiss in a dark corner, and she was his for the night. The next morning when he awoke, she was gone.

He hadn't thought much about it. She was a courtesan. Accustomed to pleasing men, and he'd paid her well. Soon afterwards, he'd become involved in the Hudson River Company and moved to New York.

The letter didn't say what had happened to Mercy after that night. Only that she'd endeavoured to raise the child for as long as she could, and now it was his turn. She wrote that she was dying. Consumption. There was no other information. No pleading. Just simple facts.

Initially, he'd angrily tossed the letter to the floor, thinking it a bag of moonshine, but as he climbed into bed, he thought back to the child's eyes. Blue eyes the colour of winter. Just like his.

Sighing, Christian came back to the present. Swallowing the rest of his brandy, he leaned forward to pour himself another generous measure. Getting foxed wouldn't help with the thousand and one things he had to take care of as the new earl, especially as it was only ten in the morning. But it helped suppress his fear for the future.

Leaning back, he closed his eyes and grimaced. His life had been so simple before Mercy had come into it and changed everything. It had been all about money. So much so that he'd gained a well-deserved reputation for being ruthless and driven. England and the Royal Navy had been another life. One he'd rarely thought about.

Raising his head, he looked around the room in distaste. The opulent furnishings gave lie to the fact that the Cottesmore coffers were practically empty. Indeed, this whole house was a testament to the damn lie his cousin had been living. But now the manor house in Surrey was a pile of smouldering ruins, it was the only thing left. It would take a large chunk of the fortune Christian had amassed in New York to rebuild the sprawling country seat, and the greater part of him wondered if it was worth it.

Especially as he couldn't even make a start on any renovations without solving the mystery that had haunted him for nearly seventeen years. And the only person who could help him with that was Nicholas Sinclair. The man who'd allowed him to escape providing he never stepped foot on English soil again.

'Whatever sympathies you might be harbouring for Mr. Stanhope, I beg you will put them out of your mind immediately, Chastity.' Grace had hardly drawn breath after they'd left the morning room before delivering the lecture Chastity had known was coming.

'I know you think me frivolous,' she protested in return, 'but you did not have occasion to speak with the gentleman, Grace. There is something tortured about him. I know it.'

'Well, the knowledge that his actions resulted in a man's death would almost certainly have that effect unless the man is entirely without any conscience at all,' retorted Grace. 'Really Chastity, he is not a kitten who needs mothering. If you are to make a good match, you simply must put these ridiculous romantic notions out of your head.'

She nodded to Bailey as the elderly butler opened the front door. 'At the very least, Christian Stanhope is a cad, and at worst a murderer. While I applaud your insistence on seeing the good in everyone, your soft heart will undoubtedly get you into trouble. Again.'

Chastity sighed as she climbed into the waiting carriage in the wake of her sister. They were to attend another fitting at the modiste. Really, it was ridiculous the number of clothes considered necessary for a Season. And not only that, but the interminable hours a person had to spend wearing nothing but undergarments while having pins stuck in the most inexplicable places. Chastity tried and failed to imagine her twin in such a position and found herself chuckling.

'I fail to see exactly what you find amusing,' Grace commented waspishly. Chastity opened her mouth to ask what on earth had her sister so up in the boughs. But abruptly noticing how drained the Duchess looked, she frowned and said instead, 'Are you quite well, Grace? You're not usually such a curmudgeon.'

Before Grace could respond, the carriage suddenly lurched forward, and both women braced themselves against the seats as the horses galloped out of the square, causing the carriage to swing violently to the left. To Chastity's concern, Grace's face turned a sickly green, and she looked as though she was about to cast her account. 'Deuced coach driver,' she muttered through gritted teeth. 'Is the word sedate completely beyond his comprehension?'

Chastity eyed her sister in concern. Joseph driving as though all the devils in hell were after him was perfectly normal. Indeed, many of the retainers in the Duke's household had idiosyncrasies which rendered them unemployable anywhere else. His grace was generally considered by most of his contemporaries to be slightly dicked in the nob given his propensity for employing men who had been cast aside by the Royal Navy due to age or injury. Very often both. Though one might question the Duke's wisdom in employing a one-legged coachman. Still it ensured that carriage rides around London were generally never dull.

Grace took a deep breath as the carriage steadied before looking over at her sister ruefully. 'As you have undoubtedly guessed, I am not feeling myself at all,' she commented. 'I have yet to tell Nicholas, but I very much suspect I'm with child.'

'Oh that's wonderful news,' enthused Chastity. Her sister grimaced slightly.

'In truth, I'd believed my childbearing years to be over,' she sighed. 'I'm approaching three and thirty.'

'But having both Tempy and Hope enceinte at the same time will undoubtedly make the time pass much quicker. Don't you think Nicholas will be pleased?'

'I'm unsure,' Grace responded with a slight frown. 'He worried so over Peter and Jennifer. He will undoubtedly insist we return to Blackmore immediately.' She raised her eyebrows at Chastity before adding, 'Which is why I have not yet broken the news to him. I cannot afford to make the journey back until after you have been settled.'

'But that could take months,' Chastity snorted. 'You should not consider me, sister. There is always next year. You must know I'm in no hurry to wed.' She paused, then added, 'Though if you're concerned, would it not be better to birth the babe here in London?'

'Perhaps,' Grace conceded, 'but I know Nicholas would feel much more comfortable within the confines of Blackmore.'

'Forgive me, but this is not about your husband,' Chastity responded tartly. To her surprise, Grace laughed. 'Truly, you just sounded like Charity,' she chuckled. 'It's good to know that you are not entirely without bite, dearest.'

'Well, if you're adamant about not yet returning to Devonshire, you would be wise to postpone breaking the news until after Father has left for home, lest Nicholas insist you share his carriage. When is Father leaving, by the way?'

Grace shook her head. 'I can tell he's getting anxious to return to Blackmore. Yesterday, he was muttering about his congregation turning into a godless rabble, but for some reason, he's been putting it off. I suspect his gout may be bothering him, and the thought of a long carriage ride does not appeal. Sometimes I forget he's getting old.'

'Mayhap he'll send Percy in his stead while the weather remains clement,' mused Chastity, 'though in truth, I would feel a lot less anxious if he wasn't questioning me about every gentleman who so much as glanced in my direction. And then there's Stepmother. Did you know she actually gave the Marchioness of Roxburgh one of the pedlar's tinctures during the ball? You know the one that caused her to come out in that hideous rash? Told her ladyship it was good for skin complaints...'

'No,' Grace gasped. 'Why didn't you tell me?' Chastity shook her head.

'There was no need. I managed to snatch the bottle back from the Marchioness's reticule before she departed.' Chastity grimaced, then laughed. 'Unfortunately, one of the vines in your ballroom has probably either died or trebled in size as I was forced to get rid of the foul stuff before Stepmother could do any further damage with it.'

Grace winced and grimaced. 'I'll speak to Father about his return before we go in to dinner this evening.'

There was no time for further conversation as the carriage skidded to a halt outside the modiste's. 'I will also be having words with my loving husband concerning his choice of coach driver,' Grace muttered through gritted teeth as she prepared to alight. 'One would almost suspect he was trying to be rid of me.'

Giggling, Chastity climbed down after her sister, the earlier conversation about Christian Stanhope entirely forgotten.

Chapter Three

'Well, Percy, it has to be said we can't put it off for much longer. If we don't return to Blackmore soon, we'll likely be facing a den of iniquity. And that's without taking into account the collection box. We'll be lucky if it's got a couple of deuced pebbles in it. Any longer and the congregation's going to need one of your specials.' The Reverend paused and narrowed his eyes before adding sagely, 'Plenty of fire and brimstone to get 'em all back on the straight and narrow.'

'So, do you think she's likely to have given up, Sir?' Percy asked, unable to entirely quash the anxiety in his voice.

'It depends on how determined she is to walk you down the aisle,' Reverend Shackleford retorted. Then he paused before adding, 'Though I have to say she's a definite improvement on Gertrude Fotheringale.'

'Sir, she's nearly six feet tall,' Percy defended desperately. 'She keeps her dead husband's gold tooth in a tin.'

'I'm surprised that hasn't been snaffled,' the Reverend mused thoughtfully. 'It must be worth a few shillings.'

'I don't know anybody bacon-brained enough to take such a risk,' Percy retorted.

'Well, if she hasn't already sold it, she must have a bit more than sixpence to scratch with,' chuckled the Reverend. 'Don't you want to get leg shackled eventually Percy?'

'No, I don't. At all. Not ever.'

Augustus Shackleford couldn't help feeling secretly relieved that his curate was not in the market for a wife. Though it had to be said, he did seem to attract the most bracket-faced trollops. Which was why the Reverend had not objected to the idea of bringing Percy to join the rest of the family in London to see in the New Year.

Unfortunately, they couldn't stay away from Blackmore for much longer. 'You're just going to have to find a deuced backbone and tell her you're not interested,' he stated. 'I'll come with you if you like.' As soon as the words were out of his mouth, the Reverend would have risked tea and toast with Lucifer himself to have taken them back. But it was too late. The curate looked as though he'd just escaped the noose.

'Tare an' hounds, Percy, she's not likely to hit you over the head, cut you to pieces and put you in the pot for her supper,' the clergyman muttered irritably.

'Well, she showed me her husband's tooth,' blurted the curate. 'And nobody knows what happened to him. What if she killed him to get it?' He shuddered. 'He could be buried somewhere in the cottage. He might even be in the wardrobe.'

'Don't be so deuced melodramatic, Percy. If she'd hidden him in a cupboard, he'd have been smelling decidedly ripe by now. What I'd like to know is how you manage to attract the attention of such peculiar females. I mean you must be doing something to make 'em think you're open to curtain lectures.'

Percy started to shake his head, then paused. 'There was one incident,' he frowned. 'Lizzy was sta...'

23

'Who's *Lizzy*?' the Reverend interrupted.

'That's her name, Sir. Lizzy Fletcher,' Percy explained. 'As I was say...'

'So you're on first-name terms with this deuced woman?'

'Well...I...she...I mean...'

'Spit it out, Percy. Either you are or you're not.' Reverend Shackleford paused and stared at his curate aghast. 'Tell me she doesn't call you *Percy.*'

The curate stared back in dawning horror.

'Are you completely addled, Percy Noon?' Augustus Shackleford fumed. 'I've neglected my flock ... nay, *abandoned* my flock, to bring you all the way to London, and *now* you tell me you're on first name terms with this...this...*Lizzy.* That's indistinguishable from a deuced proposal.'

'Well, I hardly think you've actually abandoned them, Sir,' Percy countered defensively. 'The villagers look forward to a bit of a respite every now and then.'

Reverend Shackleford opened his mouth to speak, then closed it again, entirely certain he'd end up saying something he'd regret. In truth, if Percy had been a bit closer, the curate might have found himself on the receiving end of more than a sharp tongue. And it wasn't often the Reverend was tempted to violence.

A sudden whine at their feet stopped both men in their tracks. Reverend Shackleford found his ire draining away. 'Freddy needs to do his business, and I need some air,' he muttered, climbing to his feet. 'Start packing, Percy. If Nicholas can spare us a carriage, I want to be on the road at first light tomorrow. I'll tell Agnes and the youngens. Come along, Freddy.'

And with that, the Reverend left the room–just as the first flakes of snow began drifting against the window.

∞ ∞ ∞

'He's inherited Cottesmore,' Malcolm announced as he strode into the Duke of Blackmore's study.

'The fire,' grimaced Nicholas. 'I'd heard there were no survivors.' He shook his head grimly and put down his pen. 'Very bad business. I understand very little of the house remains.'

Malcolm nodded, throwing himself into a chair. 'Apparently, Christian was the Earl's fourth cousin and only surviving member of the family.'

'And so he's come crawling back out of the woodwork.' Nicholas grated. 'He must know his past will catch up with him.'

'Aye, but only if someone decides to cry rope on the lad,' Malcolm shrugged. 'According to my sources, there wasn't much left in the Cottesmore coffers,' the Scot commented. 'Apparently, it was common knowledge the old Earl was almost cleaned out.'

'I'd have thought you of all people wouldn't put much credence in gossip,' chided the Duke drily.

'But if it *is* true, then why would Stanhope come all this way to claim a title that's mostly burnt rubble, only to risk being snubbed by his peers should his shady past catch up with him?' Malcolm countered.

'The London townhouse must be worth something,' Nicholas mused, 'but I doubt it would cover the costs of rebuilding Cottesmore House. Is Stanhope currently residing there?'

The valet nodded. 'It would seem so. He hasn't been seen in public at all with the exception of your ball.'

'And who the devil invited him to that?' the Duke growled.

'The invitation was likely intended for his predecessor.' Malcolm shrugged. 'Either that or he simply invited himself. By all accounts, Miss Chastity was the only person he conversed with throughout the whole evening. I think most people are not yet fully aware of his identity.'

'And yet he wishes to speak with me,' Nicholas frowned. 'What in God's name could he possibly think we have to say to each other?'

'Perhaps he hopes you might be persuaded to pick up where you left off,' Malcolm shrugged. 'Since it was you who helped Stanhope escape the rope in the first place.'

'On the condition I never saw him again,' the Duke bit out. 'Don't remind me of my gullibility. All those years ago, I still had faith in human nature.'

'Will you refuse to meet with him then?' the valet asked.

Nicholas leaned back against his chair, his brow creased in thought. 'I think it would be prudent of me to find out exactly what the bastard wants and to let him know that if he so much as looks at a member of my family again, I'll string him up myself.'

27 June 1798

'It's French, Captain. Sixth rate. She's turning away.'

'Can you read the name, Mr. Stanhope?'

'Looks like *Sensible*, Sir.'

'Then she's come from Malta. Prepare for pursuit.'

'Aye aye, Captain.'

'This is the last thing we bloody well need. We'll never find Nelson and the damn fleet at this rate.' The words were muttered well out of the Captain's hearing.

'I'd have thought you'd jump at the chance to break a few Froggie heads, Barnet.' Second Lieutenant Christian Stanhope eyed the Third Lieutenant knowingly.

'We ain't going to get any credit for trouncing another piddling French sixth-rater,' scoffed his companion.

Stanhope didn't answer, preoccupied with shouting commands to comply with the Captain's orders. They watched as the ship slowly began to swing round until it was facing the same direction as the fleeing *Sensible*.

'Might be some prize money,' he tossed over his shoulder before striding towards the First Lieutenant standing at the helm.

'Aye and I'm Nelson's long-lost bastard,' was the derisory answer. Chuckling, Christian Stanhope didn't respond, instead continuing to pick his way forward.

Nearly two weeks had passed since the *Phoenix* had been dispatched into the Mediterranean by Vice-Admiral Earl St. Vincent to join Nelson's squadron in his hunt for the French, but so far, they'd had little luck in locating the British fleet.

Reports had come through of Napoleon's victory in Malta, and there remained little doubt that the upstart General's intention was to invade the Turkish Khediviate of Egypt, providing support to the Sultan in his fight with the British in India and thus restoring French influence in that subcontinent. The government in London and the East India Company were naturally panicking at the prospect.

Nelson was almost certainly now on his way to Egypt hunting

desperately for the French fleet. Unfortunately, due to a vicious storm scattering the British fleet a month earlier, HMS *Vanguard* was without the support of any frigates, leaving the Admiral seriously disadvantaged, which made the *Phoenix's* search all the more urgent. In truth, they could ill afford to waste time chasing a lone French frigate sailing in the opposite direction.

∞∞∞

Present day

'I do believe your Mr. Stanhope to be a complete enigma,' Grace commented as she swept unannounced into her husband's study. 'Even the Viscountess appeared to know very little about him other than…'

'The fact that he recently inherited the Cottesmore title,' Nicholas interrupted drily, putting down his pen.

'Damn and blast, I really thought I'd got one up on you this time,' Grace grumped, sinking into a large, winged chair with a sigh. The Duke frowned. 'You're looking uncommonly pale, my love. Are you well?'

'I'm perfectly fine,' Grace responded dismissing his concern with a wave of her hand. 'I take it Malcolm uncovered the information about the title?' Nicholas nodded, still eying her with concern.

'Well, nobody I spoke to this afternoon seemed to know anything about him at all other than he was the last earl's cousin a good few times removed. So his past has not yet caught up with him as you feared.'

'I have no concerns for the man,' Nicholas snorted. 'If his murderous activities become common knowledge, then it's no more than the bastard deserves.'

'But it will not be via your loose tongue,' Grace guessed.

Nicholas sighed and leaned back against his chair. 'I will not gossip,' he agreed, 'but neither will I hide my dislike. Let us hope we do not have occasion to meet in public.'

'Do you intend to speak with him privately then?'

'I will warn him to stay away from me and mine,' was her husband's tight-lipped response. 'Other than that, we have nothing whatsoever to say to each other.'

There was a sudden knock on the door. 'Come,' the Duke yelled in case it was Bailey on the other side. The elderly butler was almost completely deaf. Fortunately, it was Mrs. Jenks. 'Will you be taking tea in here, your graces?' she smiled.

Grace looked over at her husband who shrugged. 'No, we'll head upstairs to the small drawing room. Have you seen my father this afternoon, Mrs. Jenks?'

'I believe he and Mr. Percy are currently packing,' the housekeeper answered.

The Duchess raised her eyebrows. 'Has he given any indication of when he intends to leave?' she asked.

'Well, he asked for a cold collation to be put together for tomorrow morning, so I believe his intention is to leave at first light, your grace,' the housekeeper answered, 'though I'm not sure they'll be going anywhere if this keeps up.' She nodded towards the flurries of snow beginning to settle against the window.

Sighing, Grace climbed to her feet. 'I think you might well be right, which is unfortunate as I know he's anxious to return home. Bring enough tea for six.' She paused before adding, 'And some of that chocolate tart if you have any. My father is excessively stubborn when he makes up his mind about something, and if I'm to persuade him that venturing forth in a blizzard trusting solely in the Almighty's benevolence is not in his best interest, then I'll need all the help I can get.'

∞ ∞ ∞

By early morning, the ground was entirely white over. The temperature had plummeted, and Freddy was only persuaded to go out and do his business with half a knob of leftover cheese the Reverend had found in his dressing gown pocket. Augustus Shackleford nibbled on the other half as he shivered on the kitchen doorstep watching the hound speedily cock his leg up at the nearest bush.

In contrast, the townhouse kitchen was a warm hive of activity, and hurrying back inside, both dog and master were more than content to linger in front of the roaring fire and enjoy some fresh bread and honey washed down with hot tea.

Whenever Augustus Shackleford was in London, both he and Freddy were regular visitors to the kitchen. As the Reverend piously pointed out - the Duke's servants here in Town were simply an extension of his flock back home in Blackmore and as such were every bit as entitled to his spiritual guidance. In truth, the clergyman enjoyed the hustle and bustle as well as the sweet treats the cook frequently slipped him, and while Freddy might not share the same enthusiasm for the spiritual side of things, he was equally passionate about the treats.

And as for the kitchen staff—well, since Reverend Shackleford wisely kept his sermonising for those times he was accompanied by Percy, choosing to devote the rest of the time to the latest and most entertaining gossip, he was naturally a favourite of everyone below stairs.

It also meant that he was very often the first person to find out if any trouble was brewing.

'Yer goin' to 'ave to 'ave a word wi' yer boss up there if you be wantin' to get on the road today, Revren,' commented the Cook, Mrs. Pidgeon, as she handed the Reverend his second piece of bread dripping with honey.

'P'raps 'e wants you to stay 'ere a bit longer, Sir,' commented Daisy, the scullery maid, 'given wot's 'appenin' wi' Miss Chastity.'

Reverend Shackleford paused with his bread and honey halfway to his mouth as Daisy's words sank in.

'I wasn't aware that anything *specific* was happening with Chastity,' the clergyman frowned, putting his bread down. 'What kind of *happening* might you be referring to?'

'Ain't you 'eard then, Sir?'

Swallowing a sudden onset of indigestion, the Reverend became aware that the kitchen had gone entirely silent. The bread and honey congealed into a large lump right in the middle of his breadbasket. Feeling an abrupt sense of déjà vu, he stifled a groan and shook his head slowly.

'Daisy, keep yer trap shut an' get on wi' yer chores. It ain't fer the likes o' you to be botherin' the Revren wi' any bit o' gossip.'

Entirely sure that he didn't want to know whatever it was the scullery maid had heard, Reverend Shackleford nevertheless coughed and managed, 'Please continue, Daisy.'

The young woman looked uncertainly over at the Cook who shrugged and pursed her lips.

'Well, the fing is, Sir,' the scullery maid ploughed on, 'apparently, she propo...propos...'

'Propositioned?' the Reverend interjected faintly.

'That's the word, Sir, *propositioned*. Well, they're saying that Miss Charity *propositioned* a gentleman right in the middle of the

Duke of Blackmore's ballroom.'

Chapter Four

'*Percy*, are you in there?' Reverend Shackleford banged on his curate's bedroom door urgently.

After what seemed like forever, the door opened revealing Percy dressed solely in his inexpressibles. 'Thunder an' turf, Percy, I've seen more deuced meat on a chicken,' the Reverend muttered. 'Why aren't you dressed?'

'I've just this second risen out of bed,' the curate defended. He gave a slight pause before adding, 'It's very early, Sir, but don't worry, it will take me but a minute to finish my packing.'

'Hold your horses, Percy lad, we're not going anywhere,' Reverend Shackleford sighed. 'Have you seen the deuced weather?' Without waiting for an invitation, he stomped into the room, sat on Percy's bed and stared morosely at the floor.

'Perhaps the Almighty still has work for you to do here,' the curate faltered, trying hard to hide his relief at the thought of postponing his confrontation with Lizzy Fletcher.

'Oh, He's made *that* very clear,' Augustus Shackleford replied heavily. 'And I had such high hopes, Percy. 'High hopes...'

'Err ... well ... so did we all,' responded the curate carefully, wondering what on earth his superior was talking about.

'Well, I'd better be getting along to the Duke's study,' the clergyman continued. 'Best Nicholas hears it from me. *Again.*' He shook his head sadly, adding, 'He'll be setting me a deuced bed up in there soon,' before climbing to his feet as Percy looked on, bewildered.

'I suppose I should be thanking the Almighty there's only one more to go, though I can't imagine there's a man in the whole of England beef-witted enough to take Prudence on.' The Reverend made his way to the door and pulled it open, just as Percy found the courage to ask, 'Has something bad happened, Sir?'

'I suppose it depends on what you would define as bad, Percy,' he sighed. 'In this family, it's just business as usual.'

Try as she might, Chastity could not banish the Earl of Cottesmore from her mind. Despite Nicholas's obvious belief that the man was a killer, there was something about Christian Stanhope that drew her to him. And it wasn't simply his spectacular looks. She might be flighty, overly emotional and inclined to sentimental overtures (her family's description) but she was also fair minded and reluctant to dismiss a person solely on other people's opinions.

Not that she would dare tell her brother-in-law that. But there was nothing to stop her making her own enquiries. Throwing back her bed covers, she padded to the window and pulled aside the heavy drapes. The small park opposite the townhouse was entirely covered in a thick blanket of snow. As she stared, the glass began to fog up, and she abruptly became aware of the cold.

Shivering, she was about to climb back under the covers when the sound of laughter drew her back to the window. Rubbing at the misted pane, she grinned as she spied Prudence and Anthony already up and dressed, currently throwing snowballs at each other with Freddy dancing between them.

Impulsively, she drew her nightgown over her head and quickly pulled on some clothes. Her maid would not be coming in with her morning chocolate for another hour at least, and since she was now wide awake... Well, she couldn't remember the last time she'd had a snowball fight with her siblings, especially since snow was a rare occurrence in Devonshire.

Quickly piling her hair into an untidy knot, she plonked a bonnet onto her head and shrugged into her oldest coat. Chuckling, she imagined Grace's face should she have dared use her new midnight velvet pelisse to cavort in the snow. Finally, sitting on the bed, she pulled on her trusty boots. The ones she always wore in Blackmore. Shrugging off the sudden longing for home, she threw open the door ... and ran straight into her sister standing directly outside.

27th June 1798

'Why doesn't the bastard just surrender?' muttered the First Lieutenant, Nicholas Sinclair as he stared through the telescope at the fleeing French frigate, now a mere one hundred yards away from the pursuing *Phoenix*.

'Is that a rhetorical question, Sir, or are you truly expecting an answer?' Second Lieutenant Christian Stanhope grinned at the irritated glance Sinclair tossed him.

'It's two o'clock in the bloody morning, Mr. Stanhope. Far too early for jingle-brained comments.'

'Do you think she could be carrying something the captain

wishes to keep hidden?'

'That's my guess. Her captain must know by now he can't outrun us. If he had any care for his crew, he'd raise the flag. The fact that he's still running...' Lieutenant Sinclair shrugged and sighed. 'I estimate we'll be alongside by eight bells. I'll wake the Captain at six bells. Give Mr. Barnet and Mr. Witherspoon a shake. About time they got their lazy arses out of their hammocks.'

Christian Stanhope grinned again. 'Aye, Sir.' Saluting quickly, he made his way down towards the lower deck, thinking about the First Lieutenant's comments. There could be serious prize money aboard the *Sensible*. The Knights of St. John of Jerusalem, the military arm of the Catholic Church in command of the island of Malta, were rumoured to be in possession of vast riches. Mayhap the fleeing frigate had been charged with transporting the looted treasure to France. If so, it would certainly sweeten the pot as far as Barnet was concerned, especially since the Third Lieutenant hadn't stopped grumbling since they'd taken up pursuit of the French frigate.

Ducking his head as he entered the lower deck, he weaved his way between snoring sailors until he reached his destination, wasting no time before giving both men an unceremonious shake. 'Blast and bugger your eyes,' Witherspoon muttered, pulling his blanket over his head. 'It ain't our watch yet.'

'First Lieutenant wants you both up top,' declared Stanhope without sympathy. 'We're closing in on the *Sensible*.'

Groaning, Barnet rolled himself out of the hammock. 'Get yer arse out o' bed, Withers,' he ordered, slapping the other man's exposed buttocks, 'you aint goin' to want to be caught with yer britches round yer ankles when we're knee deep in bloody Froggies.'

'Sinclair reckons the *Sensible* could well be carrying treasure from Malta,' Stanhope whispered slyly in the Fourth

Lieutenant's ear.

'The likes of us ain't goin' ter get a look in,' Witherspoon griped. Nevertheless, he rolled out of his hammock, landing on his stocking feet with a grimace.

'There'll be prize money though,' Christian Stanhope reasoned. 'Sinclair's a stickler for fairness, and he's got the ear of the Captain.'

'Don't mean to say there'll be nothin' smoky about the whole bloody business,' the Third Lieutenant grumbled, shoving sore feet into his clogs.

'There's always somethin' smoky goin' on when it comes to bloody prize money. You know that, Barnet. But I can tell yer now, I ain't hangin' back. If I get half a chance, I intend to grab me some of that bloody loot,' Witherspoon vowed.

'Aye, and you'll swing if you get caught,' Barnet scoffed as they followed the Second Lieutenant back towards the upper deck. 'And all the bloody gold in the world ain't worth shit down in Davy Jones's locker.'

Present day

The last time Chastity listened to her brother-in-law ring a peal over someone was comfortably through a closed door. On that occasion, she and her twin had thought it actually quite amusing. She was beginning to discover that it was an entirely different matter when one happened to be on the receiving end of the reprimand. Especially as this was the second time in a week.

In the past, Chastity had dealt perfectly well with her eldest sister's husband. That is to say she had very little to do with him at all. Throughout most of her childhood, he'd been a distant but stern figure to whom everyone in the Shackleford family turned when they were in a hobble.

Well it was certain she was in a hobble now. And listening to Nicholas reveal the true extent of that hobble, her heart actually went out to him. Oh how he must rue the day he married Grace. He could not have anticipated he would be taking responsibility for her whole totty-headed family. And here she was, the latest in a long line of irresponsible females to carelessly tie their garter in public, secure in their blithe expectation that the Duke of Blackmore was there to pick up the pieces.

And the fact that Nicholas rarely raised his voice somehow made it all the worse. Out of the corner of her eye, Chastity saw her father swallow a full snifter of brandy, even though it was only eight in the morning. She couldn't see Grace but could imagine her sister's face exactly.

Abruptly, she became aware that Nicholas had finished speaking and was now looking at her expectantly. Which was unfortunate as she had no idea what he'd said after, 'Your recklessness beggars belief.' She stared blankly at him.

'Tare an' hounds, Chastity,' her father exploded. 'If you had to go and make a deuced cake of yourself, couldn't you at least have chosen a gentleman with a guaranteed income of ten thousand a year who wasn't suspected of murder?'

'I...' Chastity started, only to be interrupted by Grace.

'It's no good losing your temper, Father, and *what ifs* serve no useful purpose.' Her voice was brisk and businesslike as she continued, 'Chastity dearest, as I see it, we have two possible options.' She paused, obviously waiting to ensure she had her younger sister's full attention. Inexplicably, Chastity felt her eyes well up at the term of endearment. At the very least, it showed that Grace had forgiven her foolishness.

'We can petition Christian Stanhope and hope he will do the right thing by offering for you.' She paused and winced before adding, 'Unfortunately, as it was you who propositioned *him*, he is not honour bound to do anything at all...' She glanced at her husband who nodded at her to continue, his face carefully impassive.

'And from what we know of the Earl, honour does not appear to be one of his finer qualities, so there is no guarantee he will step up. And indeed, I think everyone in this room would have mixed feelings if he did so.' She sighed and picked up her tea. 'The second option is that you return to Blackmore. Mayhap we will be able to find a local gentleman to your liking. One who has no interests in the idiosyncrasies of polite society.' Her voice turned derogatory as she said *polite society*, making it abundantly clear her private opinion of the ruling classes.

Chastity felt her throat tighten as she fought back tears. 'What would *you* have me do?' she asked Nicholas in a choked whisper.

The Duke closed his eyes momentarily, and when he opened them, his expression was no longer emotionless. In fact, the sympathy in his eyes was the final straw, and she made no move to stem the tears trickling down her face. 'I have made no bones about my feelings towards Christian Stanhope,' he said wearily, 'and as things stand, I cannot be happy entrusting him with your care. If he offers for you, and you go through with the marriage, I will be unable to intervene unless he hurts you ... physically, that is.

'I do not trust him. That said, it is ultimately up to you whether we appeal to his goodwill—if he has any.' He paused and grimaced before saying carefully, 'There is a third option. I have been approached by Edmund Fitzroy - Viscount Trebworthy, who it appears is very smitten with you.

'Obviously with what has happened, he may withdraw his interest. However, I am not without influence, and I am fairly certain I could persuade the good Viscount that to align himself with me and mine would be very beneficial to him...' He paused and raised his eyebrows at the look of sheer horror on Chastity's face, before adding drily, 'Or if not him, a suitable gentleman here in town, perhaps one with a minor title who, with appropriate recompense, might be prepared to overlook your ... indiscretions.'

'Bribe him you mean?' Chastity couldn't stifle the bitterness in her voice.

'If you wish to call it that,' Nicholas responded, his voice cool. 'I do not make the rules, Chastity, and I concur with my wife that most of them are almost farcical, which is why I choose to spend most of my time at Blackmore, well away from the absurdness of Society.' He sighed and shook his head. 'But that does not mean I can entirely disregard Society's requirements. Not if I wish to continue to provide for my family and everyone else who depends on me to put a roof over their head and food on their table.'

Chastity opened her mouth, then shut it again, swallowing her ire. She knew full well just how lucky her family had been when the Duke of Blackmore chose Grace as his bride. Closing her eyes, she pushed aside all notions of girlish romance as she endeavoured to decide which would be the most sensible course of action.

However, no matter how practical she endeavoured to be, she simply could not countenance the idea of being married to Viscount Trebworthy. The very idea made her shudder. She would rather return to Blackmore and spend the rest of her life as a spinster.

If she flatly refused to even consider the Viscount, mayhap

her brother-in-law would be successful in locating an amenable gentleman who could overlook her pariah status in return for a connection to the Duke of Blackmore.

But what about Christian Stanhope? She thought back to the first time she'd set eyes on him and her inability to erase him from her thoughts since that moment. What would happen if Nicholas approached him? Most likely he would laugh and walk away. But what if he didn't? Would he be cruel as Nicholas feared? Would he expect her to share his bed? Bear his children? An unaccustomed tremor accompanied a sudden picture of them entwined. Naked.

Shocked that she was capable of such vulgar imaginings, her eyes flew open. She opened her mouth, intending to give the Duke permission to find her a suitable, accommodating, *compliant* husband that *wasn't* Edmund Fitzroy. Instead, she heard herself saying in a surprisingly steady voice, 'Given that Lord Cottesmore is very likely to feel the backlash of my impulsive action, we would be doing him a disservice if we did not apprise him of the situation and at least allow him to make the decision as to … as to whether … if he wishes…'

'To rescue you from total ruination,' her father supplied.

Chastity frowned at his harsh, though possibly accurate, assessment of her situation. Unfortunately, he hadn't quite finished.

'Of course, your faux pas will be old news as soon as the *ton* discover your husband's a suspected killer,' he snorted, 'but at least you'll both be snubbed together.'

'So the alternative is for me to be purchased like some kind of brood mare?' Chastity cried. 'Well, go ahead and try and find a willing contender, but I tell you now, I would rather remain unwed for the rest of my life than tie myself to Viscount Trebworthy.'

Reverend Shackleford opened his mouth to respond, but before he had a chance to speak, Nicholas got there first. 'Chastity's right,' he announced to everyone's surprise. 'As much as I'd prefer it, we can't simply ignore Stanhope's involvement. Doing so could well make matters infinitely worse for Chastity.' He pushed back his chair. 'I have already invited the Earl to attend me on another matter, so we'll wait and see what he has to say.'

The Duke stood up with a wince, his old wounds received at the Battle of Trafalgar clearly paining him in the cold and damp. 'I don't know about the rest of you, but I for one am famished.' He gave a grim chuckle before adding, 'There's nothing like a family crisis to whet one's appetite.' He turned towards the Reverend. 'I trust you are not intending to start your journey home in this weather, Augustus.' It wasn't a question, and Reverend Shackleford knew better than to argue. He sighed in defeat.

'Given the circumstances, I am better placed here for the moment,' he responded heavily.

'Good man,' Nicholas responded with a faint smile. Turning towards Grace, he held out his arm. 'Shall we?'

Reasonably confident that she wasn't to be confined to her bedchamber with nothing but bread and water, Chastity got to her feet and followed the others towards the breakfast room. Despite everything, she had the strangest feeling in the pit of her stomach. A tightness that was part dread and part wild exhilaration. She didn't know which was worse.

Chapter Five

'How do you spell *bastard*, Papa?'

Christian Stanhope stared incredulously at his daughter for a second before putting down his dish of tea. 'Where did you hear that word, sweet pea?' he asked carefully.

'I heard John, the footman, say it. He said you were an upstart bastard. I think he was talking to the stable hand–I can't remember his name, sorry, Papa.'

'You don't have to remember everybody's name, Mercy,' Christian chided gently.

'But Miss Sharpham said it is the mark of good breeding to remember the names of those below you.'

'Yes, well, perhaps instead of focusing on manners, Miss Sharpham should spend more time on your letters since your spelling clearly has room for improvement.'

'It's true,' Mercedes Stanhope responded forlornly, 'I'm nearly nine years old, and I should be able to spell *bastard*.' She glanced sadly at her father before adding, 'I don't know how to spell *upstart* either.'

'Well, neither word has any place in the vocabulary of a young lady of good breeding, so you should not worry your head about them.'

'Is Miss Sharpham right then, Papa? Am I a young lady of good breeding? What does upstart bastard mean?'

'Yes, you are, sweet pea. And a young lady with such excellent breeding should never be heard uttering words like *upstart bastard*. Nor does she need to know what they mean.'

'Is John the footman in the suds now? Cook said I wasn't to listen to anything he said 'cos he's just a bloody bone picker.'

Christian winced. Really, his daughter was spending too much time below stairs. Time she should by rights be spending with her governess. The problem was, he couldn't afford to pay Miss Sharpham to be with his daughter full-time, and as the only child, Mercy was naturally lonely and gravitated towards the livelier portion of the house. He looked around the dreary breakfast room. In truth, this house was a bloody mausoleum. He hated it. But there wasn't enough in the coffers to renovate the townhouse as well as the estate.

He needed to make more money. That much was clear. Restoring Cottesmore would almost clean him out.

Whatever was left over would need to be invested, and soon. He had an excellent head for business and had no doubt he could double or triple his investments. Providing his peers would actually do business with him. But as soon as his past became common knowledge, Christian had no doubt he would be ostracised by the vast majority of Society.

He needed to clear his name. But to do that, he first had to convince the Duke of Blackmore of his innocence which would be no easy feat. He wondered how long he'd get before his grace had him thrown out?

'Perhaps you should refrain from listening to either the cook or the footman,' he suggested at length to his daughter's earnest face. 'Have you finished your breakfast?'

The little girl popped a last piece of toast in her mouth and carefully dabbed her lips. 'Miss Sharpham says that *manners maketh man*,' she announced, folding her napkin and laying it neatly across her plate.

'But you're not a man, sweet pea,' Christian pointed out, suddenly fearful that the governess might completely stifle his daughter's sparkle. He couldn't believe how important Mercy had become to him in just a few short months. Almost from the moment she'd appeared on his doorstep, his carefully cultivated life had been completely toppled. Even to the point of returning to England. The one place in which he'd sworn he would never again set foot.

'Don't be silly, Papa, she means ladies too,' Mercy scoffed, climbing down from her chair and giving her father a quick peck on the cheek. Then with a last wave, she was gone.

Sighing, Christian picked up his newspaper, intending to ring for more tea, but as he stared unseeing at the small print, he abruptly found his thoughts straying to the last time he'd seen Nicholas Sinclair.

The former first lieutenant had been pointing a pistol at his back. Christian recalled Sinclair's final words to him, spoken in a strained whisper. 'If you're going to jump, for pity's sake do it now.

27th June 1798

By four a.m., the Captain finally managed to manoeuvre HMS *Phoenix* alongside the French frigate and ordered the crew to open heavy fire from close range. Within eight minutes, the

Sensible was battered into submission.

'Mr. Stanhope, Mr. Barnet and Mr. Witherspoon, each take ten men and prepare to board,' ordered First Lieutenant Sinclair.

'Aye, Sir.'

As the three men mustered on the deck with the chosen hands, grappling hooks were thrown aboard the *Sensible* and slowly, relentlessly, the *Phoenix* was pulled towards the beaten ship until they were locked together.

With a yell, the three lieutenants leapt across the gap closely followed by their selected men. All were armed with pistols, cutlasses and boarding axes. A brief fight ensued, but within minutes, the crew surrendered. The French frigate had taken significant damage to her masts and hull, and a large number of the crew were wounded or dead.

Quickly, Stanhope as the senior Lieutenant, ordered those of the French crew still standing to be rounded up and secured and her captain taken aboard the *Phoenix*. The dead were unceremoniously tossed overboard, and the British frigate's surgeon brought across to deal with the injured. Fortunately, the *Sensible* was still seaworthy.

With Stanhope preoccupied securing the French vessel, it was left to Barnet and Witherspoon to organise the gruesome task of ridding the deck of torn body parts. Wiping his bloody hands on his britches, the Fourth Lieutenant groaned. 'I'm gettin' too bloody old fer this,' he complained to no one in particular. Behind him was the main hatch to the lower deck. Glancing round, he spied Barnet near the port rigging. If he slipped away now, no one would notice.

Heart thudding, Witherspoon backed casually towards the opening, then once he was certain he was unobserved, quickly pivoted and leapt down the hatch. The lower deck was deserted after the wounded and those still standing had been taken up to the quarterdeck, but he held his pistol at the ready as he cautiously made his way down to the hold. At the entrance, he stopped abruptly. What the bloody hell was he doing? If he was caught right now, he'd be court-martialled at the very least and likely feel the swing of the cat. But if he went through that door...

Sweat dotted his brow and pooled at the base of his spine. Barnet was right. If he took anything, he'd swing. Biting his lip, Witherspoon hesitated on the threshold, a sudden nausea taking hold. He couldn't spend the rest of his bloody life at sea. For all Stanhope's talk about prize money, they all knew that the chances of any of them seeing so much as a bloody farthing were slim. This might be his only chance.

Taking a deep breath, Witherspoon turned the handle, half hoping the door would be locked. But after a brief resistance, it opened. Glancing behind him, the Fourth Lieutenant slipped through the opening, quickly pushing the door closed.

Present day

Chastity stared at herself in the mirror. She should have been attending the opera with her family. She'd even had a new dress made for the occasion. A glorious, pale blue, which Grace insisted brought out the colour of her eyes. Tonight was to be *her* night. Queen Charlotte would be attending, and though Chastity had yet to be presented formally, her Majesty's sudden predilection towards the Shacklefords meant they would, at the very least, have likely rubbed shoulders.

But she doubted she'd ever meet the Queen now, unless some poor unfortunate could be persuaded to wed her. And quickly. Despite her earlier words, she did not see Christian Stanhope as that poor unfortunate.

Sighing, she turned away from the mirror. Truly, she'd made a cake of herself. All her twin's fears had proven well founded. And it had only taken a few weeks. She hadn't even managed one Season. Grace's last words to her before they'd departed for the opera were an earnest entreaty to remain in her bedchamber, but that was easier said than done when one's mind refused to quiet.

Seating herself in the large window seat, Chastity parted the heavy drapes and stared down at the deserted street below. The snow had ceased falling, and the new street gas lamp shed a circle of light, giving the impression that there was nothing beyond its illumination. She glanced down at her pocket watch. Ten o'clock. Unfortunately, she didn't feel in the least tired. Grimacing, she picked up her book, and stared unseeing at its pages.

If only Nicholas would allow her to speak with Lord Cottesmore. It wasn't that she didn't trust her brother-in-law to have her best interests at heart, but his dislike of Stanhope would likely end any negotiations before they'd even begun. Chastity refused to contemplate why she'd been so adamant about petitioning the Earl, but something other than his good looks drew her to him, and it wasn't simply a desire to avoid being leg shackled to Viscount Trebworthy. Despite Nicholas's conviction that Christian Stanhope killed a man in cold blood, for some reason, she didn't believe it.

She thought back to his piercing blue eyes. Even in their short acquaintance, she'd sensed an underlying ruthlessness, but there had been no cruelty. Oh she was under no illusions that a man such as he might be persuaded to love her. She had quickly learned that the marriage mart was no place for romance. But somehow, she felt that she and the Earl might deal well together. And at least he was pleasing to the eye.

But as Grace said earlier, since she had been the one tying her garter in public, he was not honour bound to offer for her. Indeed, she thought it very unlikely that he was in the market for a wife with the label of murderer hanging over his head.

If only he'd been the one doing the ruining. But then, if the Earl had asked her to dance, there would have been no ruining at all. Damn and blast, it was all so ridiculous. Just because she'd been overheard doing the asking. Truly, she might as well have been found in his deuced bed.

Frowning, she stilled. If she was found in the Earl's bed, he would have no choice but to marry her. She determinedly ignored the insistent voice in her head that sounded suspiciously like Charity declaring her completely bacon-brained for even thinking she could blackmail a man like Christian Stanhope. But what did she stand to lose? She was already in the suds. Her Season had ended before it had even begun. And for something she did in a room full of people. She ground her teeth in frustration. Bloody gossiping tabbies.

If Lord Cottesmore agreed to wed her, then the reason for their nuptials would very quickly be forgotten. Not so if another man had to be persuaded to take on damaged goods.

And if she waited for him in his bed... Well, at the very least she would get to talk to him. Alone.

That's if he didn't kill her first.

Jumping up, she began to pace the room. She'd overheard the kitchen staff talking of the Earl's residence, so she knew where it was. And with the newly raised streetlights to guide her, she was persuaded it would take her less than ten minutes to walk. It was still early enough that she would be relatively safe. Especially if she wore her oldest cloak.

Charity's voice was now screaming, 'Idiot,' at her, and she stopped pacing. Was she? Her plan was risky to be sure, but she was out of options. Somehow she had to persuade Christian

Stanhope to offer for her, no matter the animosity from the Duke of Blackmore.

But his bed? Well, mayhap that was a bit extreme. She could start by simply *asking* for an audience. At the front door. Like a normal person. If he refused to see her, well *then* she could locate his bedchamber and wait for him there. What was the worst that could happen? He would be unlikely to actually do her any physical harm. And if he threw her out of his house, the servants would undoubtedly talk, and then he *would* have to marry her.

Her mind shying away from the teeny tiny problem of *how* she would actually locate and gain entry to his bedchamber without anybody spotting her, she determinedly picked up the discarded bed cushions, positioning them under the bedclothes to look as if someone was sleeping. Then she pulled her hair back, pinning it to the nape of her neck, pulled on her boots and sought out her old woollen cloak. Finally, blowing out the candles, she pulled open the door and peeped out onto the landing.

'The thing is, Percy, I'm not getting any younger,' Reverend Shackleford declared, taking a sip of Nicholas's excellent brandy. 'My back feels as though I've been run over by a coach and four, I've got gout in me big toe and I can't see my hand in front of me without me eyeglasses. It's crucial I see Anthony take his rightful place in Society before I head upstairs to share a snifter with the Almighty. If I don't, Agnes will never let me hear the last of it.'

'Well, since you'll be dead, Sir, there's not a lot she can do,' observed Percy.

'If you think that, you don't know my wife,' muttered the Reverend darkly.

Percy frowned. His superior definitely had a point. He wouldn't put anything past Agnes Shackleford. Though if she continued taking the many potions she purchased from Blackmore's local pedlar, he suspected she'd be pushing up daisies well before the Reverend. Naturally, he didn't say so out loud.

The two men were sitting in the small drawing room on the first floor. Apart from being the cosiest room in the house, it boasted two comfortable winged chairs and a roaring fire, the latter of which was most definitely appreciated by Freddy who was currently snoring loudly in front of it.

'Tare an' hounds, Percy,' Reverend Shackleford went on sorrowfully, 'I was hoping we might even add another Duke to the family. I've been reliably informed that Chastity's a tempting armful, and from the conversations we've had, she appears to have nothing between her ears other than fresh air. There's the modest dowry from his grace. What more could any titled gentleman want?'

Unsure whether he was required to give an answer, the curate opted for nodding sagely instead.

'But what do we get? A havey-cavey earl, who may or may not have put his shipmate to bed with a mallet ... or in this case a knife according to Nicholas. And to top it all, it appears he hasn't got sixpence to scratch with, or won't have by the time he's finished rebuilding his house.' Reverend Shackleford shook his head gloomily. 'Truly, Percy, I've said it before, but the Almighty's got a deuced odd sense of humour.'

A sudden noise in the hall outside had Freddy lifting his head with a small growl. Frowning, the Reverend paused his tale of woe. After a second, the foxhound wagged his tail sleepily and lay back down with a doggy sigh.

In the silence, a muttered epithet drifted through the closed door. The Reverend glanced down at his fob watch. 'Nearly half past ten,' he murmured. 'Who the deuce could be sneaking around at this time of night? The servants are likely all abed. The Duke don't hold with keeping them awake all hours.'

'Should we investigate, Sir,' questioned Percy, notably making no move to vacate his spot by the fire.

'I suppose I owe it to Nicholas to ensure his chattels aren't being loaded into a waiting carriage as we speak,' Augustus Shackleford grumbled. Climbing heavily to his feet, he made his way to the door throwing a, 'Come, Freddy,' over his shoulder. The comatose foxhound didn't so much as twitch. Hmphing at the vagaries of man's supposed best friend, the Reverend pulled open the door a crack and peeped through. Just in time to spot a cloaked figure tiptoeing down the stairs.

'What the devil do you think you're doing?' he bellowed, stepping onto the landing.

A white, frightened face turned briefly towards him, then the figure fled down the remaining steps and hurried over to the town house's main entrance. After a brief pause, the miscreant pulled open the front door and slipped through, slamming it shut behind them.

'Right then, you varmint, if you think you're getting away with robbing this household, you're sadly mistaken. '*Percy, bring my cassock*,' Reverend Shackleford yelled, followed a second later by, '*Freddy, get your lazy arse away from the fire. It's time you earned your keep.*'

Without waiting, he hurried down the stairs, his mind awhirl with possibilities. The foremost being that whoever the thief was, he or she looked remarkably like his daughter Chastity. But then he wasn't wearing his eyeglasses.

Chapter Six

'Damn and blast,' muttered Chastity to herself as she hobbled across the square wincing at the pain in her right foot. God save her from newly polished floors. Only Grace's recently commissioned bust of her husband positioned in pride of place at the top of the stairs had saved her from ending up in a heap at the bottom of them. She found herself giggling almost hysterically at the thought of telling her sister that even a *sculpture* of Nicholas was enough to save her from herself.

On reaching the corner, she stopped and bent down to examine her foot, moving it this way and that. It was a little painful, but nothing more, reassuring her that at least she hadn't done any lasting damage. She glanced back at the townhouse, wondering how long it would be before her father roused the servants. She'd not given any thought to the possibility that he might not yet be abed. In Blackmore, he generally retired just after supper. She grimaced in frustration. Going back was no longer an option, so she had no choice but to continue on and hope that if anybody checked, they wouldn't see through the makeshift body in her bed.

To her horror, across the square, the front door to the Duke's townhouse opened to reveal her father, Percy and Freddy. 'Botheration,' she breathed. It was clear that her father hadn't waited to rouse the servants. If they were all still abed, did that mean she could circle round and go back into the house from the garden? She was beginning to have serious misgivings about her plan. What had seemed like a good idea in her bedchamber was looking increasingly jingle brained outside in the dark and freezing cold.

But did she have a choice really? If not tonight, then she'd never get the chance to deal with the Earl before her brother-in-law. She might be afraid of being forced to wed the likes of Christian Stanhope, but not nearly so terrified as she was at the thought of being leg shackled to Viscount Trebworthy for the rest of her life. And although common sense told her that Nicholas would never actually force her to wed someone against her will, she wasn't sure whether bad breath would count as a good enough reason for reluctance.

A sudden shout put an end to her ruminating. Percy was pointing directly at her. Obviously, she'd been spotted. Without waiting to see if they were following, she turned her back and limped round the corner, hopefully in the direction of the Earl's townhouse.

'Which way did he go, Freddy?'

'Would we not be better to return to the house and determine if anything was stolen?' Percy offered desperately as Freddy excitedly circled, his nose to the ground.

'Don't be so chuckleheaded, Percy,' the Reverend grunted, trying to avoid getting wrapped up in the foxhound's lead. 'This is just like old times. The two of us throwing a rub in the way of a good-for-nothing scoundrel's nefarious scheme.'

Obviously, Freddy was of the same opinion as his tail started wagging, just before he suddenly took off across the road.

'Tare an' hou...,' yelped the startled clergyman fighting to keep his feet. 'Come on, Percy lad, the chase is on.'

'But, Sir...' Percy protested, nevertheless, picking up his cassock and hurrying after his superior. 'Sir, I really think we ought to wait for...' Whatever they were supposed to wait for was lost as the Reverend disappeared round the next corner. Uttering a small moan, the curate ceased his objections and picked up his speed. The last thing he wanted was to be left on his own in the dark in the middle of London. It might well be Mayfair, but the ruffian they were chasing gave evidence to the fact there were some desperate villains abroad.

'I wish to speak with his lordship,' Chastity announced in the haughtiest tone she could muster.

'Who's askin?' The person appeared to be a footman if his attire was anything to go by, but he certainly didn't have a footman's manners. Her request and indeed her presence might well be unorthodox, but even in her limited experience, Chastity recognised insolence when she heard it. In truth, she didn't blame him. If she was honest, her visit was more than uncommon, it branded her a light skirt. Her face flaming in the dim light, she frantically sought to come up with a valid reason for her request. One that wouldn't have the footman slamming the door in her face.

'You may tell the Earl...' she started, only to have the impudent individual interrupt her.

''Is lordship's off out, so you'll 'ave to peddle yer wares elsewhere.' Then he slammed the door in her face.

'Fiend seize it,' she muttered, wondering what on earth she was going to do next. Clearly, she was not going to be allowed an audience with the Earl, and while she was not above creating a commotion to get what she wanted (she was a Shackleford after all), she didn't wish the whole street to be privy to her folly. So, the deuced bedchamber it was. *If* she could find it.

Muttering another epithet that would have impressed even Jimmy, she stepped backwards and looked up. There were two windows on the second floor, and in one of them, she could clearly see Christian Stanhope silhouetted in the candlelight. Her heart raced as she realised she may well have located his bedchamber. The Earl appeared to be tying his cravat, so evidently, he did not have a valet. A minute later, he disappeared from the window, and the flickering light was gone.

A sudden clatter at the end of the small street indicated the arrival of a coach and four. Likely it was here for the Earl. Hurriedly, she stepped away from the lamplight and into the shadows cast by a large tree in front of the townhouse. Could she hope to accost his lordship before he climbed into the carriage? As she dithered in the darkness, the front door opened to reveal the reason for her visit. Gathering her courage, she lifted her skirts to step forward but halted as she realised the Earl was not alone. An older, portly man followed him down the steps. Grinding her teeth in frustration, she watched as the two men climbed into the waiting carriage and shut the door. Seconds later, they were gone.

Chastity remained under the tree, feeling tears of defeat sting her eyes. Her one chance and she'd fudged it. It was all very well locating the Earl's bedchamber, but she still had no way of actually getting into it without being spotted, and since she couldn't remain under the tree for the rest of the night, she had no choice but to return home. Truly, she'd made a complete mull of the whole thing.

Dashing away the tears that threatened to run down her cheeks, she stepped out of the tree's shelter and looked back up towards Christian Stanhope's bedchamber. After a second, her heart gave a dull thud as she realised he'd left the right-hand window open slightly.

And a thick branch of the very same tree she'd been hiding under finished just above the sill of that particular window. Turning back, she looked up into the shadowy branches. It was some years since she'd attempted to climb a tree, but the first limb was fairly close to the ground, and thereafter, it wouldn't be too difficult to make her way up the tree as long as she took her time and was careful.

She hesitated for a few seconds, weighing up her choices. The only time she would be truly exposed would be once she accessed the branch butting the window. But the likelihood of someone noticing her this time of night were very slim. The streetlight was far enough away that it cast just enough light for her to see by without revealing her to anyone on the ground.

Pursing her lips, Chastity began to divest herself of her cloak. It would all too easily snag on the branches as she climbed. Bundling it up, she laid it in a shadowy corner, then without giving herself any time to question the folly of what she was doing, she studied the lowest branch. Taking a deep breath, she lifted her arms and swung herself up onto the limb.

'The deuced blackguard,' Reverend Shackleford muttered as he and Percy watched the shadowy figure swing himself up into the lowermost branches of the tree outside the Earl of Cottesmore's residence. 'He intends to rob the Earl. Is purloining from a duke not enough for this wretch? And all in one deuced night.'

He shook his head in disbelief and turned to Percy who was strangely silent. 'I think now might be the time to call in the Runners,' the clergyman declared. 'We've done our duty, Percy lad, there's noth…' He paused and looked down at Freddy whose tail was wagging furiously. 'What the deuce has got into you, lad?' he questioned the foxhound, puzzled as Freddy started to whine.

'I think he recognises the person climbing the tree,' Percy responded faintly.

'What the devil are you talking about, Percy?' Reverend Shackleford frowned. 'How would Freddy happen to be acquainted with a cutpurse?'

'Because it's your daughter Chastity.'

27th June 1798

Standing with his back to the door, Witherspoon waited for his eyes to adjust to the dimness of the hold. At first, he thought there was nothing of any value, but eventually he made out a number of large chests standing in the corner, sticking out behind the barrels of rum.

His throat suddenly dry, he hurried over to examine the containers. As he got closer, the chests came into focus, and he stopped, abruptly realising the enormity of what he was about to do. Clearly, this was the treasure the *Sensible* had been taking back to France.

His eyes roamed over the large chests – there were four in all. Heart slamming against his ribs, he stepped towards the first one. It was locked, but the large key remained in the lock. 'Bloody Froggy idiots,' he muttered to himself, turning the key. The chest contained gold francs. Right up to the very top. With a feral grin, Witherspoon put down his pistol and began stuffing his pockets, before pausing abruptly. *Stupid.* He'd never be able to hide the blunt, and what the hell would he do with a pocketful of French silver? Spilling the coins quickly back into the chest, he closed the lid and went on to the next. This time the coins looked to be gold. Painfully aware he was running out of time, he hurried to the third chest.

This time he struck lucky. The chest contained jewellery haphazardly piled to the top. The fourth lieutenant gave a low exultant laugh, digging his hands into the pile of trinkets. There were brooches, necklaces, bracelets, all studded with gems. Digging down deeper, he unearthed a ruby the size of a small pigeon's egg. Grinning in triumph, he tucked the gem inside his britches and closed the lid. Then picking up his pistol, he turned back towards the door.

Where Barnet stood watching him in horror.

'Wot the bloody 'ell d'you think yer doin' Withers?' the Third Lieutenant hissed, stepping away from the door. 'Put it back. They'll crop you for sure.'

'Only if they find out,' retorted Witherspoon. 'An' if you've got any sense, you'll be doin' the same. They won't miss a few trinkets.'

Barnet shook his head. 'You're a bleeding fool, Withers. Where d'you think you're goin' to 'ide it? You goin' to stick it up your arse?' He shook his head and turned back to the door. 'I ain't bein' any part o' this.'

Witherspoon watched as Barnet began to pull the door open. Without thinking, he put his hand in his pocket and slipped out his clasp knife. Soundlessly, he unfolded the blade and without taking his eyes off the Third Lieutenant, he carefully wrapped his hand around the wooden handle. 'Stop,' he ordered hoarsely.

Barnet paused briefly but didn't turn round. 'I won't see you swing, Withers. For God's sake put it back.' His whisper was pleading.

'What's God ever done to 'elp,' Witherspoon scoffed, lifting his arm high over his shoulder. A second later, the knife flew through the air and buried itself in the Third Lieutenant's back.

Chapter Seven

Present day

It took Chastity nearly ten minutes to climb up the tree. Each time she pulled herself up onto a new branch, she made sure to carefully test the limb first, being persuaded that breaking a leg or worse right at the Earl's front door would not add anything to the situation. After what seemed like ages, she finally managed to pull herself onto the branch outside the Earl's bedchamber window.

Winded, she sat for a few moments, straddling the limb. Now came the difficult part. She estimated that the distance along the branch to the window was probably about six feet. It felt like a hundred. She would need to shuffle herself along the branch until she was close enough to grasp the window latch.

Swallowing nervously, she pulled herself forward, only to find herself wobbling precariously. 'Don't look down. Don't look down,' she chanted under her breath. She could feel the roughness of the tree snagging on her drawers and petticoat and almost hysterically found herself wondering whether she'd still be wearing any by the time she reached the window. She supposed it was a trifling matter in the grand scheme of things, given that she was actually attempting to gain clandestine access to a gentleman's bedchamber in the middle of the night.

Taking a deep breath, she shuffled forward again. And then again. Slowly, the window came closer until finally, she was able to grab hold of the catch. Quickly, she pushed at the window until it was wide enough for her to slip through. Now was the tricky part. Carefully lifting her right leg, she slipped it over the sill, then grasping hold of the frame on either side of the opening, she pulled herself up and over, until at long last she was standing in Christian Stanhope's bedchamber.

For a full five minutes, she remained still, allowing her eyes to adjust to the darkness. The bed in front of her looked to be huge. Indeed, the Earl could well climb into bed and spend the whole night with her without actually realising she was there. Taking a deep breath, she slowly began undoing the buttons to her dress.

Getting to the second, she suddenly stopped. Truly, she did not have the boldness to wait for the Earl unclothed. What about in just her undergarments? Would that be a good compromise? She tried to think which ones she was wearing. As she hadn't intended to leave the house, her petticoat was her old threadbare one, and she hadn't dared inspect her drawers after shuffling along the tree branch. When the Earl pulled back the covers to the bed, the first thing he'd see would be the hole right in the front of her shift. She gave a small moan. That would be worse than being found with no clothes on at all.

Abruptly, she became aware of how cold the room was. There was no fire in the grate. Mayhap Christian Stanhope truly had found himself on the rocks. Shivering, she made a sudden decision. She was persuaded that neither her naked body nor her threadbare undergarments would likely provoke the required outpouring of lust in the Earl, so she would simply wait in his bed fully clothed.

Indeed, as she climbed under the covers, she wished she'd brought her cloak.

∞ ∞ ∞

The Reverend and Percy watched in open-mouthed horror as Chastity pulled herself agonisingly slowly along the branch towards the open window.

While the clergyman had been all for charging across the street yelling like a banshee, Percy was of the opinion that whilst such an action might well prevent his daughter from breaking and entering, it would almost certainly result in her breaking something else.

'There's no doubt about it, I've raised heathens,' Augustus Shackleford moaned as he watched Chastity finally manoeuvre herself off the branch and drop to the floor inside the room. He shook his head in disbelief as he watched her push the window back to the position it was in before she'd entered. 'What the deuce could she be about, breaking into the Earl's house at this time of night?' Percy refrained from commenting that, in his opinion, breaking into the Earl's house in broad daylight would not have made it any better, aside from the fact that she would more likely have been spotted.

'Thunder an' turf, Percy,' the Reverend muttered as a thought suddenly occurred to him. 'What if that room she's just entered is Stanhope's bedchamber?' He grabbed the sleeves of his curate's cassock fearfully. 'I mean, what if he finds her there?'

'Well, I very much doubt his lordship will retire this early,' Percy responded in his most reassuring voice.

'Oh dear Lord, mayhap she intends to seduce him,' Reverend Shackleford continued, his voice rising in panic. 'That's it, Percy, that's the totty-headed baggage's plan. I know it.' He wrung his hands in agitation. 'Where did I go wrong, Percy? Eight daughters and every last one of 'em's been involved in some kind of havey-cavey business.'

Percy didn't think that now was the time to remind his superior that much of the havey-cavey business had been instigated by the Reverend himself...

'But breaking and entering in order to seduce a gentleman...,' Augustus Shackleford groaned, shaking his head in disbelief. 'I thought we were over that kind of wanton behaviour once we got Temperance leg shackled.' The clergyman peered towards the offending window but couldn't see any movement in the room. After a few seconds, he took a deep breath, straightened his shoulders and said, 'Right then Percy, there's no time to lose. Follow me,' before marching across the road towards the Earl of Cottesmore's townhouse, an enthusiastic Freddy in tow.

His heart dropping faster than you could say, 'Amen,' Percy hurried after him. Once under the tree, the Reverend handed the curate Freddy's lead and pulled off his cassock.

'What are you doing, Sir?' Percy whispered heatedly.

'I'm going after her of course,' his superior retorted. 'It's up to me to save her from herself, Percy. There's no one else to do it.'

'But what about you, Sir? Who's going to save you if you fall out of the tree?' Percy questioned anxiously.

Reverend Shackleford paused and creased his brows as he pondered the curate's words. 'You're absolutely right, Percy,' he sighed at length. 'I'd flatten you if I landed on you all the way down here. You'll just have to climb up behind me.'

'Me?' squeaked the small man, 'but how will that help, Sir?'

'Well, you're a bit younger than me Percy, and even though it pains me to say it, a trifle nimbler on your feet.' The Reverend folded his cassock and placed it on top of Chastity's cloak. 'All you have to do if I look like I'm slipping is give me a quick push in the opposite direction.'

'But what about Freddy?' the curate asked, his voice taking on a frantic note.

'Don't you worry about Freddy, he'll be perfectly happy sitting on top of your robe. Come along Percy. No more excuses. Let's have your frock.'

For all of about five seconds, the curate actually considered refusing, but then he thought about his impending conversation with Lizzy Fletcher. If the Reverend should cock up his toes before that happened...' Hurriedly, he stripped off his cassock.

'You stay there, Freddy lad,' Reverend Shackleford murmured as he tied the foxhound to a low-hanging branch and bundled up Percy's cassock to make it more comfortable. 'We won't be long.' Then he turned towards the lowest branch, coughed and attempted a slight jump. After the third attempt, he managed to hook his arm around the limb. 'Now would be a good time for the first push, Percy,' he puffed as he swung slowly backwards and forwards in midair. 'Like old times, eh Percy,' he wheezed as the curate reluctantly placed a hand under each swaying buttock. 'That's it lad, give me a hard shove.'

Grimacing, Percy bent forward slightly and then pushed upwards with everything he had, just as the Reverend tried to help by kicking out with his feet. Unfortunately, his left boot found Percy's nose, and the curate went down like he'd been poleaxed. Seconds later, the clergyman managed to swing his leg over the branch and struggle into a sitting position.

The whole procedure had taken nearly ten minutes. 'What are you doing, Percy?' Augustus Shackleford queried in a heated whisper.

'I fink my nothe might be bwoken,' came the mumbled response from the ground below.

'I can't hear a word you're saying, Percy. Why the devil are you lying on the ground? Having a nap won't get us up this deuced tree. Chastity's honour's at stake here, and that blackguard Stanhope could be up to all manner of wickedness while we sit here prittle-prattling.'

Groaning, the curate climbed to his feet, dabbing at his nose with his kerchief while the Reverend reached up to the branch above him. 'Get a move on, Percy,' he grunted, heaving himself unsteadily to his feet. 'We haven't got all deuced night.'

Half an hour later, they were both finally seated on the branch that butted up to the open window.

'I'm not sure this will take our combined weight, Sir,' Percy panted, as the limb bounced ominously.

'Nonsense,' the Reverend mumbled, not daring to look down. Truly, he hadn't considered how high up their intended destination was.

'What do we do now?' Percy went on.

'Well, we can't stay here,' Reverend Shackleford declared. 'I think I've rubbed a hole in me breeches, and if I sit in this position much longer, it'll be me baubles next.' Wincing, the clergyman shifted slightly, then stopped as the branch groaned ominously.

'How are we going to get to the window?' Percy's question contained more than a hint of panic.

Reverend Shackleford was silent for a moment, giving the curate the distinct impression that his superior actually had no idea.

'The distance seems awfully long, Sir. Mayhap we would be better to try and climb back down.'

'Don't be so deuced lily livered, Percy. I'm certain we've been in worse situations than this.'

'When?' Percy hissed as the branch creaked.

Augustus Shackleford gripped the branch tightly and swallowed a small moan.

'Father! What in blazes are you doing?' Both men looked up in alarm to see Chastity's head poking out of the now wide-open window.

'What does it look like,' the Reverend answered through gritted teeth. The branch creaked again, and Freddy started whining from the ground below. The very same ground that looked further and further away each time the clergyman looked.

'I think we might be stuck, Miss Chastity.' Percy poked his head round the Reverend's shoulder.

'Percy!' exclaimed Chastity aghast. 'Have you both lost what little sense you had?'

'Says the bacon-brained baggage who is currently standing inside a strange man's bedchamber,' the Reverend bristled. 'If you ha...'

He stopped abruptly as another smaller face suddenly appeared at the window. Chastity jumped, giving a surprised yelp.

'Who are you, and what are you doing in Papa's bedchamber? Why are there two men in that tree?'

'Do you think Stanhope will offer for her?'

'I've no idea. Nicholas clearly dislikes him, but given that the only other man to show any interest is Viscount Trebworthy...' Grace sighed and shook her head.

'You can't possibly think to shackle her to such a dreadful individual,' Hope declared, the horror in her voice echoing the feelings of all the sisters present.

'Well, at least he isn't a suspected murderer,' retorted Grace.

'Not yet, but I can't see Chastity lasting very long if she's forced to get close enough to kiss the revolting man.' Temperance muttered, pulling a face.

Faith shuddered 'Surely Nicholas won't make her wed such an imbecile?'

'Of course he won't,' declared Patience. 'He's never forced any of us along a path we didn't wish to tread.'

There was a silence as the five women contemplated the hobble that their younger sister was in - every one of them thinking, *there but for the grace of God...*

The sisters were sitting in the family box at the newly rebuilt Theatre Royal in Covent Garden during the interval of *Pygmalion*. Their husbands had gone to obtain refreshment.

'I seem to recall that Christian Stanhope was exceedingly handsome,' commented Hope eventually.

'That won't count for much if he puts Chastity to bed with a deuced spade,' commented Patience with her customary lack of tact.

'I know very little about him,' confessed Grace, 'other than the fact that he unexpectedly inherited the Cottesmore title.' She frowned before adding, 'Nicholas is being frustratingly close-lipped, but the fact that he's giving the Earl an audience at all, tells me he is not entirely convinced that Stanhope is a lost cause.'

'Isn't there anybody else who might be willing to take Chastity on?' Temperance questioned. 'I mean she's certainly attracted a lot of interest since she arrived in London.'

'And none of the conceited popinjays will touch her with a six-foot barge pole when the scandal breaks,' Patience snorted.

Hope sighed. 'You're right, of course. They're all so far up their own posteriors, I wouldn't wish any of them on Chastity. She's far too much of a romantic to be pushed into the arms of someone who would forever consider her beneath his touch. It would destroy her.'

'Well, Stanhope certainly didn't look like a conceited popinjay,' declared Faith. 'I watched him when he and Chastity were dancing. He looked to me like he didn't give a tinker's damn what anybody thought of him. And yes, he was exceptionally handsome. So providing he's not actually a murderous goat who's too free with his fists, I think Chastity could do a lot worse.'

'What about the Queen,' Hope asked. 'Could her majesty be persuaded to overlook such a small indiscretion? With Charlotte's backing, the spiteful gossips would be stopped in their tracks.'

'I suspect the Queen has enough on her plate dealing with Prinny's appalling treatment of her granddaughter,' Grace countered.

Patience nodded her agreement. 'I don't think we can expect any outright support from Charlotte, but I'm fairly certain she would quell the nastier of the gossips should Chastity find a suitor.'

Before they could continue the conversation further, the bell rang for the second half.

'We'll simply have to wait until Nicholas has spoken to Lord Cottesmore,' Grace concluded hurriedly before the men arrived back. 'I'll send each of you a message as soon as I've managed to prize the outcome out of my frustratingly reticent husband...'

Chapter Eight

Chastity stared in disbelief at the small girl standing next to her at the window, for once, completely speechless.

'Are you Papa's friend,' she continued curiously. 'I didn't think Papa had any friends who are ladies. The scullery maid said she'd be his friend, but when I told Papa, he said...' she paused and thought for a second. 'He said it was very kind of her, but he had enough friends already. But I don't think that's true, because you're the first I've seen. What's your name? Mine's Mercy, short for Mercedes.'

'There's no deuced time for formal introductions. In case it escaped your notice, we have an emergency here. Any second now, me and Percy are going to end up splattered all over your father's front garden.' As if in answer, the branch gave another warning creak. Percy gave a small moan which was answered by a mournful woof from below.

'Have you got a dog?' Mercy questioned excitedly, peering on her tiptoes out of the window. She clearly hadn't grasped the urgency of the situation.

'He'll be a very deuced dead dog if we land on him,' warned the Reverend darkly.

'Father!' Chastity chided. 'You shouldn't say such a horrible thing in front of a child.'

Mercy frowned, giving up her attempts to detect the foxhound. 'I'm not a child. I'm nearly nine. Papa says I'll soon be having dinner with him. What's his name?'

'Freddy,' Chastity answered faintly, feeling as though she'd somehow stepped into a bizarre dream. 'And I'm Chastity. It's very nice to meet you. But as you can see … Mercy, we do have a bit of a problem. These two … err… gentlemen are stuck in the tree, and we have to think of a way to get them down.' She'd only narrowly avoided using the word *idiots,* but the glare she tossed her father spoke volumes.

'Well, they should lie down flat,' Mercy declared matter of factly. 'Everyone knows it will help to spread their weight. Haven't you ever climbed a tree before?' The last was addressed to the Reverend. Unfortunately, he didn't trust himself to answer.

'She's right, Father. If you can manage to flatten yourself against the limb, you'll be able to manoeuvre yourself along the branch towards us. Percy, hold on to the main trunk until it's your turn.'

Chastity leaned further out of the window to provide a little moral support which was mostly along the lines of, 'Get on with it, Father. You can do it.'

'I'm not sure he can,' piped up a small voice beside her. 'He's very fat.'

Hearing the low comment, Reverend Shackleford gritted his teeth. 'I'll show the little know-it-all,' he muttered under his breath. Slowly, he leaned forward until his torso was lying horizontal on the branch, or as horizontal as he could get it. Unfortunately, he feared the child was right, he had put on a smidgeon of weight. Taking hold of the limb in front of him, he dragged himself forward, inch by agonising inch. By the time he was within touching distance of the window, in what felt like hours later, he was fully convinced he was well on the way to becoming a eunuch.

Reaching out, he grasped hold of the frame and pulled himself forward until he fell in an undignified heap onto the bedchamber floor. Winded, he remained where he was for a second, until a sudden yell together with a dull thud got him struggling to his feet.

Joining the other two at the window, he groaned as he realised the branch had finally begun to split at the trunk, so the end was now resting against the sill. Percy was still gripping the trunk of the tree as though his life depended on it, which it very probably did.

'There's no time to lose, Percy,' Augustus Shackleford called. 'Just do the same as I did. I'll grab you as soon as I can.'

'Promise?' Percy's question was little more than a whisper.

'Have I ever let you down before?' the Reverend retorted, then winced. It probably wasn't the answer Percy was looking for. 'Come along lad, don't be so chuckleheaded. Where's your backbone?' He'd found that kind of encouragement usually had the desired effect. When the curate didn't move, he added, 'If you don't shift your deuced arse Percy Noon, you're going to end up headfirst in Stanhope's shrubbery, and I don't think the Almighty's ready for you yet.'

Giving a small sob, Percy let go of the trunk and gingerly leaned forward until he was flat against the branch. Everyone held their breath, but the limb held.

After a few seconds the curate began inching himself along the branch. His progress was excruciatingly slow, and the three figures at the window silently watched in trepidation. When Percy was a stone's throw away from safety, the Reverend leaned out of the window. 'Give me your hand, lad,' he ordered. With a small moan, the curate reached out his hand, just as the branch gave way.

The moan turned into a loud shriek as Percy felt himself slide down the falling limb, only to be halted as the Reverend managed to grasp his proffered hand. The branch crashed to the ground-fortunately missing Freddy who'd had the good sense to tuck himself into a corner - leaving Percy swinging in midair and yelling loud enough to wake the dead. 'Give me your other hand,' the clergyman bellowed over the din 'and I'll pull you up.'

Seconds later, the Reverend managed to grab hold of the curate's flailing hand and was just about to pull him up when Freddy began barking.

What the devil is going on?' a voice thundered abruptly. Chastity watched in horror as Christian Stanhope stepped into the circle of light provided by the streetlamp.

'Oh, hello, Papa,' shouted Mercy gaily. 'One of your lady friends has come to visit.

27th June 1798

As Barnet fell to the floor, Witherspoon hurried over. The knife was buried up to the hilt, blood already seeping into the lieutenant's shirt. Wincing, Witherspoon pulled out the knife, increasing the crimson flow which now began to drip onto the floor. Turning Barnet over, he checked for signs of life, grimacing as he heard a faint rattle. *The bastard was still breathing.* Callously, Witherspoon leaned over the prostrate man and pressing one hand against his mouth, pinched his nostrils closed with the other. Seconds later, he was certain Barnet was dead.

Climbing to his feet, the Fourth Lieutenant bent to pick up his pistol, and after checking the ruby was still in his pocket, stepped over the corpse, intending to escape while he still had time. He was about to pull open the door when the sound of running footsteps came from the lower deck. Swearing, he glanced around wildly, but there was no time to hide. As the footsteps approached, he hurriedly stepped behind the door, just as it was pushed open.

'What the...,' muttered the figure as he spotted the Third Lieutenant's body lying feet away.

Sweating, Witherspoon watched as Stanhope crouched down to examine Barnet's lifeless body. What the bloody hell was the bastard doing down here? Witherspoon knew he had seconds before Stanhope turned round and saw him. He felt in his pocket for the clasp knife, then saw it lying a few yards away from the body. *Shit.* Heart slamming against his ribs, he lifted the pistol and stepped forward. The Second Lieutenant must have heard something because he began to turn, just as Witherspoon slammed the butt of the pistol onto his head. Instantly, Stanhope slumped over the body, out cold.

Panting, Witherspoon pulled Stanhope off the dead man, then rolled Barnet's body back onto his front. Inside his head, a voice was screaming at him to run. Ignoring it, he turned to the Second Lieutenant. Blinking away the sweat dripping down into his eyes, he dragged Stanhope's prone form, and with a low grunt, lifted the man's torso, draping it across Barnet's corpse.

Wheezing, Witherspoon hurried over to the Maltese treasure, lifting the lid of the chest containing the jewellery. Quickly he pulled out a bracelet before closing the lid and going back to Stanhope who fortunately was still unconscious. He tucked the trinket into the Second Lieutenant's pocket, pocketed the clasp knife belonging to Stanhope, then went to the knife still lying on the floor and pushed it into Stanhope's hand, closing his limp fingers around the hilt. Straightening up, he felt in his pocket for the ruby, and pulled it out. After staring at it for a few seconds, he took a deep breath and popped it into his mouth. For one horrifying second he thought he was going to choke on the gem, but frantic scrabbling in Stanhope's britches revealed a small flask of grog. Desperately, he poured the liquid into his mouth and finally managed to swallow the ruby down.

Closing his eyes, he remained where he was, waiting for his heart rate to go down. What happened next would determine whether he or Stanhope were strung up from the yardarm. Then, taking a few deep breaths, he turned, threw open the door and ran towards the hatch, shouting at the top of his voice.

Present Day

Chastity felt sick. What on earth had she been thinking? And the worst thing was, Christian Stanhope was clearly aware she had been in his bed. After his thunderous entrance, the Earl had wasted no time heading up to his bedchamber, entering the room just as the Reverend managed to pull a sobbing Percy in through the window.

His face was white with fury. Which didn't seem to bother his daughter overly as she skipped over to give him a hug. Bending down, he asked in a low voice if she'd been hurt. Chastity opened her mouth to declare indignantly that she wasn't in the habit of harming children, but when he looked up again, his eyes were glacial. Hastily, she shut her mouth and swallowed nervously.

Holding on to his daughter's hand, he glanced over at the now rumpled bed and raised his eyebrows.

'Mercedes, perhaps you could show our *guests* to the sitting room while I see to the removal of the tree branch currently blocking our front door.' He bent down and ruffled the little girl's head.

'And once you've done that–bed. His tone brooked no argument, and after giving him a swift peck on the cheek, the child nodded happily and headed towards the bedchamber door.

'I assume the dog keeping the entire street awake belongs to one of you?' he went on as the three of them hastily made to follow like guilty schoolchildren. 'Then perhaps you will be so good as to fetch the hound in.' He paused, before adding, 'I trust you won't use the opportunity to leave before we've had a chance to become ... acquainted?' The Reverend simply nodded, for once completely lost for words.

After waiting as they hurriedly retrieved dog and clothes, Mercy led them to a small room which looked as though it had definitely seen better days. The furnishings might once have been luxurious, but they were now worn and tired. The grate held no fire, and the chamber had a distinctly tomb-like feel. Shivering, Chastity took a seat, slipping on her cloak for some added warmth.

Likewise, her father and Percy put their respective cassocks back on before sitting down. Bewildered, Freddy lay down by the defunct fireplace and stared at his master.

For the first half hour, they sat in silence, the only sound being voices outside the window. Clearly, the Earl had roused the staff to help him move the offending tree limb.

Unsurprisingly, they were offered no refreshment, and as the clock ticked by, Chastity began to get more and more agitated. At length, she could stand it no longer. 'Grace and Nicholas are bound to have returned by now,' she fretted. 'If they discover we are not in our beds...' She gnawed at her fingernails, unable to finish the sentence.

'Well, unless they come to tuck us in, they're unlikely to find out until morning,' Reverend Shackleford reasoned, 'and by then, we should be returned home.'

'But what if the Earl really is a … murderer?' Percy murmured the last word in an anxious whisper.

'What if he is?' the Reverend retorted. 'I doubt he'd look to see us juggling halos on his own property when half the servants are abroad.'

'And his daughter's upstairs,' added Chastity. Though she sounded less certain than her father.

'That was a bit of a deuced surprise, I must say,' Reverend Shackleford mused. 'From what Nicholas said, I'd imagined Stanhope to be nothing more than an ivory turner who'd suddenly struck lucky. But it seems there's more to him than that.' He shook his head and turned towards Chastity. 'And while we're on the subject of our host. What the devil did you think you were doing climbing into his deuced bedchamber?'

'I… I…' Chastity grimaced as she wracked her brain for a believable lie.

'And don't think to fob me off with some damn plumper,' her father, added as the silence lengthened. Chastity sagged.

'I wanted to speak with him alone,' she confessed. 'Before his interview with Nicholas tomorrow.'

'And you thought his bedchamber was a good place to hold a private tête-à-tête. Because…'

Chastity's face flamed, but she didn't answer.

'Well, if you were hoping to seduce the fellow, you're certainly not dressed for it,' the Reverend responded matter-of-factly.

'Sir, you're a man of the cloth,' protested Percy, aghast, 'surely you cannot approve of such wanton behaviour.'

'Whether I approve or not has never made a blind bit of difference to any of 'em before now, Percy. But I have to say, of all the schemes my offspring have come up with over the years, I think this one might be the most totty-headed.' He shook his head and sighed. 'And to think Percy and I nearly ended up in matching plots trying to save you from yourself.'

'I was desperate,' defended Chastity. 'The alternative is Viscount Trebworthy.'

'Well, I think even I might have chosen me in such circumstances...' All three sets of eyes swung to the door at the sound of the dry comment, and Chastity coloured up.

'But what I'd like to know,' Christian Stanhope went on briskly, striding into the room, 'is why you thought to choose *me* as an alternative to the good Viscount. Clearly I am not swimming in lard.' He gestured to the worn furnishings. 'And I'm almost certain the Duke of Blackmore has wasted no time blackening my character.' He shook his head. 'Truly madam, as flattered as I am that you've taken such extreme measures to capture my attention, I can assure you, I am not a good catch.' He seated himself in the only available chair and crossed his legs, clearly waiting for an explanation.

'Well, that might be true if...'

'And you are?' the Earl quizzed.

'Her father, my lord.' He nodded towards Percy who was busy trying to make himself invisible. 'And this is my curate, Percy Noon.'

The Earl quirked a dubious brow. 'It's not often I find myself nonplussed, but I must confess I'm entirely mystified as to why a man of the cloth might decide to aid and abet his daughter in breaking into a man's bedroom ... via a *tree*.' He gave an incredulous shake of his head. 'I assume Sinclair does not know what you're about?'

Augustus Shackleford sighed. 'No, he does not. But the fact of the matter is, my daughter faces ruin because she was overheard foolishly asking you to dance with her during my son-in-law's New Year's Eve ball.'

The Earl of Cottesmore stared at him disbelievingly for a second. Whatever he'd been expecting the Reverend to say, it clearly wasn't this. He turned towards Chastity who like Percy was busy trying very hard to become part of the furniture.

'I have only been back in London for a short time but have already heard of the eccentricities of the Shackleford family. It seems that you are a chip off the same block, Miss Shackleford. Did you not think to simply come and speak with me this eve?'

Chastity had been staring down into her lap, wishing for a hole to simply swallow her up. At the Earl's address, she gritted her teeth and looked up. It was the first time she'd really looked at him since he'd entered the room. For a brief second, Christian Stanhope's sheer masculine beauty stopped her breath. She realised he was clad only in a shirt and breeches. His sleeves were still rolled up from shifting the infamous tree branch revealing tanned forearms that for some reason seemed ridiculously intimate. She met his eyes. They were alert, but no longer furious. The silence lengthened, and she realised he was waiting for her side of the story.

Twisting her hands in the fold of her cloak, Chastity took a deep breath. 'I tried, but your butler informed me you were not at home to visitors.' She paused and bit her lip. 'I saw you go out, my lord, and I didn't know what to do. I... I ... was going to return home ... but you have an audience with Nicholas tomorrow ... and...' She shook her head, fighting tears. Christian Stanhope merely waited, watching her, much as she imagined a cat would a mouse.

'I appreciate that it is concerning another matter,' Chastity managed to continue, 'but it is my understanding that my brother-in-law intends to bring up the ... contretemps I find myself in.' She paused again, trying to find the right words, though she suspected that there weren't any words that would make this night's debacle sound any better.

'I simply wished to appraise you of the situation before your meeting tomorrow,' she said at length. 'To ask that you consider ... that you consider ... err...'

'Marrying you, thus saving you from the even worse alternative, which appears to be Edmund Fitzroy,' the Earl provided drily. Chastity's face flamed anew.

'Well, I have no doubt that the Viscount is the Duke's preferred option. Indeed, I am surprised he's prepared to consider my suit at all,' the Earl went on, 'given that he believes me the foulest of murderers.' He gave a grim chuckle, 'And you Miss Shackleford must be desperate indeed to put your life in the hands of someone you've been told is a cold-blooded killer. I'm persuaded Lord Trebworthy cannot be *that* bad.'

'Are you not then?' Chastity's question seemed to take him aback, and he stared at her impassively for several uneasy moments.

'No, Madam, I am not,' he answered eventually, his voice weary and surprisingly sad.

'Then let us help you prove it,' Chastity blurted.

'Steady on,' Reverend Shackleford protested, 'What's all this we. I really don't think Nicholas will wish us to be involved in such smoky business.'

'I appreciate the offer, Miss Shackleford, but it appears you have your own problems at the moment.' Unbelievably, the Earl gave a wry grin. 'The truth is, as it stands, we're both in the suds.'

'I have to say, my lord, that your assessment of the situation does unfortunately seem to be accurate.' Percy's sudden, unexpected contribution drew all eyes to him. He gave a self-conscious cough before continuing, 'And if that is the case, I believe Miss Chastity's suggestion to have merit.'

Reverend Shackleford stared at his curate as though he'd grown two heads, but before he could say anything, Percy ploughed on. 'Sir, your daughter's best option is to marry the man with whom she… she… behaved… err… *indelicately*. You know that, as do I. And most certainly, the Duke will be cognisant of that fact.' He turned towards the Earl who was staring at him coolly. 'Lord Cottesmore, if you are prepared to offer for Miss Chastity, it is to her benefit to assist you in clearing your name.' He gave a slight pause before adding, 'We will help, even if the Duke of Blackmore will not.'

There was an uncomfortable silence during which the Reverend went an interesting shade of puce. At length, it was the Earl who spoke first. 'Forgive me, Mr. Noon, but I fail to see how a mere chit of a girl and two men of the cloth will be able to help me in such an endeavour. Your offer is undoubtedly well meant, but I feel I must decline. Despite your breaking and entering *expertise*, I have no wish to see any harm come to any of you. I have enough on my conscience already.'

Despite wanting to gag his curate mere seconds ago, Reverend Shackleford felt unaccountably miffed at the Earl's dismissal of their aid. He drew himself up indignantly. 'I'll have you know, my lord, that Percy and I have solved stranger cases than yours.'

'What about your daughter?' Chastity interposed quietly. 'What kind of life will she have if knowledge of your supposed crime becomes food for the gossips?'

'And what if we are unable to solve this particular mystery— which, forgive me, but you really know nothing of?' Christian Stanhope bit out. 'Are you still prepared to be wed to a pariah?'

'I believe you when you say you are innocent, my lord,' Chastity declared hotly, strangely no longer afraid of his anger. 'Let us help you prove it.' She paused before adding, 'And yes, being wed to a mere pariah is infinitely preferable to Viscount Trebworthy.'

Chapter Nine

Chastity woke to the sound of the maid drawing the curtains. For once the sun was shining in through the windows, and she revelled in the unaccustomed warmth focused directly onto her bed. She felt as though yesterday had taken place weeks ago. So much had happened since she'd watched Prudence and Anthony throwing snowballs at each other in the park.

Sipping her hot chocolate, she watched the maid build up the fire in the grate. Everything was so different here compared to the vicarage. Back in Blackmore, there was no one to wait on her, no one to help her dress, arrange her hair. It was like two different worlds. Her older sisters all appeared to enjoy the trappings of wealth, but she noticed that when they returned to Devonshire, they always came back to the vicarage. Tempy had said it was in case she ever forgot who she was.

Thanking the maid, Chastity leaned back against the pillows. Her sisters had all been fortunate enough to marry well, some of them far above their station, and while their courtships had, for the most part, been somewhat... unconventional, the one common factor was love. They were all in love with their husbands, and their husbands were in love with them.

She thought back to her final conversation with Christian Stanhope, before she, her father and Percy had finally taken their leave.

'I hope you are certain about this, Miss Shackleford,' he'd murmured, watching her with enigmatic blue eyes. 'We are talking about the rest of your life. I am not a demonstrative man, so do not expect hearts and flowers. This is a business arrangement and will never be anything more.' He paused before adding levelly, 'I have a child and have no expectations of another. That said, if being a mother is important to you...' He left the sentence unfinished, and her face coloured up at the implication. Clearly, he was leaving the decision as to whether there would be any intimacy between them up to her.

Sighing, Chastity leaned back and closed her eyes. It was better this way. She'd been a foolish child with her notions of romance. Her sisters had been fortunate, but marrying for love wasn't the way of the world, and it would be too much to expect that all of them would be so lucky. At least she wouldn't have to cover her nose with a kerchief every time she got close enough to have a conversation with the Earl. Resolutely, she buried the thought that simply looking at Christian Stanhope made her heart race and her stomach do somersaults.

Climbing out of bed, she washed in the now lukewarm water left by the maid, before dressing hurriedly. Fortunately, on returning home in the early hours, they had not encountered either Nicholas or Grace, so she was not concerned that breakfast might be a constrained affair. Even so, she was determined to reinforce her preference for the Earl of Cottesmore as a suitor–her brother-in-law would almost definitely express his doubts that Stanhope would even be prepared to offer for her. The knowledge that the Earl had already agreed to do so, she'd naturally keep to herself.

She hated to lie to the Duke, but she was persuaded that admitting to her reprehensible actions over the past twelve hours would do nothing to further her cause. Her father was of the same opinion, with the additional emphasis that, in his opinion, omission was not the same as pitching the gammon.

She was exceedingly disappointed therefore when she discovered on entering the breakfast room, that the Reverend had chosen to take his breakfast in bed. 'Deuced chucklehead,' she muttered as she helped herself to bacon and eggs. As she sat down at the table though, she had a sudden thought. What if he really was indisposed? Climbing trees in the middle of the night was not the kind of activity a gentleman of his age would be inclined to indulge in. She put down her knife and fork, feeling a sudden onset of panic. There was no sign of Percy either, which was a good sign, but everyone else was here. Prudence and Anthony were arguing over the last piece of toast, Grace was helping Jennifer peel an apple and Nicholas was closeted behind his newssheet, clearly hoping to avoid any further discussions about his upcoming meeting with the Earl of Cottesmore.

She was just about to excuse herself when all of a sudden, the front doorbell rang. Everyone looked over at the door in surprise, and the table fell silent. A social call this early in the morning was highly unlikely. The Duke lowered his newspaper as a knock sounded on the breakfast room door, opening a second later to reveal the stooped form of Bailey.

'You have a visitor, your graces,' he intoned formally. Before Grace could ask who it was, a slight figure stepped around the elderly butler with a broad smile.

'Felicity!' exclaimed Grace, jumping to her feet in pleasure. 'We weren't expecting you until the end of the month. She hurried over to her friend, and abandoning formality, threw her arms around the matron in delight. Laughing, Felicity Beaumont returned the Duchess's hug. 'It's good to see you too, your grace,' she responded when Grace finally let her go.

'You know better than that, dearest friend,' Grace said reproachfully at Felicity's use of her title. 'Please, join us,

Bailey will see to your luggage.' She looked over at the butler with a grateful smile. He nodded and bowed his head before withdrawing.

'How are you, Miss Beaumont,' Nicholas asked with a warm smile, his affection for his wife's former tutor genuine.

'I am well, thank you,' she responded, smiling in thanks as the maid brought her a dish of tea.

'Whilst we are eternally grateful for your early arrival,' the Duke went on drily, 'given that as usual, things are going rapidly to hell in a handcart in your absence, may I ask what brings you to us a month earlier than planned?'

Felicity gave a small rueful chuckle. 'In truth, I'm not sure, your grace. I woke yesterday and simply felt that I should come.' She paused, then added, 'I have learned not to ignore my intuition.'

'Well, it's a good thing you're here, Miss Beaumont,' Prudence declared matter-of-factly. 'Chastity's well and truly tied her garter in public, so she's going to have to marry either the Earl of Cottesmore who murders people with a knife, or Viscount Trebworthy who murders people with his breath.'

27th June 1798

When Christian came to, he was locked in the brig. Wincing, he felt the top of his head, feeling an egg-shaped lump crusted with dried blood. What the devil had happened? Why the bloody hell was he locked up? Groaning, he staggered to his feet and limped towards the front of the cell. Pressing his face against the bars, he realised he was back on HMS *Phoenix*. The inside of his mouth felt as though something had died in it. A wave of nausea rocked him, and he felt inside his pocket for his flask of grog. Unsurprisingly, it was gone. Closing his eyes, he gripped the metal and waited for the sickness to pass.

Feverishly, he thought back to the last thing he could remember. There was a body in the hold. Barnet. The sudden shock of recollection sent him to his knees. Groaning, he crawled to the brig wall and collapsed with his back to the damp wood.

Ignoring the pounding of his head, Stanhope sought to retrace his steps. He'd spied the Third Lieutenant going down the main hatch. After ten minutes, when Barnet didn't come up again, he'd decided to investigate. After ordering his men to carry on, he made his way down the hatch. At first, it had seemed as though Barnet had vanished, but after hearing a sudden thud aft, he made his way towards the hold.

The last thing he remembered was pushing open the door and seeing Barnet's lifeless body. He crouched down, and then ... nothing.

Christian put his head in his hands. He felt as though his brain contained nothing but fog. He couldn't think straight. Creasing his brow, he fought the urge to cast his account and strained to remember. There had been a knife wound in the middle of the third lieutenant's back, but no knife... No, that wasn't right. There had been a clasp knife on the floor about a foot away from the dead man. The blade had been covered in blood. He began to sweat as the pain in his head reached a crescendo. A noise. Someone behind him. Still crouched beside the body, he'd started to turn... He remembered the sight of a raised hand followed by a blinding pain in his head.

Abruptly, Stanhope leaned forward and threw up. Dear God, was he having a seizure? That was his last thought as he slumped to the side and passed out.

Present day

Lizzy Fletcher stared out at the driving rain. The weather for January had been unusually wet, even for south Devonshire. She supposed it indicated that further north they were knee deep in snow. Shivering, she pulled her woollen shawl tighter and huddled next to the fire. She bloody hated the rain. If she'd had any sense, she'd have taken herself nearer to London. Definitely drier up there, and nearer to her brother. Useless good-for-nothing bastard he might be, but he was the only flesh and blood she had left.

Her husband gone these two years and no children–at least none that had survived long enough to walk, she didn't know why she was still here.

It had been Charlie's idea to come to Blackmore. He said the new Duke of Blackmore was the finest man he'd ever served under. He'd promised to let no man starve, even if he only had one arm. So they'd come to Devonshire, with nothing but the clothes on their back. And true to his word, the Duke had made sure they had employment. Rented them a small cottage on the edge of the village. They scraped by, although there wasn't much call for sailmakers, especially those missing an arm. But her Charlie was quick-witted, and still handy with a needle. They'd taken in sewing, mending and the like. From the big house and from those in the village who could afford it.

Then one morning, he announced he was off to London. Said he had to see a cull about some money he was owed. She never saw him again.

And now all she had left of him was his gold tooth. Charlie had pried it from his mouth just before he left. If something happened to him, he said she was to keep it for a rainy day.

Lizzy gave a dark chuckle. If ever there was a bloody day wet enough, today was it.

Her thoughts turned to Percy Noon. Gawky, thin as a bleeding rake, but still, there was something about him. She thought perhaps it was his kindness. It certainly wasn't his looks. But then, she was no bloody oil painting, and at nearly six feet, she towered over most men, including her Charlie.

The curate had taken to popping in on his parish rounds, and they'd share a glass of milk and talk. They talked about anything and everything. He was used to hobnobbing with his betters, and at first, she was flattered he seemed to like talking to her. But gradually, she began to hope there might be something more.

She still didn't know why she'd shown him the tooth. Looking back, it had been a bird-witted thing to do. What man would want to be shown another man's tooth, especially one still stained bloody from where he'd pulled it from his mouth?

She thought perhaps she'd wanted to show him she wasn't a woman without means, and there was a fair bit of gold in Charlie's tooth.

Percy hadn't seen it that way though. He'd given her one horrified look and made up an excuse that he needed to get back to the vicarage, and she hadn't seen him since. She knew he was in London with the Duke's family, but that was all.

Lizzy sighed. Percy Noon had gone from her life. In truth, he hadn't ever really been in it. A glass of milk once a week hardly counted as a courtship, even if she had asked him to call her Lizzy.

Hope was a fickle thing. In truth, she was better off without it. She hadn't realised just how much she'd been hoping–until she stopped.

Mayhap it was time to sell Charlie's tooth, but she didn't know who to take it to. There was no one in Blackmore who had the blunt. She looked outside at the rain, still hammering against the windows. Was it raining in London? More likely snowing or Reverend Shackleford would have returned home by now.

Leaning closer to the candlelight, she attempted to thread her needle, her mind still deep in thought. Her brother John would know where to sell the tooth. She couldn't send it to him for him to sell though. She'd never see the bleeding coin if she did. But there must be plenty of places in London she could take it herself. All she needed was some names. Surely John wouldn't begrudge her that?

She hadn't seen her brother in ten years, not since she and Charlie came to Blackmore, but he sent her the occasional letter, and she knew his address. But how would she get there? A stagecoach would cost too much, and she wasn't even sure it would be running in this weather. She'd have to get to Torquay first. Abruptly, her fingers stilled as she recalled a conversation with Mrs Higgins up at the big house the day before.

Lizzy had been taking back some napkins she'd darned when the cook had happened to mention that Jimmy Fowler was off to London to deliver some papers to the Duke. Apparently, Jimmy had been insufferable, bragging that the Duke needed him in Town. When did she say he was going? Putting down her needle, Lizzy thought back to the conversation. Tomorrow. Mrs Higgins had said he was going tomorrow.

In sudden reckless excitement, Lizzy climbed to her feet. Would he let her share the carriage? It wasn't something usually done, but if she could persuade Jimmy of her need, then he might agree to let her accompany him. She'd be more than happy to share the box with the coachman. She didn't think the Duke of Blackmore would object, but could she ready herself in time?

Hurrying into the small kitchen, Lizzy grabbed her cloak and bonnet. Without giving herself time to reconsider, she shoved the bonnet on her head, shrugged on the cloak and headed out into the rain.

Chapter Ten

30th June 1798

When Christian Stanhope next woke, he could feel the movement of the ship underneath him. The *Phoenix* was obviously under sail. He was lying on the floor, a filthy blanket his only covering. Beside him, someone had placed a cup of brackish water. Lifting himself onto his elbow, he picked up the cup and drank greedily.

'If you drink it too quickly, you'll only bring it up,' warned a voice from the shadows. Startled, Christian slopped the liquid onto the floor. 'Who's there?' he questioned, his voice coming out as a whispered rasp.

A figure stepped forward. It was Nicholas Sinclair.

Stanhope struggled into a sitting position. He felt as weak as a kitten, but the agony in his head had reduced to a dull ache.

'Why am I here?' he croaked.

The First Lieutenant stepped towards the bars and eyed him in distaste. 'You don't remember murdering a man?' he snapped.

Stanhope frowned. 'Barnet,' he said at length.

'Aye, *Barnet*,' Sinclair bit out. 'What happened? Did he catch you stealing the bracelet?'

'What bracelet? What the devil are you talking about?' Christian answered, struggling to his feet.

'The one we found in your pocket,' Sinclair retorted. 'Did you really think you'd get away with it?' The First Lieutenant shook his head in disgust. 'Enough that you were caught stealing, but to *murder* a man to hide it. I thought you a better man that that, you craven bastard.'

Christian Stanhope simply stared wordlessly at the First Lieutenant, as he fought to understand exactly what had happened. Sinclair's expression turned sickened as he spat out, 'He was your *friend.*' He turned away in disgust and strode towards the door.

'I didn't murder anybody,' Stanhope rasped. 'Barnet was dead when I arrived. And I didn't steal a deuced bracelet–or anything else for that matter.'

Nicholas Sinclair paused as Stanhope continued, his voice an agonised whisper. 'You *do* know me, Nick. And you know I wouldn't do this.'

The First Lieutenant shook his head but didn't turn round. He rapped on the door to be let out.

'Who is my accuser?' Stanhope croaked harshly as the key turned in the lock. 'Who witnessed my supposed crimes?'

For a second, he thought Sinclair wasn't going to answer, then he turned back, his face a mask of anguish. 'It was Witherspoon. Swore you stole the bracelet then killed Barnet to cover it up.'

'So Witherspoon was there?' Christian Stanhope growled angrily, gripping the bars. 'Tell me this, Nick. Who would you trust with your life? Me or that lazy, good-for-nothing bastard?'

The First Lieutenant's mouth tightened. 'You know I would have chosen you every time Kit,' he murmured hoarsely, but Fletcher claimed he saw you too.

'They're both lying,' Stanhope bit out. 'You're going to string me up on the word of a couple of bloody loose screws?'

Sinclair stared back at him, his face expressionless. 'You'll get your chance to speak,' was all he said in the end before shutting the door behind him.

Present day

Christian Stanhope stared unseeing into his morning coffee. As he mulled over them, the events of the night before began to seem more and more like some kind of fanciful dream. Why the devil had he agreed to allow a clergyman, a curate and a chit of a girl to help him locate a killer? In what world could that ever end in anything less than a bloody disaster?

If he had any sense at all, he would advise Nicholas Sinclair of exactly what had transpired, and beg him to forbid the three amateur detectives from involving themselves further.

What a deuced mess. He should never have attended the Duke of Blackmore's ball. Oh he'd been well aware that the invitation had been sent in error, but it had seemed like a good way to inform Nicholas Sinclair that he was back in England. He chuckled darkly. At least it had seemed so at the time, reasoning that in a room full of people, his grace was less likely to draw his cork on sight.

He had no idea how he was going to finally convince the Duke that he really was no murderer. But more than that, he'd hoped to enlist Sinclair's help in locating the true culprit. And so far, all he had to go on was a bill of sale dated the 3rd February 1799.

It stood to reason that Barnet must have observed Witherspoon doing something forbidden, which got the Third Lieutenant killed. That something could only have been the theft of an item from the Maltese treasure chests - something small and easy to hide.

Whatever it was, Witherspoon couldn't risk stashing it somewhere aboard the *Sensible* as he might never have chance to retrieve it. And hiding it on his person would have been suicide. So his only alternative was to swallow it.

It had to have been a gem. One valuable enough to fetch plenty of coin, but not easily traced.

Since he'd been back in England, Christian had visited every jewellery shop in London that he knew had been in business back in the late 1700s, searching for one who had sold something small and valuable in 1798 or 1799. Naturally, since selling small, valuable items was a jeweller's business, there were an abundance of transactions. But Stanhope was specifically looking for an item with no previous history. Which was more of a rarity than one might think since it usually indicated a stolen item, and no jeweller is likely to admit to selling on pilfered goods.

Eventually, he visited a jewellery shop in Belgravia who had sold a particularly fine ruby to one Lady Winthrope. The jeweller in question stated that this particular ruby had been offered for sale by a military man who claimed the gem had been a gift from Egypt.

Whilst always on the lookout for obvious signs that a stone had been thieved, the jeweller was also an astute businessman who knew he couldn't afford to look such a gift horse in the mouth. Consequently, he agreed to find a buyer as long as he received a twenty percent cut. And that, as far as he was concerned, was that.

When Christian had questioned whether he could remember what the seller had looked like, the jeweller had scoffed that it had been sixteen years ago.

However, as the Earl was leaving, the man stopped him just as he was about to walk through the door. 'There was one thing,' he mused, his brow creasing as he endeavoured to remember. 'The fellow had a scar over his right eye. Not very big but it sliced right through his eyebrow. Didn't do anything for his looks, especially as I recall him being a bit Friday faced, even without the disfigurement. Looked like he hadn't had it that long. It was still red and angry, like it had gone bad at some point.'

Christian took a sip of his coffee. Witherspoon hadn't had a scar when last he saw the bastard, but if he'd come by it before leaving the navy, Nicholas Sinclair would likely know about it. And mayhap it would finally tip the scales in his favour.

2nd July 1798

'Stanhope… Stanhope… *Stanhope!* Initially, Christian thought he was hearing things, but eventually he realised the insistent voice was actually somebody speaking to him. Blinking, the Second Lieutenant lifted his head and stared groggily through the bars into the darkness. As far as he could tell, it was the middle of the night. Definitely past midnight–he could remember hearing the bells signalling the watch before he finally fell into a fitful sleep.

Groaning, Stanhope rolled over and climbed to his feet.

'We're nearing Crete,' the disembodied voice hissed. 'Can you swim, Sir?' Christian frowned, trying to make sense of the question and the voice, and grunted in frustration. 'Withers means to see you hang,' whoever it was pressed urgently. 'He's promised Fletcher a reward once we put ashore if he backs his story. Your only hope is to swim for it, but even if you can't, I'd say drowning's a better way to go than swinging from the bleeding yardarm while the bastards are aiming kicks at your feet.'

'Who are you?' questioned Christian, peering into the shadows. He could see the outline of a figure but couldn't place the voice.

'Best you don't know, Sir. I'm goin' to unlock both these doors, but then you're on your own. I ain't risking being cropped alongside you.' The figure stepped up to the bars, his cap pulled low over his head, shielding his face. Swiftly, he unlocked the door, then with a whispered, 'God speed, Sir,' he was gone.

For a few seconds Stanhope stood rooted to the spot. The bastard who'd killed Barnet was Witherspoon. The snake had undoubtedly pilfered something valuable from the Maltese treasure. Likely, it was Barnet who caught him at it.

The second lieutenant placed his hand on the bars and pushed. The door opened with a squeal. He made to step through before hesitating. If he fled now, he'd never get to prove his innocence, but then he knew more than one dead man who'd gone to the gallows swearing they weren't guilty. Cursing under his breath, he tiptoed towards the outer door, expecting it to be thrust open at any second.

The room was almost pitch black, the only light guiding him coming from beneath the door. Pausing on the threshold, he waited for his heart rate to stabilise, then pulled it open slightly, enough to peep through into the small square room on the other side. The weak light came from the top of a short set of stairs. Taking a deep breath, he stepped out of the brig and crept towards the steps. He knew they lead aft, behind the main mast. If he was careful, he'd be able to slip overboard without anyone the wiser.

Heart in his mouth, Christian carefully placed his foot on the first stair, then the next. It took him nearly five minutes to climb the ten steps, and by the time he got to the top, the sweat was dripping into his eyes causing them to sting painfully. The cold of the brig was in complete contrast to the stifling heat up top. He could feel the ship was moving but sluggishly. As he reached the top step, he cautiously poked his head out of the hatch turning a full circle. He could hear voices but saw no one. There was no sign of the French frigate. Likely she'd been despatched under a prize crew to Admiral St. Vincent in Spain.

He could see the dark shape which he assumed was the Island of Crete in the distance. And it was a bloody distance. It was certainly a good thing he could swim, else he'd stand no chance at all. Warily, Stanhope stepped out onto the deck. He couldn't afford to dither too long, or the distance would cease to be even remotely swimmable. He gave a dark inward chuckle. He would almost certainly be jumping to his death. But his anonymous rescuer was right. Better the fishes had him on his terms rather than the bloody Navy's.

Crouching down to minimise the possibility of discovery, Stanhope crept to the starboard side of the ship, rising to his feet only as he reached the railing.

'I never thought you a damn coward, Stanhope.'

Christian froze at the sound of the low voice behind him. Nicholas Sinclair.

'You know better,' he murmured back without turning round. 'But I could shout my innocence to the bloody world for all the good it would do.'

'Step away from the railing,' the first lieutenant went on levelly. Christian looked back over his shoulder. In the dim light, he could see the pistol Sinclair was pointing at his back.

'There's only the slightest chance I'll make it to Crete. We both know that,' the Second Lieutenant bit out, a sudden fury at his position gripping him. 'For the sake of what friendship we had, let me go ... *Sir*.' He spat out the final *Sir* and Sinclair raised his pistol, his own anger momentarily getting the better of him.

The two men watched each other silently, warily. Then the First Lieutenant closed his eyes briefly, his next words coming out in a strained whisper. 'If you're going to jump, for pity's sake, do it now.'

Present day

It had been decided-mostly on Grace's insistence-that the discussion with the Earl of Cottesmore would take place in the presence of herself, Chastity and their father. While Nicholas had balked at first, his wife refused to be moved.

'Chastity has a right to know who and what this man is, should he agree to offer for her,' she'd declared, 'and as for me, I simply couldn't countenance not knowing first-hand what my sister could be letting herself in for.' She'd paused before adding, 'And I am certain my father feels the same way.' Her husband had raised his eyebrows indicating his doubt concerning the Reverend's enthusiasm for tackling the Earl, but he'd not argued, merely requested he be given a few minutes alone with Stanhope to explain the situation before Augustus Shackleford arrived to put his two pennies worth in.

A half an hour before the appointed time, Chastity sat in the small drawing room nervously twisting her hands as she listened to Grace telling Felicity what had transpired.

'Goodness,' was the matron's mild comment when the Duchess had finished. 'I shall endeavour not to stay away quite so long next time.'

'I'm so sorry,' breathed Chastity.

'Oh you don't need to apologise to me,' Felicity Beaumont chuckled. 'I can honestly say, hand on heart, that the Shackleford family has without doubt provided the most stimulating experiences of my life.' She turned to Grace. 'So, this Earl of Cottesmore. Is he a total rogue as his grace believes?'

'In truth, I'm not sure. It's unlike Nicholas to be so intractable, which leads me to believe there is more to their past than he has admitted to.'

'And you, my dear,' Felicity murmured to Chastity. 'What is your opinion of Christian Stanhope–putting aside the fact that he apparently has the face of a fallen angel?'

Chastity bit her lip. Should she confess her actions of the last evening? Admit that she had not only met with Lord Cottesmore, but also his daughter? In truth, she hated lying. She'd never been very good at it. Not like Tempy and Prudence. She opened her mouth to reveal her imprudent actions, when Felicity added, 'Though I would imagine you know very little about him given that you only met him the once.' She gave a low chuckle. 'Indeed, we must be grateful your behaviour has not yet rivalled that of Temperance and Patience at their worst.'

Feeling suddenly sick, Chastity swallowed. At length, she finally managed, 'You are right, Miss Beaumont. I have not had occasion to spend much time with the Earl. Yet despite our brief acquaintance, I do feel most strongly that he is innocent of the crime he's been accused of.'

'And are you willing to gamble your safety on that belief?' Felicity questioned gently.

Chastity nodded, just as the doorbell rang.

'Well, proof of the pudding...,' Miss Beaumont concluded, drinking the last of her tea. 'I will leave you to your... negotiations, though in truth, I would love to be a fly on the wall.' She sighed and shook her head. 'As you can see, my tendencies towards inquisitiveness have increased. I think it must be my age.' Getting to her feet, she gave a warm smile to Chastity. 'Try not to worry, dearest. All will be well. Now, if you'll excuse me, I will go to see to my unpacking.'

Shaking out her skirts, the matron made her way to the door, where she paused, throwing drily over her shoulder, 'Though I expect a full accounting at dinner.'

Chapter Eleven

Christian Stanhope had no idea what to expect on entering the Duke of Blackmore's study. He hadn't seen Nicholas Sinclair for seventeen years. Since returning to London, he'd had occasion to observe his former First Lieutenant from a distance, but close to, he was surprised at how little the Duke had changed.

After being shown into the room by a butler who looked as though he must be nearing ninety, the two men had stared at each other for a few seconds before Christian executed a formal bow, murmuring, 'Thank you for agreeing to see me, your grace.' Nicholas's aloof expression did not change, and neither did he rise from behind his desk. That said, his nod and invitation to sit down was not entirely hostile. *Score one for me*, the Earl thought as he took a seat facing the desk.

'Before we discuss whatever it is you think we have to talk about,' the Duke said steadily, 'there is another matter of which you should be aware.' He paused, clearly searching for the right words. Christian, knowing exactly what the Duke intended to say, almost felt sympathy for him. Almost.

'You may recall that when you attended our New Year's Eve ball in this house, you happened to dance with my sister-in-law,' he said carefully at length.

'How could I forget?' Christian responded smoothly. 'Especially as it was the first time I have been asked to dance by a beautiful woman.'

Nicholas narrowed his eyes. 'If you are aware of what I am about to say, then I would ask that you confess it.'

Christian sighed, his desire to bait the Duke disappearing as quickly as it arrived. 'I am assuming Miss Shackleford has been accused of risqué behaviour by those detestable tabbies who were hanging on her every word,' he commented, 'but I can assure you it was not my intention to compromise her.'

'No,' Nicholas grimaced, 'she did that all on her own.' The Duke's dry comment was so much like the old Nick that Christian had to swallow an unexpected lump in his throat.

'What is it you wish of me?' he questioned flatly, determined to make Sinclair spell it out.

The Duke gritted his teeth. 'Right at this moment, what I want is the truth. Beyond that, we will see.' Nicholas paused and took a deep breath. 'I assume your request for an audience is to finally give me your version of what happened on *Sensible*?'

'Naturally,' Christian managed to respond in a relatively calm voice. What he really wanted was to plant a facer on the sanctimonious bastard's face. However, the Duke's next words took the wind out of his sails.

'I trust you won't object to others hearing your account?'

The Earl frowned, taken aback. At length he shook his head warily. Right on cue, there was a knock on the door. Swivelling round as Nicholas barked, 'Come,' Christian watched with raised eyebrows as the Duchess of Blackmore sailed in, closely followed by Chastity Shackleford, her father, and lastly an older man who looked suspiciously familiar.

'I'd like tae say well met, laddie, but it wouldnae be the truth.' The Earl narrowed his eyes, trying to place the Scottish lilt. The man didn't bother to enlighten him, and suddenly, Christian felt as though he was on trial. His anger bubbled up.

'Mayhap you'd like to bring the rest of the family in while you're about it,' he drawled. 'Or possibly the entire membership of White's? In for a penny as they say.'

'I am entirely happy to share whatever you wish with whomever you wish,' the Duke countered, his voice taking on a hard edge.

'Would you care for some tea, Lord Cottesmore?' the Duchess of Blackmore cut in smoothly, before Christian could retaliate.

'If I'm to be on trial, I would rather my last drink be something a little stronger, if it please you, your grace,' he growled.

'Pour four brandies will you, Malcolm?'

Malcolm! No wonder the man looked familiar. Malcolm Mackenzie had been the leading steward aboard the *Phoenix*.

Gritting his teeth, Christian took the proffered brandy, nodding his head in thanks. After taking a welcome sip, he glanced over at Chastity and her father. Both had had a lot more to say for themselves the night before. Idly, he wondered where the curate was. His musings helped calm him somewhat, and by the time tea had been brought in for the ladies, he'd mostly recovered his equilibrium.

'So,' the Duke of Blackmore declared abruptly as soon as the maid had left the study. 'I dare say your side of the whole smoky business is long overdue. Though if I think you're lying, I won't hesitate to have you thrown out.'

I'd like to see you try, the Earl thought grimly. Out loud he said, 'Before we begin, your grace, I would like to remind you that there is no formal charge against me. I am here at your invitation. As a peer of the realm, albeit a recent one, no matter your private thoughts, I believe you owe me at the very least, civility.' He paused and glared at the Duke before adding, 'What happened to innocent until proven guilty?'

Nicholas took a deep breath. 'As you say, my lord,' he offered formally, 'you have yet to give your account of what happened, and given that you jumped ship before your innocence or otherwise could be established…' He trailed off, clearly waiting.

The two men stared at each other. Christian longed to ask why Nicholas had let him go all those years ago. Had it been for the sake of their friendship? The Earl wondered if he'd ever find out. Taking a deep breath he told his side of the story.

By the time he got to the part where he jumped overboard, even Freddy was hanging on his every word.

'When I leapt into the water, I truly believed I was jumping to my death.' Christian shook his head, forcing back the ever-present nightmares about drowning. 'The only reason I survived was a floating piece of flotsam. I managed to grab hold of a large fragment of timber from who knows where and used it to propel myself towards the shore.

'Once I reached land, I managed to find menial work–enough to keep me alive at any rate. Three weeks later, I made my way to Heraklion. As I arrived, a merchant ship had just docked. She was going to the Americas with a cargo of tea and had put in for repairs. The captain allowed me to work my passage to Boston.' He paused, taking a sip of his brandy, clearly lost in the past.

'In Boston, nobody was interested in my life history,' he said at length. 'It didn't matter what had gone before. There was a sense of freedom I'd never experienced. Safe to say I prospered, and within five years had enough money to purchase my first house.' He shrugged. 'The rest as they say is history and not relevant to our discussion.'

'Did ye nae think o' coming home tae clear yer name?' Malcolm questioned when it became clear that the Earl had said all he was going to.

'How would that have gone any better than onboard the *Phoenix*?' Christian argued. 'They would have locked me up as soon as look at me. America was a new start. An opportunity to make something of myself without any disgrace dogging me. At the time, I had no intention of ever returning to England.'

'So why did you?' Nicholas questioned sharply. 'If you were prospering in the Americas, why come back and risk being ostracised or worse? You had no need of a bankrupt title in a country you turned your back on?'

'I have a daughter,' snapped Christian. Nicholas stared incredulously at him for a second, then sagged back into his chair.

'The whys and wherefores are none of your bloody business,' Christian went on grimly. 'But know this. I will move heaven and earth to ensure she has what is rightfully hers.'

'How old is she?' Grace questioned softly.

Startled at the interruption, the Earl looked over at her. 'She'll be nine on her next birthday,' he offered gruffly.

The Duke gave his wife a warning look. Clearly, he did not want to get sidetracked. 'So you are looking to finally clear your name?'

'I must,' Christian answered simply.

'So how the deuce do you plan to do that?' Reverend Shackleford spoke for the first time, thinking it past time they got to the heart of the matter. He'd been waiting since the early hours to discover what the Earl's plan was. Truth be told, life had been a little boring since the shenanigans in Dartmouth, and he found himself unexpectedly eager to do a bit of investigating. And if it saw his daughter wed at the end of it? Well, all the better.

'I need to track down Witherspoon,' the Earl answered. 'If the varmint is still alive.'

'Why should I believe it was Witherspoon who killed Barnet and hit you over the head?' Nicholas questioned. 'From your account, you didn't actually *see* your assailant. The only witnesses were Witherspoon and Fletcher. And they both told the same story.'

'The same pack of lies, you mean,' Christian bit out, running his hand through his hair in frustration. 'Witherspoon planted that bracelet on me to conceal the fact that he was the thief. Ask yourself why I would be so stupid as to put the bloody thing in my pocket?'

'Barnet interrupted you,' Nicholas reasoned. 'Mayhap you didn't have time to hide it.'

'I've told you that Barnet was dead when I came upon him. As I bent down to check his pulse, there was someone behind the door. That someone was Witherspoon.'

'We found nothing on him to suggest he'd pilfered anything,' countered Nicholas, watching the Earl carefully.

'That's because the bastard swallowed it,' Christian ground out. He turned towards Grace and Chastity. 'My apologies, ladies,' he offered tightly before giving a sigh. 'I have given this much thought. It had to have been a gem. Small enough to swallow, but easily recoverable after my demise.' He grimaced in distaste. 'Once I was dead, he was home free. It didn't matter whether by hanging or drowning.'

'If you're right, then surely he would have sold the gem once back in England.' Chastity blurted, unable to sit silent any longer. Ignoring her brother-in-law's irritated glare, she hurried on. 'There may be a record if he used a reputable jeweller.'

'My thoughts exactly,' the Earl responded with a slight hint of a smile. 'I have already located a jeweller who was sold a very fine ruby in February 1799. The seller was apparently a military man who claimed the gem was a gift.' He turned back to the Duke. 'Tell me this, your grace. Did Witherspoon sustain an injury after my abrupt departure?'

Nicholas frowned as he thought back. Finally, he nodded. 'He caught the end of a heaving line. The *monkey's fist* hit his face as I recall.'

'I remember it,' added Malcolm. 'It was shortly before we docked in Portsmouth. Surgeon thought he was going to lose an eye. It...'

'...sliced through his eyebrow,' Christian finished triumphantly. 'The jeweller told me that the man who sold him the ruby had a nasty scar above his right eye. One that hadn't been done long. When did you dock?'

'It was the middle of January,' the Duke answered decisively. 'I went from the *Phoenix* to my first command.'

There was a silence as everyone in the room digested the Earl of Cottesmore's account.

At length, Nicholas shook his head and gave a weary sigh. 'Would you do the honours, Malcolm?' he said, holding up his empty brandy glass. As the valet refilled the four glasses, the Duke stared at nothing, clearly deep in thought. His face was troubled, and Grace struggled against a sudden urge to go over and kiss his cares away.

Nobody spoke. Any judgement had to come from Nicholas as the assumed head of the family. The only sound came from Freddy snoring by the fire.

Chastity stole a look at the Earl. He was watching the Duke of Blackmore, his face carefully blank. His expression implied he didn't care what the Duke's verdict was, but tension radiated from his body, and she could see his empty hand curling into a fist as it lay on his lap.

She thought back to the little girl she'd met last night. If the Earl of Cottesmore agreed to wed her, she would become a stepmother. The thought was disquieting given that her experience of stepmothers was limited to her own. While Agnes had no malice in her, she spent most of her time either on the chaise longue or in bed. She'd never been particularly interested in any of her husband's offspring aside from Anthony. And she only had time for him at three o'clock on a Friday over tea and crumpets.

But then in her stepmother's defence, the Shackleford brood had been enough to drive even the stoutest soul to their bed with a stiff sherry...

Her thoughts came to an abrupt halt as Nicholas slowly got to his feet. Heart in her mouth, she watched as he walked round the desk to stand in front of the Earl. In answer, Christian Stanhope rose out of his chair. 'It seems I owe you an apology, Lord Cottesmore,' the Duke said after a second, his voice husky with suppressed emotion. He inclined his head. 'It's my hope that you'll accept my assistance in clearing your name, but whether we are able to locate Wetherspoon or not, I will make it clear to my friends and acquaintances that you have both my support and my backing. And whatever they decide, I should be honoured to do business with you.'

Chastity saw the moment the tension left the Earl of Cottesmore's body. A lump came into her throat, and for a second, she thought she might cry.

'You have my thanks,' Christian responded, his own voice equally rough. He held out his hand, and Nicholas gripped it without hesitation. 'I may be wrong, your grace' the Earl continued ruefully after a second, 'but it's my belief we have something more to discuss?'

'Nicholas,' the Duke amended, 'or even better, Nick, as you used to. I have not changed my opinion of the snobberies of polite society. And you are quite correct, we do have something to discuss. However, at this stage, I believe it is best done in private … Kit.' The two men grinned at each other, in perfect accord for the first time in seventeen years.

'Well, given that your discussion is likely to concern the latest of my daughters to tie her deuced garter in public, with your permission, I'd like to remain.' Chastity's face flamed at her father's blunt words as the Duke turned to the Reverend with a rueful chuckle. 'It seems we've been here before, Augustus,' he countered drily. 'Indeed, by now we should be experts.'

Christian Stanhope turned towards Chastity. He didn't speak, but simply smiled at her in reassurance, but rather than comforting her, it had the opposite effect. His smile was devastating, and her heart began pumping wildly. Dear God, how would she ever be able to share a life with this man without losing her heart? Her girlish ideas of love finally vanished completely to be replaced by a longing so profound, it almost brought her to her knees.

And as she stared back at his starkly beautiful face, Chastity realised she was in terrible trouble.

Chapter Twelve

Jimmy Fowler didn't know quite what to make of Lizzy Fletcher. He'd had misgivings about allowing her to share the Duke of Blackmore's carriage but knew Nicholas Sinclair would have done the same thing. But then he was at liberty to do so. It was his carriage.

Jimmy came from a different world. One where you gave nothing away lest it come back to bite you in the arse. The Duke's partiality for charitable actions had taken a long time for Jimmy to understand.

Initially, when the Duke had given him things, Jimmy would simply hoard them, whether needed or not. It had never occurred to him to pass such items onto others. The desperate desire to simply survive meant that any care for one's fellow man could be abandoned at the drop of a hat for something as little as a loaf of bread.

Gradually though, over the years, Jimmy had come to respect his mentor. But more than that, he worshipped him. The Duke could be harsh, but he was always scrupulously fair. He believed that an accident of birth did not make one better and indeed that the wealthy had an obligation to those who had nothing. The villagers in Blackmore did not starve. His grace made sure that even the meanest of them had a roof over their head and food in their belly. And he could always be appealed to for help. If the Duke believed a claim valid, he never withheld his assistance.

Did that stretch to allowing a servant to lend out his carriage to a woman who looked as though she didn't have sixpence to rub together? Jimmy believed so.

But that didn't make the journey any easier or go any faster. After attempting on the first day to make polite conversation (it didn't hurt to get the practice in), Jimmy had subsided to uneasy silence for the following two. He didn't know Lizzy Fletcher. Oh he knew *of* her. Her husband had served with the Duke, and most people thought him too ripe and ready by half. When he disappeared, there wasn't many who missed him. Since then, Lizzy had kept herself to herself, so her asking to come with him to London was a bit of a turn up. He wondered why. As far as he knew, she'd not left Blackmore since the day she arrived.

Still, it was none of his affair. He'd drop her off at Whitechapel and be on his way.

Chastity sat in her bedchamber and brooded. Whatever Nicholas, her father and the Earl were talking about, it seemed to be taking an inordinately long time. It shouldn't be taking this long surely. But mayhap he was having second thoughts. When they'd spoken in the early hours, he'd been desperate. Except, now he had the Duke of Blackmore's backing, he no longer needed her to help him clear his name. But then she reasoned, he might no longer have her brother-in-law's support if he declined to make an honest woman of her.

Unfortunately, there was no certainty of that. Her situation was entirely of her own making and in truth, Stanhope owed her nothing. The Duke would see it so, she knew.

Round and round her thoughts went, until she felt like screaming. The knock, when it finally came, almost had her jumping out of her skin. 'His grace requests your presence in his study, Miss Chastity,' Bailey intoned from outside the door. Her heart gave a dull thud.

'Tell his grace I'll be with him shortly,' she answered breathlessly. Then smoothing down her skirts, she looked into the mirror. She was deathly pale. Almost a ghost in the late afternoon light. Pinching her cheeks and biting her lips to give them some colour, she took a deep breath and headed to her fate.

Her nerves threatened to get the better of her as she stood outside the door, but the sudden arrival of Grace helped to calm her. 'It seems we've been summoned,' her sister declared drily. 'Chin up, darling. Things are looking decidedly better than they did this morning.' Chastity nodded her head and managed a slight smile. Grace touched her shoulder lightly, then, without knocking, pushed open the door and swept into the room, trilling, 'You called, your grace?' She then proceeded to give a deep, mocking curtsy.

Nicholas regarded his wife's exaggerated entrance with amused exasperation. 'Please take a seat, ladies,' was all he said. To Chastity, who'd followed meekly on behind her sister, he gave a reassuring smile.

As they entered, the Earl prepared to stand, until the Duke stopped him. 'As you may well have observed with my wife's theatrical entrance, we do not stand on ceremony in this family. Naturally, it may have something to do with my wife's lowly birth.' Christian's eyes widened at the implied insult, but to his surprise, the Duchess didn't appear at all affronted. 'Lawks, ain't you the cocksure gent,' she grinned as she took her seat.

The Reverend snorted and shook his head. 'Are you certain you wish to join this family,' he sighed. 'All dicked in the nob. Every last one of 'em.'

'Then mayhap my daughter and I will fit in better than I'd expected,' was Christian's only wry comment. As the room fell silent, his eyes sought out Chastity. During the banter, she'd been staring mutely down at her skirts, but at the sudden hush, she looked up, her own eyes locking on the Earl's.

Despite the earlier, lighthearted banter, when he finally spoke directly to her, Stanhope's words were formal, even stilted. A far cry from the arrogant rake with whom she'd made such a cake of herself little more than a week ago. 'I have spoken with his grace and your father, Miss Shackleford, and it's been agreed that a union between us should suffice to keep the gossipmongers at bay. All that remains is for you to accept my offer of marriage.'

Chastity stared at the Earl's unsmiling face. As a proposal, she thought perhaps she'd give him credit for actually opening his mouth, but she supposed she should be simply grateful he was prepared to get her out of the suds. She found herself nodding. Then, clearing her throat, she added an almost inaudible, 'Thank you.'

'I will put an announcement in the Morning Post,' the Duke interjected briskly. 'It should silence the gossips before they get a chance to cause any real damage.'

'Perhaps you would like to bring your daughter to dinner tomorrow evening?' Grace added, having recovered her poise. 'It would be an opportunity for her to get to know us a little.'

'Not sure that's a good thing before the deuced ceremony's over with,' Reverend Shackleford hmphed. While relieved at the thought of getting Chastity leg shackled, it had to be said he was feeling particularly miffed at the thought he would likely now be excluded from any snooping.

The Earl nodded his head. 'That would be delightful, thank you.'

'I will arrange to have dinner early so the children can attend. Would five o'clock suit you, Lord Cottesmore?'

'Christian, please, if we are not to stand on ceremony. And yes, five will be perfect.' Climbing to his feet, he looked over at the Duke who correctly interpreted his anxious expression.

'I'll have Malcolm begin making enquiries as to Witherspoon's whereabouts immediately,' Nicholas assured him. 'In the meantime, do you have the stomach to brave White's with me this evening? Four of my brothers-in-law will be there to offer their support.'

The Earl laughed ruefully. 'I'm not sure which will be worse, facing the gossips or being examined for flaws by the rest of the family.'

'Oh you have no worries about the men,' Grace commented. 'Total sweethearts, all of them. It's their wives you'll have to impress.' She looked over and smiled at Chastity who was quietly watching the exchange.

Chastity dutifully smiled back. It was all very jolly. Old animosities had been put aside, and they were all happily agreeing on the next steps. And not once had anyone thought to consult her. The Earl had hardly looked her way since his proposal as though her approval of the proceedings was a forgone conclusion. She supposed at the end of the day it didn't matter what she thought. By tying her garter in public, she'd become merely a problem to be solved. And solve it they had. Clearly to everyone's satisfaction.

As the Earl made his farewells, lifting her fingers to press a perfunctory kiss on her knuckle, Chastity wanted nothing more than to land him a prime facer.

Her foolishness had got her into this mess, but if he thought her simply the price he had to pay in return for the Duke of

Blackmore's support, he was going to find himself very quickly corrected.

She might have lost her belief in romance, but she'd be damned if she'd be any man's afterthought.

∞∞∞

'D'you know 'ow to find your way to your brother's from 'ere, Mrs Fletcher?' Jimmy asked, eyeing the area the carriage had stopped in apprehensively. 'I mean, it's dark and...' his voice trailed off.

They had been travelling for nearly three full days, and despite the matron's earlier reserve, Jimmy had managed to coax her into conversation. Indeed, by the time they reached the outskirts of London, he learned that Lizzy Fletcher possessed both intelligence and wit. In fact, he was sorry when they finally arrived at the location she had requested.

Peering through the carriage window, Lizzy conceded that the area did not look quite as she remembered, but putting on a brave front, she nevertheless began to open the door. The horses were dancing nervously, causing the carriage to rock violently, and as Jimmy leaned forward to help, he spotted two likely gallows birds loitering in the shadows. Making a quick decision, he slammed the door shut and rapped sharply on the carriage roof. The coach driver needed no further urging, and within seconds, the carriage was turned round and heading back towards the river.

'Whatch you up to, Jimmy Fowler?' Lizzy protested in a shrill voice.

'I ain't abducting you, Mrs Fletcher, if that's what you're thinkin'. I'm lookin' to save' you from the bloody varmints 'angin' around that street corner.' He shook his head. 'If I left you in a place like this, 'is grace'd 'ave me baubles. I'm taken' you to 'is 'ouse. Someone there'll 'elp you find your brother, I'm certain of it.

'He ain't dead!'

Witherspoon looked up in distaste as the statement was followed by a bout of coughing. Christ, the bastard'd be bringing his bleeding lungs up at this rate.

'Who ain't dead?' he questioned when the hacking finally subsided.

'Don't play silly buggers wi' me, Wivers,' rasped his companion. 'You know who I mean. Stanhope. Against all the bleeding odds, the bastard's alive and kicking and back in London.'

Witherspoon sat back on his heels and fought down the sudden panic that threatened to swamp him. 'Says who?'

'I seen 'im wi' me own eyes. All toffed up, walkin' bold as you like down 'aymarket. You reckon e's lookin fer you?'

'Well if he is, he ain't goin' to be lookin' down here is he? If we keep our heads down, we'll be safe enough.'

'It ain't me Stanhope'll be lookin' for. You were the one who stuck a knife in Barnet and left 'im to take the blame.'

'Just remember which side your bread's buttered on, Fletcher. We've got a good set up here. I'd hate for you to lose out because you thought to make a quick few bob.'

'I ain't goin' to be 'ere long enough to make more 'an bloody sixpence. I won't rat you out, Wivers, but I ain't goin' to take a fall for you neiver. Not this time. I've already done my bit. Just fought you ought ta know. Stanhope's back, and the way 'e wos dressed ses 'e ain't exactly purse pinched. Chances are, 'e'll want to clear 'is name, and that means e'll be lookin' for 'is ol' mate Wiverspoon. An' if 'e catches yer–well, if 'e don't kill you 'isself, old Derrick'll do it fer 'im.' He gave another hacking cough, this time expelling a globule of bright red spittle on the floor.

Witherspoon stopped what he was doing and looked up, his face deadly serious. 'Make no mistake, Fletcher,' he growled. 'If I end up with the morning drop, you'll be swinging alongside me.'

'Wot do I care about that?' his companion wheezed. 'This bloody churchyard cough'll finish me off soon enough. I want wot you owe me Wivers afore I kick the bucket. I've done everythin' you asked since we left the Andrew. Even lost me bleeding arm saving your skinny arse from the Upright Man after we got this place.'

Witherspoon gritted his teeth, fighting the urge to run the whinging bastard through. He'd probably be doing him a favour. Better than bloody dying slowly of the white plague.

'I told you, you'll get it,' he snapped. 'Give me until the end of the month. You know we've got a big fight coming up. We'll be swimming in bloody lard once the culls have handed over the blunt. Until then, stay out of o' Stanhope's bloody way. I'll send a request to the Upright Man. He owes us a favour. It's time we put the bastard down like the vermin he is, even if we have to pay someone to do it.'

Chapter Thirteen

'I don't think we should be consigned to the periphery of this investigation, Percy, after all we've been through. After all, if it wasn't for us, both the Duke and the Earl would likely still be at odds.'

'I'm not sure I quite follow, Sir.'

'Well, if we hadn't seen fit to take matters into our own hands, laying the foundations for today's interview so to speak, it might have been a very different story.'

'I doubt Lord Cottesmore would count almost being brained by a falling tree limb right outside his front door as laying the foundations for anything other than an early demise,' Percy argued. 'Surely the Duke will not want us involving ourselves in such a potentially dangerous situation.'

'Tare an' hounds Percy, you've changed your deuced tune a bit since last night,' Reverend Shackleford declared irritably.

'That was before the two gentlemen sorted out their differences,' the curate protested. 'I doubt very much that we will do better than Malcolm in locating this blackguard, and I'm persuaded the Duke has the matter entirely in hand.' He didn't end with *thank the Lord* but the Reverend knew he was thinking it.

'Chucklehead,' Augustus Shackleford muttered, helping himself to a bit more cake, making sure to drop a piece to Freddy.

All of a sudden, the drawing room door burst open to reveal Chastity. 'This is *not* acceptable,' she announced, marching into the room. 'I am not simply an object to be sold. Especially not to such an ... an ... uncouth, ill-mannered individual.'

The Reverend raised his eyebrows as his daughter flung herself into a chair. 'That's not what you said last night,' he observed bluntly.

'He didn't even say a dozen words to me earlier. How can I marry someone who doesn't even deem me worth the time of day?'

'Well, he had plenty to say to you last night,' her father reasoned. 'Thunder an' turf, Chastity, don't throw a deuced rub in the way. Remember the alternative is Edmund Fitzroy.'

'At least he thought me attractive,' Chastity muttered, peeved.

'And that's a good thing?' Augustus Shackleford questioned doubtfully.

'Yes...no, oh I don't know. The fact is I'm just a means to an end, Father. If he has nothing to say to me now, then what will happen after the wedding?'

Her father shrugged, obviously nonplussed. 'Agnes and I get along perfectly well together, and I can't remember the last time we actually spoke. There are worse things, Chastity, believe me. You could have ended up with a gabster.' He shuddered.

'But he thinks me in possession of nothing but fresh air between my ears,' Chastity protested in a softer tone.

'Oh, I'm sure that isn't the case,' Percy piped up vehemently. The Reverend nodded his head in enthusiastic agreement despite the fact that he'd been thinking the exact same thing mere days ago.

'I mean, last night,' Percy went on earnestly, 'he was prepared to accept your offer of help in clearing his name. So surely that says he believes you to be reasonably intelligent?'

'Or he was desperate,' muttered Augustus Shackleford under his breath.

'Perhaps you are right. I am likely overreacting,' Chastity responded, chewing her nail thoughtfully. 'But now Malcolm is on the case, I presume we three are now surplus to requirements.' She sighed, picking up a piece of cake.

'That doesn't have to be so,' declared her father. 'I'm certain there are a myriad of tasks we can undertake to facilitate Malcolm's enquiry.' Both Chastity and Percy stared at him open mouthed.

'Goodness, Father, I had no idea you had it in you to be quite so articulate,' Chastity remarked, her good humour slightly restored. 'Do you have any ideas?' She nibbled on her cake as she waited.

In truth, the Reverend hadn't got a clue, and he was just about to bluff it out when there was a knock on the door.

'Come,' shouted the Reverend, the relief in his voice unmistakeable. Mrs Jenks stuck her head round the door. 'Forgive me for disturbing you, but their graces are out, and I've no one else to ask.'

'What's the problem, Mrs Jenks?' Chastity asked with a frown.

'There's this young man at the door. Says his name is Jimmy Fowler and he works for the Duke back in Blackmore.'

'I seem to remember Nicholas mentioning Jimmy was on his way here,' the Reverend recollected. 'Is Malcolm at home, Mrs Jenks?'

'I think he went out earlier, Sir. Would you like me to check?'

'Why don't you send him up here to us?' Chastity interjected. 'I'm certain Nicholas won't object. I haven't seen Jimmy for ages. It will be nice to see how he is. Would you be able to get him a room ready for tonight, Mrs Jenks? I doubt he will return to Blackmore until he's had occasion to speak with the Duke.'

The housekeeper nodded. 'There is one small problem Miss Chastity. He's not alone. He has a... lady with him.' Her pause before the word lady, spoke volumes.

'Well, I doubt he'd be bringing a deuced lightskirt with him,' Reverend Shackleford grunted. 'Did he say who she was?'

Mrs Jenks shook her head. 'No he didn't, but my goodness, she's uncommonly tall.'

There was a sudden crash as Percy dropped his plate on the floor. Flustered, the curate got onto his knees to pick up the pieces with Freddy's enthusiastic help. 'Please don't worry, Mrs. Jenks,' Chastity murmured waving the housekeeper away. 'It may be that the err ... lady will require a room as well.'

'I'll ready two just in case.' Mrs. Jenks responded. 'Would you like me to bring a small repast perhaps?'

'Excellent idea,' the Reverend declared absently, eying his curate with a frown.

'What the devil's got into you, Percy,' Reverend Shackleford muttered as the housekeeper shut the door. Both he and Chastity watched in astonishment as the curate stood up and looked around wildly. As footsteps came up the stairs, he gave a small moan and began squeezing himself next to the bookcase.

'Are you addled, Percy?' the Reverend demanded, truly mystified. The curate responded to his superior's question by squeezing his eyes shut.

After a quick knock, the door opened again. With one

last bewildered glance at Percy, Chastity stood up. 'Jimmy!' she smiled, eying the now twenty-year-old with not a little admiration. The former ruffian had changed considerably since the Duke of Blackmore had taken the boy under his wing. Indeed, he was no longer a boy.

Jimmy had filled out and was now well over six feet tall. He was also exceptionally handsome, and she found herself actually blushing slightly as he stepped forward and gave a small bow. 'Miss Chastity, it's a pleasure to see you,' he grinned, making an effort to speak as the Duke of Blackmore had taught him. Then, turning towards the Reverend, he added, 'And you, Sir.' He looked around. 'Is Percy not here?'

There was a small silence. Jimmy waited for a second, then, with a small cough turned to his companion. 'This is Mrs. Lizzy Fletcher.' he revealed. 'She's come up to London to see her brother. She wa...'

Augustus Shackleford interrupted with a snort. 'So that's why the chucklehead practically had an apoplexy. 'You can come out now, Percy, the widow's not here for you.'

Lizzy Fletcher narrowed her eyes at the Reverend's words. 'That's right Percy Noon, I ain't 'ere for you. You've got a bleedin'–beggin' yer pardon Miss–'igh opinion of yerself if you think I'd come all the way to London chasin' your skinny arse.'

Jimmy winced and hurriedly interrupted as the curate sheepishly stepped out from the side of the bookcase. 'I was takin' Mrs. Fletcher to her brother's house,' he explained. 'But I... I couldn't leave her in the 'ands of the gallows birds roaming the streets around Whitechapel.'

'Of course not,' Chastity declared, aghast. 'Please Mrs. Fletcher, do sit down and make yourself comfortable.'

After one last glare at the flushing Percy, Lizzy Fletcher sniffed and sat down carefully on the edge of her seat. 'It's very kind of you to allow me to rest 'ere awhile,' she conceded. Once I've got me breath back, I'll be on me way.'

'We cannot possibly allow you to go wandering around the streets of London in the dark,' protested Chastity. 'Especially not Whitechapel.' She paused before adding delicately. 'You're certain your brother has his residence in that particular neighbourhood?'

'It ain't the best, I'll grant yer,' Lizzy sighed, 'but I don't recall it bein' quite that bad last time I was 'ere. But then I had Charlie, so likely I din't pay much attention.'

'Is that the name of your husband, Mrs. Fletcher?' Reverend Shackleford enquired carefully.

Lizzy gave a tight-lipped nod.

'And is he...?'

'Dead. I reckon anyway.' Percy visibly flinched at the widow's abrupt response.

Glancing over at his white-faced curate, the Reverend endeavoured to look suitably sorrowful before adding. 'Err, you don't seem entirely certain of his demise, Mrs. Fletcher.'

'I ain't seen 'is body, it's true,' Lizzy answered with a gruff sigh. 'But 'e's been gone these two years now...' She cast another indignant glare towards Percy before adding, 'An' 'e gave me 'is gold tooth. Pried it right out of 'is mouth afore 'e left. I reckon that meant 'e din't think 'e'd be comin' back...' She suddenly paused and shook her head.

To his infinite surprise, Percy felt a sudden urge to spring to his feet and comfort the overcome widow. He gripped the arms of his chair in case his feet should decide to do something foolish.

A second later, Lizzy gave a small sniffle and looked back up. 'I ain't touched it since the day the bastard walked out,' she sighed, 'but I reckon it's time I put it to good use. That's why I'm 'ere. My brother knows people, an' can tell me who to sell it to.'

'Couldn't you just 'ave sent him the tooth to sell on your behalf?' asked Jimmy with a frown.

Lizzy gave a derisory snort. 'Did I mention 'e was a lying bastard who'd sell 'is own mother fer a shillin'? No, I needed to see 'im face to face. I could always tell when 'e was shammin' it.'

'Forgive me,' Chastity faltered, 'but he doesn't sound like a very nice man.'

'That's cos 'e ain't. Me ma thought bein' in the Navy might 'ave given 'im a few values, but he were no better when 'e came out. Still a bloody ivory turner.'

'He was in the Navy?' Reverend Shackleford asked, intrigued in spite of himself. 'Did he serve under the Duke of Blackmore?'

Lizzy nodded. 'Along with Charlie. That's how we met. They both came out at the same time. Sixteen or seventeen years ago now.'

'Which ship did they serve on?' asked Percy abruptly. Lizzy narrowed her eyes, and for a second, he feared she wouldn't answer. Then she shrugged. 'The *Phee* ... something I think it was called. They never really talked much about it.'

'What's your brother's name?'

Lizzy blinked in surprise at the unexpected brusqueness of the clergyman's question. Uncertainly, she looked between Reverend Shackleford and Percy.

"Is name's John,' she answered hesitantly after a few seconds. 'John Witherspoon. But everyone calls him Withers.'

'I think we should tell his lordship.' Percy's voice was adamant.

'Now let's not be too hasty to cry rope, lad. I say we take old Lizzy to visit with her brother and see how the land lies. That way we can present Cottesmore with all the facts.'

'We might also vanish off the face of the earth if what we know about Witherspoon is true,' Chastity reasoned.

'Tucked up with a spade,' agreed Percy grimly.

'Well, we're not deuced well going to walk in and ask him if he knifed his shipmate seventeen years ago,' was the Reverend's exasperated response. 'We'll let him think we're just there as an escort for his sister. He likely doesn't even know Stanhope's back in England.'

Both Chastity and Percy regarded the stout man dubiously. It was nearly ten o'clock, and for the past hour, Augustus Shackleford had been practically bouncing on his chair after Mrs. Fletcher's jaw-dropping revelation. Being forced to say nothing whilst Jimmy and Lizzy availed themselves of Mrs. Jenk's excellent cold repast had put him on the verge of an apoplexy. Indeed, he'd all but shoved their unexpected guests out of the drawing room the second their plates were empty. Clearly, Lizzy at least thought him foxed.

'Only two hours ago you were bemoaning the fact that your intended considered you empty headed,' Reverend Shackleford pressed. 'At the very least this will force him to sit up and take notice.'

'And thinking me dicked in the nob would be preferable?'

'Oh, I'm certain he's already of that opinion considering you climbed a deuced tree to get into his bedchamber.'

Chastity frowned, then gave a small huff. 'He might lock me up and throw away the key once we are wed,' she declared.

'One can live in hope,' retorted the Reverend, helping himself to the one remaining lemon tart.

'We could at least inform Malcolm,' interjected Percy a trifle desperately.

'Might as well go straight to Nicholas,' snorted Reverend Shackleford, spraying crumbs over a delighted Freddy's nose.

'So your intention is to do nothing aside from simply perusing the premises?' Chastity eyed her father doubtfully. The Reverend nodded vigorously.

'But what if it turns out that Lizzy is her brother's accomplice? Her husband was clearly the Fletcher who lied for Witherspoon on the *Phoenix*. She could be leading us into a trap.'

'She doesn't know anything about the whole havey-cavey business,' scoffed the clergyman.

'So, she could be in danger,' piped up Percy, his voice unexpectedly concerned. Both Chastity and the Reverend turned to look at him in surprise. 'I mean... I... I wouldn't want any harm to come to her, naturally,' the curate added, clearly flustered.

'Do you swear to do nothing aside from perusing the premises?' Chastity gave her father a narrow-eyed stare. At his nod, she added a stern, 'If it should emerge that Mrs. Fletcher may be in some kind of danger, we will immediately withdraw, taking her with us?' Another nod.

'Won't the Duke find out about Lizzy's brother once he speaks with Jimmy tomorrow?' countered Percy.

'Thunder an' turf, I never thought of that,' Augustus Shackleford muttered.

'Nicholas is unlikely to be abroad until midmorning after a late night at White's,' Chastity responded. 'If we set off early enough, we could be there and back before he even comes down for breakfast. It's likely that Mrs. Fletcher will be keen to finish her journey anyway. We just need to persuade Jimmy to allow us to accompany her in his stead.'

'I doubt the lad will be happy with that,' the Reverend frowned. 'He'll go straight to Nicholas as soon as we're out of the deuced door.'

Chastity screwed up her face in thought. 'Well, he'll just have to come with us then. You can tell him that as Lizzy is one of your parishioners, it is your duty to ensure she reaches her destination safely. Which it is.'

'What about you?'

'Chaperone,' Charity declared triumphantly.

The Reverend gave a slow nod, followed by a satisfied smile. 'Well then,' he beamed, rubbing his hands together, 'I think our strategy's as watertight as it's going to get. I'm off to take Freddy to do his business, and then I'll retire. We need a good night's sleep if we're to throw a rub in the way of that scoundrel Witherspoon.'

As he climbed slowly to his feet, Chastity frowned and added, 'Just to be sure, Father, by *throwing a rub in the way*, you're referring to the valuable information we'll be *passing on* to Lord Cottesmore?'

The Reverend nodded happily. 'By noon tomorrow, Chastity, we'll be the toast of the hour. You mark my words...'

Chapter Fourteen

As he entered the Cottesmore townhouse, Christian Stanhope felt as though a huge weight had been lifted from his shoulders. He hadn't realised how much he'd been affected by the loss of Nicholas Sinclair's friendship. In truth, he'd never allowed himself to dwell on it.

He'd told himself that he needed the Duke of Blackmore's support to clear his name, but that had only been a part of it. Seeing Nicholas today told him just how much he'd missed his friend and mentor.

Climbing the stairs to his bedchamber, he imagined Witherspoon's face when he finally came face to face with the bastard. Likely, the former Fourth Lieutenant thought him dead. Though strangely, the thought of bringing Witherspoon to justice did not bring him the same satisfaction as before.

Christian pulled off his shirt and called for a bath, his thoughts turning to this evening. In arriving at White's with the new Earl of Cottesmore, Nicholas was clearly stating his position to those who thought to spread rumours about the Earl's character. While it wouldn't stop some from giving him the cut direct, those who allied themselves with the Duke would almost certainly consider him in their business propositions. And once he hopefully gained a reputation for being a shrewd investor, the sticklers would undoubtedly come running.

Grinning to himself, Christian stepped into the steaming bathtub set by the fire. *What a difference one day could make*, he reflected, settling back into the tub. Last night things had looked dire indeed. He thought back to his first meeting with Chastity Shackleford. He had to admit he admired her spirit. And in truth, she was exceedingly pretty. His thoughts suddenly ground to a halt, and he sat up in abrupt realisation.

In all his musings since arriving home, this was the first thought he'd given to his future wife. At no point in the proceedings had he even given the slightest consideration to how she might be feeling. He'd made no attempt to converse with her. Indeed, he'd hardly even looked at her. He swore softly. She was to be the future stepmother of his daughter. Theirs might be a marriage of convenience on both sides, but he did not wish Mercy to grow up in a cold, unhappy household.

His thoughts went back to his words to her in the early hours of the morning. *I am not a demonstrative man, so do not expect hearts and flowers. This is a business arrangement and will never be anything more.* And worse. *I have a child and have no expectations of another, but if being a mother is important to you…*

Christian ran his fingers through his damp hair in agitation. He'd basically implied he'd accept her offer of selling herself to hide her shame, but not to expect anything in return. He'd even inferred that they would be intimate only if she wanted to become a mother.

The Earl groaned. Fiend seize it, he'd made a bloody mull of things so far. And he had no idea how to put it right. He wasn't in love with her, nor she with him, but that didn't mean they had to live in the kind of sterile relationship he'd described. In truth, he'd been so consumed with his problems, he hadn't been thinking straight.

Absently, he began to soap his shoulders. She'd actually been waiting for him in his bed. Clearly, her desperation to avoid being leg shackled to Viscount Trebworthy was very real. He found himself chuckling at the look on her face. If she'd hoped to seduce him, she hadn't really thought it through.

Suddenly, and entirely unexpectedly, he felt himself harden at the thought of Chastity Shackleford lying in his bed waiting for him. Frowning, he stilled, conjuring her face in his mind's eye. Long chestnut hair. Curly he guessed, remembering the few wayward tendrils escaping her coiffure. Blue eyes with clear skin. He pondered the spots of colour that had been decorating her cheeks. Too late, he wondered whether they might have been there due to annoyance rather than discomfiture.

His mind wandered down to her ample curves. Her dress had been modest but clung as though she'd been poured into it... Christian stopped. The temptation to relieve himself was entirely unexpected and unwelcome. It was simply that he hadn't been with a woman for some time. Shaking his head to clear it, he quickly finished washing and, reaching for a towel, climbed out of the tub.

The important thing was to rectify his boorish behaviour when they met for dinner on the morrow. The marriage had to be a success, if only for Mercy's sake.

∞∞∞

It was still dark when Chastity climbed out of bed the next morning. Shivering in the cold, she hurriedly donned her warmest dress and undergarments. It was still bitterly cold outside, and the snow on the ground showed no signs of thawing, so she decided on her serviceable boots along with an extra pair of stockings. Finally, pinning her hair under her bonnet, she picked up her cloak and made her way downstairs to the kitchen.

As predicted, Mrs. Fletcher had already risen and was fully dressed, her bag at her feet, nibbling on a hot buttered scone. She looked surprised at spying Chastity. Clearly she had not expected them to meet again. Hurriedly, she climbed to her feet. 'I...I was waitin' fer Jimmy,' she faltered.

'You be wantin' a scone, Miss Chastity?' the cook shouted from her place by the stove. Like her father, Chastity was no stranger to the kitchen staff. Indeed, she found its warm, bustling confines a welcome respite from her sister's determined efforts to turn her into a lady. Oh she had no illusions that the staff were oblivious to her fall from grace, but here there was no censure.

The Duke's servants might consider the Shackleford family a little on the eccentric side, but since so many of Nicholas's servants had their own odd quirks, the family's foibles were not viewed as anything out of the ordinary.

'That would be lovely, Mrs. Pidgeon,' Chastity answered honestly. 'My father and Percy will be along presently, and I'm certain they would appreciate a little something too.'

She sat down next to Lizzy. 'We will accompany you to your brother's house, Mrs. Fletcher,' she announced, holding up her hand as the widow opened her mouth to protest. 'It is the least we can do.'

'But you 'eard Jimmy, Miss. It ain't the safest o' places. Wot would their graces 'ave to say if anythin' 'appened to you.'

'I'm persuaded we will come to no harm in broad daylight,' Chastity declared firmly. 'There is after all safety in numbers, and I'm certain your brother will be grateful to have you delivered to him safe and sound.'

Lizzy gave a rude snort. 'I doubt 'e'd care one way or another,' she scoffed.

'Then all the more reason for us to accompany you,' answered Chastity, patting the matron's hand.

'I ain't sure about that Miss Chastity.' Having overheard the last part of the conversation as he walked into the kitchen, Jimmy had entirely abandoned his Ps and Qs in his anxiety. 'The Duke'll string me up 'isself if I let anythin' 'appen to you.'

'Are you suggesting the Almighty will not protect his own?' boomed the Reverend from behind him in the slippery-slope-downstairs tone he saved for special occasions.

Jimmy visibly paled. 'No, Sir, of course not,' he faltered, 'but...' He trailed off and looked desperately at Chastity who smiled helpfully.

'That's settled then,' Augustus Shackleford responded, abandoning the fire and brimstone. 'Mrs Pidgeon, my curate and I will be delighted to take advantage of your good nature and excellent baking skills. Would you be kind enough to wrap up two scones? Percy is even now out braving the freezing cold to summon a hackney coach to take us to our destination.'

Less than five minutes later, they were squashed into a hired carriage whose last occupant had clearly not been on intimate terms with a bar of soap for quite some time, if ever. Either that or he'd been dug up, was the Reverend's muttered verdict from behind his kerchief.

Flinching, Percy improvised with the hem of his cassock whilst Chastity was fortunate enough to have Freddy on her knee. The foxhound's coat might have been less than fragrant, but it was better than the foul air in the carriage, and she gratefully buried her nose in the warm fur to block out the worst of the smell.

Both Lizzy and Jimmy appeared unperturbed by the stink, and staring over Freddy's head, Chastity couldn't help but wonder if her nose had become more delicate since she began mixing in more exalted circles. Mayhap she had been a little hard on Edmund Fitzroy...

Still, on the positive side, it kept conversation to a minimum, or more specifically Jimmy's protests. Unfortunately, it also meant that the three conspirators were less observant than they would have been under other circumstances. Thus, it was only the quick thinking of Jimmy that prevented the theft of Chastity's reticule the very second they stumbled from the carriage. As it turned out, that wasn't the only shock.

As Jimmy gave chase, expertly manhandling the ruffian to the ground and planting him a prime facer, Lizzy let out a loud screech, and picking up her skirts, ran over to the prone man and walloped him around the head with her bag which connected with an ominous crack.

'Blast and bugger your eyes, Charlie Fletcher,' she shrieked. 'Where the bloody 'ell 'ave you been these two years, you good fer nothin' bastard.'

∞∞∞

'Does that mean Miss Shackleford is going to be my new mother?'

Christian stared down at his daughter, searching for any signs of distress at his words. Fortunately, Mercy's expression was one of curiosity. 'She will be your stepmother, sweet pea,' he answered carefully. 'You already have a mother, even though she's in Heaven now.'

'But she'll live here, with us?' the small girl prodded. Christian swallowed, but before he could find a suitably delicate answer, she added, 'Can I have a new dress for the wedding?' Unable to stop himself, the Earl grinned down at her. 'Will Freddy come and live with us too?' she continued, slipping her hand from his and skipping around him.

They were taking their customary early morning stroll in Hyde Park. The day was cold but dry, and thanks to the hour, there were few people around to disturb them. It was the most treasured part of Christian's day. 'I think Freddy belongs to Miss Shackleford's father,' he explained gently. 'But I'm certain you'll see him this evening as we've been invited for dinner with Miss Shackleford's family.'

'Will there be a lot of people?' Mercy asked after a moment.

He wondered if he'd been wise in accepting the Duchess's invitation for dinner quite so soon. If the whole family came... But no, surely her grace would not think it appropriate. But considering the father... He thought back to their first meeting, and for the first time, he truly wondered what the devil he'd let himself in for. He glanced down at Mercy who was now busy digging at the snow with a stick.

'Miss Shackleford is very good at climbing trees, Papa. Do you think when she lives with us, she'll climb the one in the back garden too?'

∞∞∞

Felicity Beaumont put the finishing touches to her hair and sighed, staring at herself in the mirror. She looked tired... and old.

Far too old for a ridiculous crush on a man who was never likely to look at her as anything other than a family friend.

Tutting at herself, she turned away from the glass and bent down to pick up her shawl. It was early still, and the maid had not yet been in to stoke up the fire. Felicity knew she'd been foolish to rise at such an ungodly hour. Breakfast would not be served until ten. But lately she'd been having trouble sleeping. Her back ached something fierce when she stayed in one position for too long. Mayhap if she went down to the kitchen, she could request a hot chocolate be brought to her in the small drawing room, and perhaps a crumpet.

Decision made, she wrapped the shawl around her shoulders and made her way below stairs.

In contrast to the rest of the house, the kitchen was already bustling. Mrs Pidgeon immediately ordered the scullery maid to build up the fire in the drawing room and bade Felicity warm herself next to the huge fireplace while she waited. Pressing a large dish of hot chocolate into the matron's hands, the cook commented that she'd never seen her kitchen so busy with visitors this time in the morning. When questioned, she admitted that had Miss Beaumont come down not ten minutes earlier, she would have bumped into the Reverend, Percy and Miss Chastity.

Frowning, Felicity wrapped her cold hands around the dish. 'Where are they now?' she murmured, an unpleasant feeling curling in the pit of her stomach.

'Well, they took that poor woman to see her brother,' Mrs. Pidgeon answered giving a large pan of porridge a stir. 'I did wonder why it needed four of 'em, but it's not my place to question the ways o' me betters.'

Felicity stared at the cook in bewilderment. 'I wasn't aware there had been another visitor to the house,' she said carefully at length.

'Last night, late it was,' Mrs. Pidgeon confided, always happy to share a bit of gossip. 'Jimmy Fowler arrived from Blackmore with this woman in tow.' She shook her head. 'I ain't seen the lad in an age. My, he's goin' to break a few 'earts that one.' She placed the lid back on the porridge and wiped her hands on her apron. 'Jimmy reckoned this female lives over in Blackmore too. Up 'ere to visit wi' 'er brother.' She gave a sniff before adding, 'Bit above 'erself if you ask me. I mean the cheek of 'er askin' to share 'is grace's coach.' She shook her head. 'And then she gets a bloody escort to Whitechapel. Be gettin' ideas above 'er station afore long.'

More baffled than ever, Felicity nevertheless thought it best to bring the conversation to a close. The last thing she wanted was to be accused of gossiping with the Duke's staff. Thanking the rotund cook, she finished her dish of hot chocolate and made her way back towards the drawing room where Mrs. Pidgeon had promised to send her a hot buttered crumpet as soon as they came out of the oven.

Mulling over the cook's words, Felicity didn't notice there was someone standing at the top of the stairs until she spied a pair of feet above her. With a small gasp, her eyes flew upwards. It was Malcolm. Her heart slammed against her ribs. Really she was too damn old to react so.

'Miss Beaumont,' he greeted her in his gruff Scottish burr. 'I ken yer looking well. The Duchess said you'd nae be arriving until the end of the month.'

Felicity's face reddened at the thought that the valet might have asked when she was coming. Taking the last step onto the landing as he inclined his head, she murmured, 'I had an inkling I might be needed a little earlier.' She gave a slight chuckle before adding ruefully, 'It seems I was right.'

'Ye certainly were, Miss Beaumont, though some might say it's nothing out of the ordinary.' Felicity laughed as Malcolm grinned down at her, for a second in complete accord as only outsiders who mixed regularly with the Shacklefords would understand.

'How long are ye planning te stay?' the Scot added as Felicity took a step towards the drawing room. She turned back, face flaming anew at the thought he might be interested. 'I shall stay as long as I'm needed,' she answered with a smile.

'Aye, well, if that's the case, you'd do well to move in.' Heart thudding, Felicity stared up at the valet. Was she imagining the intent look in his eyes? She searched for something witty to say, but nothing came to mind.

'I'd best be off.' Malcolm broke the odd connection first, giving another slight bow before starting down the stairs. Felicity fought the urge to stamp her foot. When was the last time she'd had no witty comeback? Truly she was behaving like a chit just out of the schoolroom.

Sighing, she picked up her skirts, intending to continue on to the drawing room, just as her thoughts went back to her conversation in the kitchen. Should she tell the Scot? Would she simply be spreading gossip? She was still hovering indecisively at the top of the stairs when she heard the front door open and close. Her chance had gone.

Chapter Fifteen

Witherspoon lifted his head at the sound of the sudden commotion outside. Frowning, he climbed to his feet, then suddenly stilled as he recognised a female voice he hadn't heard in years. *What the bloody hell was Lizzy doing here? Damn it.*

With a muttered oath, he jumped to his feet and hurried outside, just in time to see his sister turn into the arms of...was that a bloody vicar...giving noisy sobs. Witherspoon frowned. The poor bugger looked about to collapse with Lizzy's weight leaning on him, especially as she was about a foot taller. He glanced down at the comatose figure in the road, where... was that another bleeding vicar...appeared to be slapping the unconscious man's face in between shouting, 'Down Freddy,' to a dog currently trying to give the cove a Brutus haircut with his teeth. After a second, Witherspoon recognised the prone figure as Charlie, and his heart sank to his boots. This was all he bloody well needed.

Grimacing, he strode over before more gawpers had time to gather. Bloody hell, it was like Paddington Fair Day.

'Lizzy!' he shouted with every evidence of delight, 'what brings you to our fair city?'

'Don't you Lizzy me, John Witherspoon. 'ow long's 'e been 'ere?'

She pointed to her still unmoving husband.

Witherspoon slowed to a halt, weighing his options. More people were gathering by the second. Everyone loved a good domestic. 'Get 'im inside,' he ordered the two natty lads trailing behind him. 'And don't empty his bloody pockets, or I swear I'll string you up meself.' Then, he turned to the two clergymen who were now standing side by side like a couple of bloody crows. The dog was being held on a tight lead by a tall youth who looked to be the one who'd brought Charlie down. 'These friends o' yours, Lizzy?'

There was a slight pause. Then his sister sniffed and said, 'They took pity on me is all. Saw me wondering 'round the place and worried I might end up in the 'ands of a mutton-monger, or worse.'

Chastity was standing to one side, slightly behind Jimmy as she watched the proceedings. She didn't know why Lizzy had lied about knowing them but was nonetheless glad she had. Her father naturally got into the swing of things before the rest of them. He pointed to the figure who was propped up via his single arm and being dragged none too gently across the filthy cobbles.

'This poor lady was set upon by this…this…ruffian who callously…' He ground to a halt, suddenly remembering that the ruffian in question was actually Lizzy's missing husband and she'd been the one doing the setting upon. He glanced wildly around for Chastity and was relieved to spy her standing behind Jimmy, her reticule now firmly in her grasp.

'The bloody idiot tried to snaffle 'er purse,' Lizzy finished the story, her voice now weary and sad. ''Ow long's 'e bin 'ere, John?'

'I thought you knew he was here, I swear,' her brother defended. 'When he turned up he said you was finding it difficult to make ends meet with him having only one arm and all. I've been giving him money. He said he was sending it to you.'

Lizzy shook her head. I ain't seen a penny since 'e walked out.' She laughed mirthlessly. 'That's why I'm 'ere. All the bastard left me was a bleeding gold tooth. I was lookin' to sell it.'

With a cool glance at the Reverend, John Witherspoon stepped forward and took Lizzy's hand. 'Thank you for your timely assistance, gentlemen,' he said brusquely, 'but I'll take care of my sister from here.'

Unexpectedly, Percy stepped forward. 'Are you happy for us to leave you…' he paused, then stammered, 'Miss?'

Lizzy turned her head as her brother put his arm around her shoulders and began propelling her towards the large warehouse her husband had just been dragged into. 'I'm fine. Thank you for yer kind assistance. P'rhaps we'll bump into each other again one day.'

Chastity impulsively stepped forward to intervene, but Jimmy swiftly blocked her passage. She offered him a brief glare but obediently halted. Seconds later, the door to the warehouse closed, and Lizzy was gone.

'We can't just leave her there,' Percy protested.

'Well, you've changed your tune a bit, the Reverend responded irritably. 'Only last night I thought you were about to have an apoplexy at the mere thought of the deuced woman.'

'That was when I thought she'd murdered her husband.'

'One gold tooth and you decide she's put him to bed with a deuced spade? Seriously Percy, I'm not sure what the Almighty will have to say about it when you finally come face to face. Didn't you think to ask her? I mean, she might be on the large side, but that doesn't mean she's capable of seeing her husband off. Not to mention extracting the deuced molar.'

They were seated in a mercifully much sweeter smelling

hackney carriage on their way back to the Duke's town house. Chastity was quiet, listening to the conversation as much of it was entirely new to her. She'd had no idea there was any personal history between Percy and Lizzy. She'd thought the curate simply shy at the thought of meeting a strange woman. But now she came to think of it, hiding behind a bookcase did seem a bit extreme.

For Jimmy, the conversation could have been in French for all he understood it. He stared in bewildered silence at the two clergymen as they finally approached the corner of Grosvenor Square.

'I know it's not in my nature to give up,' Reverend Shackleford announced heavily as the carriage slowed down. 'But I think we've done as much as we can. I am no happier leaving Lizzy with her blackguard of a brother than you are, Percy, but the decision was hers to make.' He shook his head before adding, 'In truth, I don't believe she will be there for long, but we need to speak with Nicholas and Malcolm as soon as possible.' Sighing, Augustus Shackleford rose to his feet before climbing laboriously down from the carriage.

'What about the Earl?' Chastity asked, hurriedly climbing down after him. 'Surely he will be the one to decide which course of action to take.'

'Let's go and find out shall we?'

'Are you certain he didn't recognise any of you?' Christian Stanhope's question was terse.

'Why would he? As far as old Witherspoon was concerned, we were simply strangers who happened to be passing.' The

Reverend shook his head. 'I've never seen him before, have you Percy?' The curate gave a subdued shake of his head.

'It's hard to believe that this Fletcher woman is connected to Witherspoon. That's some damn coincidence.'

'Not really,' Nicholas shrugged. 'A lot of my former ship's company have sought me out over the years. They know I'll never see them starve. In truth, I'd forgotten about Fletcher's connection to Witherspoon. The man still had his arm when he left the service. I assume he met Lizzie through her brother and decided to settle in Blackmore.' The Duke grinned, clearly delighted their quarry had been found so soon.

'What do ye wish te do about the blackguard?' Malcolm asked. 'Ye canna just leave him running free, and at the moment, he's no idea we know where he's hiding.'

Christian sighed and shook his head. 'As much as I'd like to see the bastard pay, as yet, I have no proof. Unless someone admits to seeing him stick that knife in Barnet, it's my word against his.'

'Your word'll carry a sight more weight than the owner of a bloody gambling den,' growled Malcolm.

'That as may be, but if I show my hand and fail to see him swing, I'll spend the rest of my life watching my back...' He paused before adding softly, 'and those of my wife and child.'

'Ye'll be doing that anyway once he kens you've returned,' argued the Scot.

The Earl nodded wearily, running his fingers through his hair in frustration.

'What about Fletcher?' the valet suggested. 'Could he be persuaded te open his mouth?'

Reverend Shackleford shrugged. 'I reckon it won't be long before Lizzy's husband's pushing up daisies,' he commented. 'In truth, he looked to have one foot downstairs already.'

The three men were sitting in the Duke's study along with the Reverend. After recounting everything that had happened since Jimmy and Lizzy Fletcher's arrival the night before, Augustus Shackleford was, for the most part, content to sip his brandy and allow the younger men to decide what action to take. In truth, he was done to a cow's thumb and not for the first time, longed for the rain and rolling hills of Devonshire. Though he would never admit it to anyone but Percy, the truth was he'd begun to feel his age. His mind might still be as sharp as a well-creased cravat, but it had to be said his body had seen better days. He finally understood how his old horse Lucifer must have felt before being put out to pasture.

'As I see it, we have two options,' Nicholas was saying, leaning back in his chair. 'We either ignore Witherspoon and hope he stays holed up in his bloody sty... Or...' He leant forward and steepled his fingers. '...we set a trap and watch the bastard fall into it.'

∞∞∞

Despite Chastity's frustration the day before, her longing to see Lord Cottesmore again was so acute it was almost painful. She'd taken great pains with her toilette, finally wearing the iced blue dress that had been intended for the opera. Her hair was pinned high on her crown, only to fall in a cascade of ringlets over her left shoulder. As she eyed herself in the mirror, she had to concede that if Christian Stanhope did not find her even remotely ravishing this evening, then he never would. Smoothing her gloves over her elbows, she abruptly imagined the Earl's long fingers sliding from her wrist to her upper arm. Unexpectedly, she felt a tingling in her breasts. Startled, she looked down.

Oh, she was well aware that gentlemen had a penchant for women's bosoms. Too many bad poets waxed eloquently about *the pillows of Venus* for any woman to be completely oblivious. But she'd never before given them more than a cursory thought. Certainly not in connection with a man's fingers–gentle or otherwise.

Unbidden, a sudden giggle arose as she thought back to the whispered conversations between her older sisters that she and Charity had eavesdropped on. She remembered them both being horrified at the time–but now, looking down at her sudden tingling bosoms, she thought perhaps the actions her sisters had described, bizarre as they'd sounded to a sixteen-year-old, most certainly bore further consideration.

Perhaps one didn't need romance after all. She certainly hadn't felt a desperate desire for Obadiah Simpson's hands to be anywhere other than in his pockets.

Picking up her reticule, she took a deep breath and prepared for her first dinner with her betrothed.

It was bitterly cold as Christian helped his daughter into the hackney carriage that would take them to Sinclair's townhouse. He owned no coach of his own and currently could not spare the coin to buy one. However, the maid had provided Mercy with a hot brick wrapped in flannels to warm her feet on, and the little girl was wearing her warmest pelisse.

In actual fact, Mercy didn't seem to feel the cold and spent the majority of the journey bouncing up and down in excitement or attempting to balance on the covered brick. Leaning back against his seat, Christian smiled at her antics and thought back to his own boyhood. It had been very different to hers. He'd been brought up in the country. Norfolk. His mother had died in the birthing of him, and his father had been the local blacksmith. They lived well enough, and Christian had spent most of his childhood sailing the Broads.

Though Mercy now led an indulged life, her existence up until the point she'd been left on his doorstep had been meagre indeed, from what he'd been able to pry from her.

In the beginning, he'd tried to find her mother, searching the poorhouses and hospitals of New York, but to no avail. He suspected she hadn't wanted to be found, was perhaps dead even then. According to Mercy, she coughed all the time and her kerchiefs were bright red.

But, though they'd clearly been living hand to mouth, his daughter still had many stories to tell of laughter and fun. Though he was certain she missed her mother terribly, Mercy's nature was not to brood, and gradually, over the months, she came out of her shell, changing his life completely. Looking back, Christian considered the man he'd been before Mercy's unexpected arrival.

Arrogant, impulsive and driven. In truth, it was no wonder Witherspoon had been able to frame him for murder. He was ripe to be brought down. He would never have made a good naval captain.

In many ways, the brashness of the Americas had suited him, and when he arrived in Boston, Christian truly thought he'd put his past behind him. He looked through the carriage window at the twilight streets. This was the London of wealth and privilege. Underneath it all was a seething mass of poverty, dirt and death. Yes, New York and Boston both had the same squalid underbelly, but there was always the sense that a person could rise if he wished. The rules of class did not keep a man down in the dirt as they did here.

His musings came to an abrupt halt as they arrived at Grosvenor Square. 'How do I look?' he asked his daughter. She considered him seriously. 'You look very handsome, Papa,' she decided after a few seconds. 'Please don't embarrass me will you?' Christian raised his eyebrows as he watched her alight the coach. Seriously, nearly nine years old and she was asking him not to *embarrass* her? Mayhap times were changing. Sighing, he climbed down and paid the coach driver.

As the carriage moved off, they were left in sudden silence. The snow remained crunchy underfoot, and the air was still and freezing cold. Candles blazed through the windows of the house giving a warm, welcoming feel. All of a sudden, he felt nervous. The only thing he knew of his bride-to-be was her proficiency at climbing trees. Not an essential talent required in a young lady of breeding. But then, in truth, she wasn't a lady, any more than his own daughter.

He felt Mercy's small hand slip into his. 'Don't be scared, Papa,' she whispered. 'Miss Shackleford is a very nice lady, and I know she is going to be even better than your other friends.' Christian grinned down at her ruefully. 'Mayhap it would be a good idea not to mention my...err... *friends* at the dinner table, sweet pea. The truth is, whatever the maid said, I've never really had any.'

'Wasn't Mama your special friend?' Christian's heart somersaulted. 'Yes, darling, she was,' he answered gruffly. 'She was my only *special* friend.'

'Until now.' Mercy smiled up at him, and together they climbed the stairs.

Chapter Sixteen

'I know they said my name's Prudence, but you can call me Pru.'

Mercy gave a small curtsy as Miss Sharpham had taught her. To her chagrin, Prudence let out a peal of laughter. 'You don't have to curtsy to me,' she chuckled. 'The truth is, I'm just a vicar's daughter, so it should be the other way round.' She spread her skirts and gave an exaggerated dip of the knee, almost to the floor.

The two girls were closeted in the corner of the large drawing room. Prudence had seized Mercy's hand the moment they were introduced and dragged her away from the *tediously boring* adults.

'You don't behave like a lady,' Mercy conceded doubtfully.

'That's 'cos I'm not one and never will be,' Pru answered, plonking herself down on her chair. 'Mercedes, that's a very interesting name. I don't know anyone with it at all. Apart from you that is.'

'It was my mother's name,' Mercy answered shyly.

'I take it she's dead,' Pru said bluntly. Mercy nodded, receiving a shrug in return. 'I never really knew my mother,' the older girl confided. 'There's only ever been Agnes–she's my stepmother.'

She pointed over to a stout matron with a large doily covering her head.

'Is she kind to you?' Mercy asked, having been read many stories about wicked stepmothers.

Prudence blinked. 'I'm not sure she even knows my name,' was her answer at length. 'The only one of us she's really interested in is Anthony. He issued from her loins,' she declared loftily.

'What's a loin?'

Pru frowned, opened her mouth, then shrugged. 'Not important. Wait until you meet Anthony,' she enthused. 'He's a good sport. The only one in the whole family who still knows how to have fun. Apart from me. And now you.' She cocked her head on one side. 'You do know how to have fun, don't you?'

'I...I think so,' Mercy responded, frantically sorting through her head for Miss Sharpham's opinion on fun.

Belatedly, Prudence realised that Mercy's question about stepmothers might have been prompted by her concern that she was about to inherit one. 'Oh, you need not worry about Chastity,' she offered airily, 'she's as soft as syllabub and most definitely knows how to have fun. I'm entirely certain you and she will deal famously together.' She paused and looked over the younger girl's shoulder.

'Ah, here's Anthony now.' Mercy turned towards the door in time to spy a tall slender youth with a riot of curly hair, the colour of burnished copper. 'We think Agnes's hair might once have been that colour,' whispered Prudence with a grin as she watched her brother being introduced to the Earl, 'though Lord knows where he got his skinny build from.' Mercy blinked noting the rotund form of the boy's parents.

After the introduction, Anthony wasted no time listening to the small talk being conducted on the adult side of the room but headed straight for his sister. To Mercy's delight, he had Freddy in tow. As the boy got closer, Mercy could see his eyes were a vivid green, the colour of the small newts living in the pond at the bottom of their garden. 'Hello, Mercy,' he grinned, 'I hear you're to become part of the family. I warn you now, we're all completely dicked in the nob, though in the spirit of telling the truth from the outset, I should tell you that of everyone, I'm the most normal.'

Prudence snorted. 'And if you believe that, you'll believe anything.'

∞∞∞

Laying down her knife and fork, Chastity looked around the table, certain that her eldest sister could count the dinner party a great success. There were eight around the table which was a perfect number to facilitate the light banter the Duke and Duchess were so good at. Though Peter and Jennifer should have been there, they were both suffering from slight colds, so Grace had evidently thought it best they stayed in the nursery.

Chastity eyed her sister. They'd had no further opportunity to discuss whether Grace was enceinte, and clearly she'd said nothing to Nicholas. Chastity pursed her lips. This wouldn't do. For good or ill, she was now betrothed, and it was time for Grace to consider her own needs.

Betrothed. That had a very formal ring to it. Chastity gave a covert glance to the Earl seated to her left. He looked exceedingly handsome in his evening dress, so much so that the tingling she'd felt earlier had spread. In truth, it was making her a little uncomfortable. So far they'd not had much opportunity to speak beyond the usual pleasantries, but every time she looked at him, she became distracted by his mouth, wondering how his lips would feel covering hers. There it was again. She squirmed awkwardly.

'Are you well, Miss Shackleford?' Damn it, his voice did strange things to her too.

'I'm just a little hot, that is all,' she responded, hating the breathlessness in her voice.

Christian opened his mouth to say something more, but to Chastity's chagrin, he was interrupted by the Duke addressing the table.

'Given the reason for our gathering, I'd like to suggest we enjoy our port with the ladies. Would that be acceptable?' Though he spoke to everyone, Nicholas's suggestion was clearly directed towards Christian, and the Earl bent his head in ready agreement.

A few minutes later, Grace rose from the table and led the way into the large drawing room. Once there, the obvious temptation was to continue discussing the problem of Witherspoon, but mindful of younger ears, they stayed away from the dark subject. Chastity smiled at Mercy, happy to see her playing a game of cards with Prudence and Anthony while surreptitiously feeding Freddy the marzipan coins under the table. At least Pru hadn't suggested they play for real money - it wouldn't be the first time.

Indeed, everyone seemed in very high spirits aside from Percy who Chastity noted had been quiet throughout dinner. She observed her father casting the curate more than one concerned glance too, so evidently she wasn't imagining it.

Inevitably, the conversation turned instead to their betrothal, and Chastity found herself once more casting covert glances towards the Earl. To her disappointment, his face gave nothing away, and she felt a sudden anxious tug in her stomach.

'Naturally, I'd prefer to conduct the nuptials myself at the church in Blackmore,' her father was saying.

'I think mayhap a spring wedding would be lovely,' Grace enthused. Devonshire is especially lovely in May.' *It would also enable her sister to be back at Blackmore before her lying-in*, Chastity thought.

'The announcement is due to go in tomorrow's Morning Post,' Nicholas declared, 'although we were in two minds whether we should make such a public announcement given the situation with our former associate.' He shook his head. 'But at the end of the day, both Augustus and I agreed with Christian that hiding from the confrontation will not make it go away, and this way we at least have some control over the situation.'

Chastity, who hadn't been privy to the earlier conversation as a result of their discovery of Witherspoon's whereabouts, frowned in confused concern. Surely, they could simply send someone to arrest the blackguard and be done with it? She determined to ask her husband-to-be as soon as they were alone. And if he thought to keep anything from her... Well, he hadn't reckoned with the fact that she'd had years of honing her prying skills from her six older sisters.

'I assume the wedding taking place at Blackmore will necessitate keeping it reasonably small?' questioned Christian.

'Yes,' agreed Chastity with relief. 'Please. I don't want a large affair like Hope or Patience.' The Earl turned and finally smiled at her, once again eliciting the butterflies that so plagued her in his presence.

'I'm not sure if you are aware, Miss Shackleford,' he stated after a second, 'but I have yet to begin the repairs to the Cottesmore Estate. However, that's something I hope to rectify as soon as the weather begins to improve.' He paused before continuing carefully, 'Once the refurbishment is complete, it is my plan to spend the majority of the time there. With your father's permission, I would very much like to take you for a visit, given that it will be your home too.'

Chastity swallowed a sudden lump in her throat as she nodded. Then she gave a slight chuckle, murmuring, 'Though I have to admit, my lord, I have no idea where it is.'

'It's near Ringwood. On the borders of the New Forest,' he answered. 'Not so far from your sisters I believe.'

'While I applaud your intention, Kit, could I request that you postpone such a visit until our mutual friend is safe and sound in *Newman's Hotel*.' The Duke deliberately used the diminutive term for Newgate Prison. Even the youngest ears were familiar with London's most infamous gaol.

The Earl nodded grimly. 'That would be wise, I agree...' He paused before continuing, 'Would it be appropriate for Miss Shackleford to accompany me for a stroll in Hyde Park? Unfortunately, it will have to be on foot as I'm not yet in possession of a curricle.'

'Can I come too, Papa?' piped up Mercy, showing clearly she'd been listening to the conversation.

'I'd be happy to chaperone you,' Prudence added with an impudent wink.

'I'm entirely certain a sixteen-year-old would not be considered a fitting escort,' countered Felicity drily. She turned towards the Earl, adding, 'I would be delighted to act as your chaperone, my lord, and of course, a companion to Prudence and Mercedes should they accompany you.'

In the end, it was agreed that Lord Cottesmore would call for Chastity at two p.m. on the morrow and they would be accompanied by not only Felicity, Prudence and Mercy, but also the Duchess, Peter and Jennifer. Fortunately, Anthony was to attend a fencing lesson.

'A veritable family outing,' muttered Chastity sourly. Overhearing her, Christian fought to hide a grin. She'd sounded much more like the woman who'd gone as far as climbing a tree to speak with him. To his abrupt surprise, he discovered he actually wanted to get to know that side of his wife-to-be. How odd. He gave a bemused shake of his head.

Soon after, he spied Mercy giving a particularly large yawn and reluctantly took his leave. Nicholas wouldn't hear of him hiring a hansom carriage, insisting that the evening was still early, and his coachman would be more than happy to do the honours.

As they were leaving however, Grace took the Earl aside to confess that the coach driver's skills were somewhat erratic. A ride in Joseph's carriage was always stimulating but very often unpredictable and took a little getting used to. She therefore advised his lordship to sit Mercy next to him and hold on to her tightly, otherwise she could well end up in the gutter.

Her grace didn't feel now was the time to mention the driver only had one leg...

'What the deuce is bothering you, Percy Noon, and don't you dare say nothing, you've been Friday faced all night? Reverend Shackleford finally cornered Percy halfway up the stairs on his way back from letting Freddy out for his last wee. 'Is it the widow?'

'She's not a widow,' retorted Percy dully continuing up the stairs.

The Reverend raised his eyebrows. 'Well that's good isn't it?' he demanded in exasperation. 'I mean, at least if she's still got her old one, she'll stop looking for another, so you've had a reprieve.' He paused before adding a rueful, 'Though it likely won't last long, given the fact her husband looked as though he'd been dug up.'

'He's an ivory turner,' declared Percy vehemently as they reached his bedchamber. Augustus Shackleford frowned. 'Yes, well, he was a Jack tar and most of 'em aren't noted for their noble bent.'

'What if he's violent?' Percy insisted.

'He's only got one arm,' Reverend Shackleford countered. 'I doubt very much he'd be able to get the better of Lizzy Longshanks even if he didn't have one foot in the hereafter.'

'And what about this Witherspoon fellow?' Percy's voice was getting louder. 'He's even worse.'

'He's also her brother,' the Reverend reasoned. 'Look, lad, I think Lizzy Fletcher is more than capable of looking after herself. She might be a bit bracket faced, but she's no fool.'

'And anyway with a bit of luck, old Withers'll be for the morning drop before he gets the chance to do any damage...' He paused and looked round before lowering his voice. 'I think Malcolm's going to set a trap for the blackguard.'

'What kind of trap?' queried Percy, pushing open his bedchamber door.

'I don't know yet,' the Reverend retorted, following the curate in, 'but I'm certain they'll need our assistance once they're ready to spring it.' He waited until Percy sat down on the side of the bed before seating himself next to the smaller man.

'So why is all this troubling you so much... really? Come on Percy, don't give me any deuced moonshine.'

There was a silence, only broken as Freddy jumped up onto the bed between them and made himself comfortable. For once, Augustus Shackleford didn't say anything, content to simply wait until the curate was ready to unburden himself.

'I can't stand by and do nothing. Not again,' Percy exclaimed.

'I'm not sure I'm following you,' the Reverend muttered, creasing his brow in confusion.

'I didn't help my mother,' Percy finally blurted. 'I could have, but I didn't.'

Reverend Shackleford raised his eyebrows. 'I'm not sure how you've come to that conclusion, Percy lad. Last I heard, she was running that pub in Salcombe.'

'But that was Jago,' protested Percy. 'And you and he saved her from the rope. All I did was pray.'

'Now just a deuced minute,' the Reverend sputtered in outrage. 'Since when did you begin underestimating the power of prayer, Percy Noon? The Almighty's got us out of more scrapes than we've had hot dinners and why do you think he's done that? It's not because I've spent my life running around like a deuced headless chicken. You've always been the steadfast one, not me. It's you, standing behind me giving the Almighty a good talking to, Percy. That's how your mother's still here, that's how we're still here and that will be how Lizzy Fletcher gets out of the hole she's found herself in.' He shook his head and began rummaging around inside his cassock.

'I'm not saying action's not called for, lad, but without a few Hail Mary's behind it...' He trailed off with a shrug.

'But we're not Catholic,' frowned the curate, puzzled.

Reverend Shackleford finally located what he was searching for and brought out his small flask of brandy in triumph. Unscrewing the top, he gave a long sigh and said, 'You know what, Percy? I don't think He really cares...'

Chapter Seventeen

Lizzy Fletcher looked round the squalid room her so-called husband had been living in for the last two years and wanted to scream. The object of her affections was lying on the filthy mattress complaining that his head hurt, and she'd probably damaged his brain.

'Well, since most o' your thinkin's done in your bleeding nutmegs, it ain't much of a bloody loss,' she responded callously, picking up something that appeared to have started life as a vegetable and slinging it out of the open door. 'I don't know 'ow you've lived like this for so long, Charlie,' she muttered hoarsely, fighting back tears. For pity's sake, she thought she'd cried her last tears, bloody years ago. 'Ow could this be better than wot we 'ad?'

'E owed me money, the bastard. I came up to get it,' the prone man mumbled.

'Who owed you money, Charlie?'

'Your bastard brother, that's who.' Groaning, he struggled into a sitting position, a sheen of sweat dotting his brow.

Against her will, Lizzy stepped over and felt her husband's brow. He was cold and clammy to the touch. She shuddered, stepping back. 'Well, if John owed you money, 'ow come it's taken two bloody years to get it back?'

'He says it's all in *there*.' Charlie shot back savagely, stabbing his finger in the direction of the *Flying Horse*. 'He told me if I waited, we'd be rich. Me an' you, Liz. Rich. No more charity from Duke high an' bloody mighty.'

'Wot the 'ell are you talking about Charlie? You tol' me the Duke of Blackmore was the best you'd ever served under. Them's were your exact words. That's how you dragged me all the way to bloody Devonshire.'

'That's wot 'e tol' me to say,' Charlie muttered, rubbing his head. 'Fact is Liz, 'e din't want you 'ere. Your ma cocking up 'er toes an' you turnin up like a bloody bad penny. He wanted you gone. Said you wos too ripe and ready by 'alf. He knew you'd see through 'im, start askin' questions, get in the bloody way.' He paused and swayed before continuing. 'Sinclair was out by then too. 'E wanted me to keep an eye on the bastard. So we killed two birds wi' one stone.' He finally collapsed back onto the bed. 'Get me some grog, woman,' he mumbled.

Lizzy grimaced. She picked up the small bottle of rum but held it high above her husband's head. 'Not 'til you tell me wot the bloody hell this is all about Charlie. I swear on my life, I'll pour this 'ole bottle in the gutter if you don't tell me the bleeding truth.' Charlie howled and made a feeble swipe before falling back and groaning.

'You've bloody killed me, you bitch,' he muttered.

Lizzy said nothing, just continued to hold the bottle high over his head, waiting.

''e said 'e'd split it if I lied for 'im,' Charlie finally slurred.

'Lied for who? John? Wot did 'e do?' Lizzy demanded.

'Killed 'im. Stuck a knife right between 'is shoulder blades. 'E tol' me if I said it wos Stanhope did it, 'e'd see me right.' Lizzy blinked trying to make sense of her husband's words.

'But the bastard jumped,' Charlie suddenly cackled. 'E jumped afore 'e could swing. So there wos John, left wi' a ruby up 'is arse...' Lizzy watched in distaste as her husband started laughing, until suddenly he began to cough, a line of crimson dribbling from the corner of his mouth.

'Course we could 'ave split it when 'e sold the bleeding ruby,' he rasped. But, no, 'e 'ad big ideas. Bought this bloody place instead.' He gave a pained shrug. 'I told 'im we was doin' alright. We din't need 'im peddlin' 'is bleeding fancy ideas. But did the bastard listen?' He started to cough again, his chin now stained a dark red.

Hastily, she lowered the grog and pulled out the stopper, but before she had the chance to put it to his lips, a huge gout of blood suddenly shot from his mouth. Sobbing, Lizzy tried to lift his head up, but the bright crimson liquid continued to slide down his chin. In the end, all she could do was watch in horrified fascination as her good for nothing husband, eyes bulging, choked to death on his own blood.

And then, abruptly, it was over. Slowly, without taking her eyes from his sightless, staring ones, Lizzy lifted the bottle of grog and put it to her own lips.

Waking up to bright sunshine, Chastity lay back against her pillows and sipped her hot chocolate. How much had changed in less than forty-eight hours.

Despite Lord Cottesmore's earlier avowal that their marriage would be a business arrangement only, she finally dared hope that it might become more than that. Perhaps she hadn't entirely given up on romance, but even if he did not wish to pursue the... physical side of marriage, she still needed them to be friends. She could not countenance living the rest of her life in a frosty atmosphere. She would just have to ignore the part of her that reacted so strongly to his presence. It wasn't *that* difficult to do. Indeed, she'd become quite accomplished at it, though it was admittedly usually for the exact opposite of reasons. Unbidden, her mind conjured up thoughts of Viscount Trebworthy.

Hurriedly, she threw back the covers and climbed out of bed. This morning, as soon as breakfast was finished, she would seek out her sister and enquire after her health. Though the fact that Grace felt well enough to accompany them to Hyde Park this afternoon indicated that perhaps the nausea had subsided.

Without bothering to wait for the maid, Chastity pulled on one of her sisters' hand-me-downs, giggling at the thought of her maid Rose's outrage should she lay eyes on her. This afternoon she'd be spending more than enough time primping and polishing, and really, she needed to give her ribs a rest from the deuced stays. They were unlikely to have any visitors before then, so though Grace might tut at the sight of her, at least she'd be able to breathe for a few hours.

Breakfast was a lively affair, despite the spectre of John Witherspoon hanging over them. Percy was a little more cheerful after Malcolm reported that he'd spotted Lizzy alive and apparently well, helping her husband out of her brother's gambling den, which Witherspoon had whimsically named the *Flying Horse*. Clearly, the thought of her was what had been concerning him during the dinner.

As they were finishing, Nicholas read out the announcement of their betrothal, and Chastity couldn't help but feel a small thrill at hearing the words. Naturally, she couldn't help wondering whether Lord Cottesmore would even have given her a second glance if she hadn't tied her garter in public, but then to her knowledge, at least two of her sisters' marriages had begun equally inauspiciously and had flourished since. No, today, she was determined she would not fall prey to uncertainty. Forever second-guessing oneself was exceedingly tiresome.

As soon as breakfast was finished, she followed her eldest sister up to the nursery.

'How are you feeling?' Chastity asked as soon as Briony had left them alone. 'I must say you have much more colour in your face than you did a few days ago.'

Grace didn't answer immediately, being busy fastening up the dress on the doll Jennifer had given to her. 'I swear this deuced dress has more buttons on it than mine,' she muttered, handing the doll back. Watching her daughter toddle off towards her dolls house, she finally turned and smiled. 'I do feel better, thank you dearest. And I don't believe there is any doubt that I am increasing.'

'Have you told Nicholas?'

Grace shook her head. 'I plan to tell him as soon as we've got this business with the Earl over with.' She held up her hand as Chastity opened her mouth to object. 'Felicity knows and she is making sure I eat my greens and don't do too much. You and she are all the confidantes I need at the moment.' She paused and chuckled. 'Once I've told Nicholas, he will immediately go into mother hen mode. I simply wish to hang on to my freedom for as long as I can. Now let's talk about your wedding dress.'

The rest of the morning passed in a blur. After spending an hour in the nursery with Grace, Chastity sat down to write a letter to her twin. She hadn't written since Christmas, and it was difficult to know exactly where to start. Indeed it was even harder to consider that the person who'd always been closest to her actually had no idea of what had transpired, and as she scribbled away, Chastity feared her sister would lose the will to live before she even got to the important part.

She was just placing the missive in an envelope as Rose knocked on the door. Glancing down at her watch, Chastity gasped. It was almost one. So much for primping and polishing. But then, did it matter really? It was unlikely the Earl would get within ten feet of her with their entourage.

Forty-five minutes later she was seated in the drawing room, nervously waiting. She watched Prudence as she played a game of dominoes with Peter. Grace and Felicity sat calmly side by side with their embroidery. Chastity forced back a laugh. If anyone had suggested needlepoint to her sister when she first wed Nicholas, Grace would have thought them addled. In truth, most of her pieces ended up in the servants' quarters even now.

The fact was none of the Shackleford sisters had achieved any real proficiency in the skills considered so essential by ladies of the *ton*. Especially musically. Indeed, collectively they could give an alley full of cats a run for their money, though Patience was the worst. Her singing voice was truly awful. Their father had frequently given her a shilling just so she would mime when she was in church.

Her thoughts on Patience, she was reminded of the last time they were seated in a drawing room waiting for the Marquess of Guildford to call. Her eyes caught those of Felicity, and she could tell the matron was thinking exactly the same thing. Both of them burst out laughing. Grace and Prudence looked over at them enquiringly.

'Please my dear, if you could refrain from uttering any profanities in the Earl of Cottesmore's presence, I would be most grateful.'

Chastity shook her head, endeavouring to get her mirth under control. Just as the doorbell rang.

∞∞∞

Lizzy spent the entire night sitting with her dead husband, and it was only as the first streaks of red appeared across the horizon that she finally heaved herself out of the chair and covered him up.

As she pulled the sheet over his head, she spied her hands, still caked in crimson. With a small moan, she wiped them on her skirt, but the gore was dried and incrusted. Looking down, she realised Charlie's blood was all over her. She fought the urge to cast her account, forcing herself to breathe deeply despite the overwhelming acrid stench of copper. There was no way she could leave until she'd changed her clothes. Rummaging around her bag, she pulled out a small, cracked piece of glass – part of a mirror her mother had given her when she was a girl. Holding it up to her face, she gulped back a sob. She looked as though she'd been rolling around in a bloody abattoir.

She hurried outside Charlie's room which was little more than a shed at the back of her brother's gambling den. *You've got a lot to bloody answer for, John Witherspoon*, she thought, gritting her teeth. Whatever happened next, she wanted some bleeding answers.

Looking round in the early morning light, she spied a bucket containing some brackish liquid. Lifting it to her nose, she sniffed cautiously. Water, though a few days old. With a last glance around, she took the bucket back into Charlie's room and stripped off her outer garments. Using her bodice as a cloth, she wiped herself down as best she could, then pulled on her Sunday dress. Looking at the stained garments she'd taken off, she was sorely tempted to simply throw them away, but she had no other clothes. Somehow, she'd have to get the stains out. Shaking her head, she rolled the bodice and skirt up together and shoved them into her bag.

Next, she searched the room for any coins, knowing she was likely wasting her time. The only wealth Charlie had possessed lay in her purse. As she searched, she thought back to his words just before he'd cocked up his toes. Something about a ruby and splitting it.

She'd always wondered how her brother had been able to afford this place. Clearly he'd snaffled the gem and promised to share what he got for it with Charlie. Her poor gullible idiot of a bloody husband. John had kept him hanging on all these years.

Well it was time for an accounting. She'd have her say or die trying, and if the scab thought to lay a hand on her...she'd scream the bloody place down.

Her anger holding back the fear, Lizzy marched out of her husband's tomb and shut the door behind her. John had rooms at the top of the warehouse from what she heard him say yesterday. Quietly now, she walked across the yard and slipped in through a door on the side. It had been locked, but a sharp tug had opened it easily enough. Typical bleeding John. Never did anything properly-always looking to save a few bob.

She came to a shadowy corridor, leading to a narrow set of stairs. She took a step forward, intending to march up the stairs yelling her brother's name. Then, abruptly she paused. She would have done that not hours ago. Back when she thought her brother was just a good-for-nothing fatwit. But now she knew different. He was dangerous.

Everything was silent and she shook her head to clear it. What the bloody hell was she doing? John Witherspoon'd see her dead and buried without a tear. There was no way she could call him out.

By rights, she should just cut her losses and escape while she still had a bloody pulse. She took a hesitant step backwards, her bag, with its pathetic purse inside, knocking against her hip. She thought of Charlie's tooth. The only thing worth a damn she had in the whole bloody world. And that bastard upstairs *owed* her.

Cautiously, she tiptoed back towards the stairs, looking up into the shadows. Slowly, she placed a foot on the first step, testing it to see if it creaked. Then another. The sweat began trickling down her back, and suddenly, her fear ran white hot as she heard voices. Heart slamming against her ribs, she stopped, hardly daring to move.

'It's in the bloody Morning Post. The bastard's getting wed.'

'Blast and bugger his eyes. Who's he getting leg shackled to?'

'Some damn chit out of the schoolroom, only this particular chit happens to be the Duke of Blackmore's sister-in-law.'

Lizzy heard a chair scrape back before crashing onto the floor. 'Then it's time we got rid of the bastard once and for all. Did you contact the Upright Man? Tell him I'll double his price, but I want it doing today. That bastard's dogged my life for long enough.'

Lizzy didn't wait to hear any more. Whimpering, she stepped quietly back down the stairs. She was under no illusion. If John discovered her listening, he'd slit her throat.

Once at the bottom, she pulled open the door and stood for a second, her back pressed against it. Closing her eyes, she bit her bottom lip, for a brief second wondering what on earth she was going to do. Then she thought back to the words she'd overheard.

The Duke of Blackmore's sister-in-law had to be Miss Chastity. Was she betrothed? There had been no mention of it. But at the end of the day, it didn't matter. John was paying the Upright Man to commit murder. If it wasn't the Duke, it was someone his grace knew. She didn't quite know the why of it yet, but she'd throw a bloody rub in the way if it was the last thing she did.

Pushing herself away from the door, she looked fearfully upwards, then hurried towards the large gate.

Chapter Eighteen

'Do you enjoy painting, Miss Shackleford?' Lord Cottesmore asked politely as they strolled along the footpath next to Hyde Park's Rotten Row. Chastity resisted the urge to laugh considering her musings before they left.

'I enjoy it,' she conceded, 'but I doubt I'll ever be the next female Botticelli. In fact, Prudence once declared my Pan bore a striking resemblance to Freddy.'

'He did,' declared Prudence, unashamedly eavesdropping from behind them. 'I think Freddy thought so too. He growled every time he went past the picture. In the end, stepmother had it moved into the scullery.' She turned to the Earl. 'That's the painting, not the dog.'

'I wondered where it went,' Chastity huffed. 'It wasn't my idea to hang it by the front door.'

'I think Grace was going through a phase of nurturing our artistic talents,' Prudence answered with a grin. 'It was before she married Nicholas,' she explained to the Earl. 'I think she was trying to make up for leading us astray during our formative years.'

'How would you know,' Chastity scoffed. 'You weren't even eight when Grace got married.'

'I'll have you know I remember it well,' Prudence declared. 'It wasn't only Freddy who was disturbed by that painting. I still have nightmares about it now.' She looked down at Mercy who was tugging her hand. 'Miss Felicity has given us some bread for the ducks,' the little girl enthused, holding up an unrecognisable lump that may or may not have been organic matter. 'She said would you mind helping Jennifer?'

Prudence raised her eyebrows knowingly. 'I've been summoned,' she grinned, allowing herself to be pulled towards the small pond. 'Remember, you adorable lovebirds, you're not wed yet, and every Town Tabby within a hundred-yard radius undoubtedly has their quizzing glass trained upon you right this second.' She laughed gaily as Mercy asked her, 'What's a Town Tabby?'

Reverend Shackleford was just about to settle down with a dish of tea and a piece of Mrs. Pidgeon's lemon tart, when there came an urgent banging on the front door. He didn't move for a minute or two, hoping against hope that Bailey wasn't dozing in his cubby hole again. Unfortunately, the banging came again. This time accompanied by the clanging of the doorbell. As far as the Reverend knew, the Duke was out on business, and Malcolm– well, in truth, Malcolm could be anywhere in London. Even Percy had decided to take Freddy out for a quick ramble around the park opposite.

Sighing, Augustus Shackleford got to his feet and laboriously made his way down the stairs as the banging continued. Clearly this wasn't a social visit. Finally reaching the bottom, he quickened his steps and hurried across the entrance hall, yelling, 'I'll be there in a second. Keep your shirt on.'

Fumbling with the doorknob, he finally managed to drag it open, just in time to watch Lizzy Fletcher faint into Percy's arms.

'AGNES!' bellowed the Reverend as Percy looked in grave danger of expiring on the Duke of Blackmore's front doorstep. Hurriedly, he stepped forward to help prop the matron up. Where the deuce was Agnes? He tried to remember the last time he'd seen her. It must have been at dinner last night.

'MY DOVE...' he yelled again, grunting under the strain of keeping Lizzy's head from bouncing off the top step. Percy was beginning to turn an interesting shade of purple.

'DEAREST...' It had to be said that his last effort was more of an agonised whimper, and never in the whole of their marriage had he been so glad to see his wife unexpectedly appear together with her customary waft of ammonia.

'Salts,' he croaked.

'Oh, my goodness,' Agnes enthused, totally in her element. With a flourish any physician would envy, she whipped her smelling salts from the depths of her reticule and waved them expertly under the unconscious woman's nose. Seconds later, Lizzy groaned and came round, staring up into Percy's now streaming eyes. 'Please don't cry,' she murmured, raising her hand to his cheek. In truth, Agnes had likely been a little too enthusiastic with the salts, but Reverend Shackleford didn't think it would help the situation to mention it.

Eventually, the two men managed to help Lizzy to her feet while Agnes hovered around waving her cure all at anyone who paused for so much as a second. Clearly it was the most fun she'd had in ages. Together they finally succeeded in manoeuvring the matron onto the recently vacated chaise longue in the morning room.

Wheezing, Augustus Shackleford staggered to his feet and rang the bell summoning assistance from below stairs.

While his back was turned, Lizzy suddenly sat up and grabbed hold of Percy's collar. It was the choking sound that alerted the Reverend that all was not entirely well. 'You 'ave to tell 'im,' she sobbed. 'The Upright Man's got someone goin' to 'ush 'im. Today.'

'Who's goin' to kill who, Lizzy?' Fortunately Jimmy was the first on the scene, and his matter-of-fact demand seemed to bring the frightened woman back to herself. She took a deep breath and struggled into a sitting position.

'Me brother, John,' she clarified in a whisper. 'I...I...don't rightly know who they're goin' to 'ush, but it's whoever Miss Chastity's getting leg shackled to.'

∞∞∞

Christian watched Mercy lead Chastity's younger sister away in bemusement. 'Is she always like that?' he questioned doubtfully.

'No, mostly she's worse,' Chastity murmured, seating herself on the bench facing the Serpentine lake. 'In truth, my lord, I'm entirely certain you have no idea what you're letting yourself in for.' She said the last ruefully. 'The only reassurance I can give you is that I am relatively normal. That is, when compared to many others in my family, not the general population.'

The Earl gave a bark of laughter as he sat down next to her. 'You think I am jesting,' she continued flatly.

'I have no idea what to think,' confessed Christian. 'I only know that since our first meeting, my life has been turned upside down, and I have the feeling that things will never be as they were.'

'Oh, I'm certain of it,' replied Chastity glumly.

'Why so Friday faced?' he questioned softly, turning to face her. She regarded him through her lashes for a second before coming to a sudden decision.

'I should tell you first that I have completely turned my back on affairs of the heart,' she declared loftily, watching for his reaction. To her disappointment, other than raising his eyebrows quizzically, he said nothing.

'My point is that I am not in need of the hearts and flowers you are clearly reluctant to dispense.'

'Ah,' murmured the Earl. She glanced over at him and waited for a second, however it appeared he'd said all he was going to.

'*But*,' she continued, putting a great deal of emphasis on the conjunction, 'at the very least, I expect us to be civil to one another...' She paused and bit her lip before shaking her head. 'No, that's not correct. I wish us to at least be friends. Mercy needs that, and *I* need that.' She looked over at him. 'I cannot live in an icehouse,' she added quietly.

∞∞∞

It took another full five minutes to get the full story from Lizzy.

'Where's Malcolm?' queried the Reverend, suddenly feeling very old.

Jimmy shook his head. 'We can't spare the time to look for him,' the young man determined after thinking for a second. 'We have to warn his lordship and her grace and the rest of 'em.' He grimaced anxiously. 'Did they intend to walk the length of Rotten Row?'

Reverend Shackleford shrugged. 'I assume so. Tare an' hounds, what a deuced scrape. Surely there won't be an attempt on his life in such a public place?'

'This is not the busiest time of day in Hyde Park, Sir,' Percy interjected. 'It would be the perfect time to shoot someone and simply slip away before anyone realises what has happened.'

Jimmy looked over at the clock on the wall. 'I estimate we have nearly two hours until the light begins to fade,' he predicted. 'Once dusk sets in, it will be too late for even the best marksman to use a pistol. So if he intends to strike, he will do so very soon.' He turned to the Reverend. 'I'll head towards Rotten Row this very minute. There's no time to have a horse saddled, so I'll go on foot. Sir, you stay here and wait for Malcolm and his grace. Get two horses ready in the meantime. As soon as either returns, direct them to Hyde Park. Hopefully, at least one of them will arrive back before it gets dark.'

With that, he nodded his head, pulled on his cap and ran out of the front door.

∞∞∞

'I should very much like us to be friends, Miss Shackleford,' Christian Stanhope offered quietly. Chastity stared back at him, fighting an irrational disappointment. What did she expect? That he would get down on one knee? Then she stopped thinking altogether as he reached down and took her hand. It was the first time they had touched.

'My life before Mercy came into it was almost devoid of any female companionship save that of necessity,' he stated bluntly. 'I was an only child. My mother died in the birthing of me so for the majority of my childhood, it was just me and my father. He purchased a commission for me at fifteen, which took everything he had. From then on, I spent most of my life at sea until I was forced to make a new start in the Americas.' He paused, and she became aware that his thumb was stroking the inside of her palm. She resisted the urge to lift her other hand and cup his cheek.

'I first went to Boston, then on to New York. I freely admit I was driven, working seventeen hours a day for seven days a week. Gradually, my wealth increased which only served to make me more determined. I was ruthless, ambitious and single minded. The occasional dinner party was the only time I was actually present in any lady's company.' He paused and smiled causing her heart to do a sudden flip. 'Until Mercy.' He stared intently at Chastity. 'She changed my life. Gave me something to live for other than money.'

'So you were not married to her mother?' Chastity questioned softly. Christian shook his head.

'A dalliance of one night. She died of consumption not long after leaving Mercy on my doorstep.' He gave a rueful chuckle. 'Perhaps you can imagine the difficulty I had in the early days,' he murmured. 'But I would lay my life down for her in an instant.' He looked down at their entwined hands, and Chastity felt as if the world had vanished save for the two of them.

'I am telling you this to explain my harsh words to you the other night,' he explained carefully. 'I've had no dealings with women. In truth, the whole female species baffles me–Mercy included– and quite frankly, the thought of being wed terrifies me.' He raised his eyes until they met hers. 'I'm unsure how to be a husband, but it's my hope you will teach me.'

Chastity stared back at him, her heart beating wildly in her chest. She wanted to throw herself into his arms. 'I do not have all the answers,' she said huskily at length. 'And indeed my experience of men is as lacking as yours with women.' She chuckled softly. 'We must needs teach each other I think, my lord.'

A sudden shout brought them both back from their cocoon. Looking over Christian's shoulder, Chastity saw Jimmy running towards them. She frowned as the Earl swivelled round to look. Jimmy was gesticulating frantically. Then everything seemed to happen in slow motion. She watched her fiancé let go of her hand and turn to glance over his right shoulder, then she felt his hands on her arms, dragging her off the seat to the ground. As she fell backwards she caught sight of a tall man standing under a tree. Her brain struggled to process the sight of a pistol aimed directly at them.

Twenty yards away, Grace straightened and turned, wondering at the commotion. She took an incredulous step forward as she saw the Earl push her sister to the ground, not noticing the man standing behind them. Felicity's eyes however were immediately drawn to the glint of the pistol, and she instinctively stepped in front of the Duchess, shielding her from what was clearly a madman.

At the same time, there was a loud crack, and less than a second later, Miss Beaumont slid gracefully to the ground.

Chapter Nineteen

After making sure she was unharmed, Christian shouted a harsh, 'Stay there,' to Chastity. Then, after giving an anguished glance towards the fallen Felicity, he leapt over the bench and chased after the shooter who was even now fleeing the scene. As he ran, all thoughts of anything other than his quarry, left the Earl's mind.

The assassin didn't waste time looking behind him, but immediately headed away from Rotten Row towards the end of the Serpentine. The fact that he hadn't discarded his heavy pistol told Christian it was double barrelled, leaving one bullet left.

Gradually, the Earl gained on him as the man began to slow. Clearly he was not accustomed to being chased, being more used to working in the shadows and slipping away unnoticed. Indeed, had Jimmy not warned them, that is exactly what would have happened.

Christian forced his mind away from the sight of their chaperone falling to the ground. He couldn't afford to get distracted. He had to catch the man while he was still in the park, lest he lose him in the alleyways beyond Tyburn. As the Earl ran, he watched carefully for the moment the blackguard realised he was being outpaced and decided to use his one remaining bullet. It came quicker than he'd anticipated. The man abruptly stopped, turned and dropped to his knees. Christian could see his hand trembling with exhaustion as he lifted the pistol and pointed it.

Swearing, the Earl threw himself to the ground, just as the deafening rapport cut the early evening air. The cutthroat didn't wait to see if his shot had hit its target but threw his now defunct pistol aside and immediately staggered to his feet. Seething now, Christian put on a last burst of speed. He knew he had the bastard.

Seconds later, he finally caught up and launched himself onto the varmint's back. They both went down hard. Christian had the advantage being on top, but the killer was heavyset and much taller. For a few precious seconds they grappled as the assassin endeavoured to twist the Earl onto his back. Christian managed to hold him down but couldn't pull his arm back to get in a punch. In the end, desperation won out and the Earl managed to lift his head back high enough to head butt the man with his forehead. The sound of the bastard's nose splitting gave him a savage satisfaction, and he followed it up with a prime facer, instantly rendering the man unconscious.

'How is she?' Grace's words showed the depth of her anguish as Malcolm finally entered the drawing room.

The Scot sighed. 'Fortunately, the bullet missed any o' the vital organs and came out through her back. Ah've cleaned and dressed the wound. She's sleeping comfortably enough, and it's ma belief, with plenty o' rest, she'll make a full recovery.'

Grace gave a small, relieved sob as Chastity gripped her hand. 'Felicity saved my life,' the Duchess whispered.

'Aye, she's a brave one,' Malcolm commented, his voice unaccountably gruff, 'and it'll be up te you te keep her in bed fer as long as possible. The stubborn woman will no hear it from me.' He shook his head and poured himself a large brandy. 'Any word from Nick or Jimmy?'

Grace and Chastity shook their heads. 'Lord Cottesmore arrived back from Bow Street a little over an hour ago,' the Duchess informed him, 'but left immediately with a contingent of Runners to assist in apprehending Witherspoon.'

'Lizzy told them everything she knew,' Chastity added. 'Hopefully, it will be enough to convict him. She's remained in Bow Street while she gives a statement. Father and Percy are with her.'

'How is she?' Malcolm asked taking a sip of his brandy.

'Naturally shocked on discovering the extent of her brother's criminal activity,' Chastity responded. 'But I think the horror of watching her husband die in such an awful manner put paid to any lingering affection she might have harboured.' She put her hand down to Freddy who was leaning against her, taking comfort in his rough fur. 'He hasn't left our sides since we got back from Hyde Park,' she commented bending down to give the foxhound an affectionate kiss on the nose.

Grace glanced outside. 'It's nearly dark,' she murmured, gripping her sister's hand.

Nicholas and Jimmy alighted from their hackney round the corner from Witherspoon's establishment. Both were armed with pistols and dressed in nondescript clothes. Indeed, looking at the Duke's unkempt apparel, nobody would have guessed his true rank.

Once the carriage had disappeared, they walked nonchalantly towards the gambling den. The gates were open, but as it was still early, the yard was almost deserted.

Glancing over at Jimmy, Nicholas nodded towards the main entrance. His meaning was clear. They would start there. The last time the Duke had laid eyes on Witherspoon was nearly seventeen years ago, and assuming the bastard hadn't worn well, the older man knew he could well be relying on Jimmy for any identification.

They stepped into the dark interior of the cavernous building and waited for their eyes to adjust. At length, Jimmy tapped the Duke on the shoulder and tipped his head towards a tall skinny man who was holding court with a couple of likely gullgropers.

'Bloody hell, I'd never have recognised him,' Nicholas muttered, eying the hideous scar that slashed through the man's eyebrow.

'What do we do?' Jimmy murmured. 'We can't take 'im with these culls around. By the look of 'em, they're more'n likely to wade in.'

The Duke was silent for a second. 'We'll wait here,' he said at length. 'It's dark enough that it's doubtful he'll recognise either of us. We just need to keep the bastard in our sights.' He looked over at Jimmy. 'No heroics,' he cautioned the youth. 'Your hotheadedness will not serve you here. With luck, the Runners should arrive within the hour.'

'Will the Earl be with them do you think?'

'I think wild horses wouldn't stop him,' answered Nicholas drily.

After knocking the cutthroat unconscious, Christian accepted the aid of passers-by who, in turn, flagged down a passing curricle. A length of rope had been found and used to secure the man before he began to come round. Within half an hour, the Earl had been able to return to the scene of the shooting where he was assured that the injured lady had been taken care of. After paying a lad to deliver a message to the Duke's residence, Christian imposed upon the curricle's owner once more to deliver both him and his prisoner to Bow Street.

Soon after, to Christian's relief, Reverend Shackleford and Percy arrived with Lizzy Fletcher in tow. The matron was keen to give a statement to the Runners describing exactly what she knew. Any loyalty to her brother had evidently long since withered. While their prisoner was unlikely to corroborate Lizzy's story, the Runners now had enough evidence to raid Witherspoon's warehouse and arrest him.

As he rode in the carriage with the uniforms, Christian reflected that what they had still might not be enough to see Witherspoon hang. There remained no proof that he'd murdered his shipmate, aside from Charlie Fletcher's garbled account, but Christian doubted Barnet's was the last murder the former Fourth Lieutenant had ever committed, and he had to hope that someone would be willing to cry rope in return for a suitable reward.

In the event, Witherspoon didn't put up much of a fight, though he eyed both Nicholas and Christian with mocking contempt, spitting at their feet as he was dragged past. It was clear he didn't think he'd remain incarcerated for long.

The raid on his quarters upstairs revealed nothing untoward, and on the face of it, Witherspoon appeared to be a legitimate businessman. All they had to convict him was a failed assassination attempt and his sister's word. If anyone else had been involved with the gambling den, they'd vanished into thin air.

∞ ∞ ∞

'Even if he is freed, surely he won't risk coming for you again?' Chastity demanded, trying to force down her fear.

'I think he truly has other things to worry about at the moment,' Christian responded, his grin almost savage. 'And since Fletcher was the one backing his story...well, I suspect Witherspoon is going to want to lie low.'

'It's unlikely he'll risk trying for you again,' Nicholas agreed. 'He certainly won't wish to draw attention to himself. And anyway, I doubt he'll be walking the streets anytime soon. We can only hope the hired killer will point the finger in the right direction.'

They were sitting in the dining room having just finished dinner. Both the Earl and Mercy had been invited to spend the night-an offer Christian was more than happy to accept given the circumstances. Briony had been given the evening off, and the children surrendered into Prudence's less-than-motherly ministrations.

'And I cannot imagine anyone will mention your name in connection with Barnet's murder now that Fletcher is dead and Witherspoon has no one to back his story,' Nicholas added with a small smile.

'As soon as Felicity is well enough, I should like to return to Blackmore,' Grace declared suddenly, drawing all eyes to her. 'I think she will recover much more swiftly in the cleaner air of the countryside, and of course, we have a wedding to plan.' She smiled faintly at Chastity.

'It's certainly about time I got back to my flock,' the Reverend announced. 'If Percy and I are away for much longer, they'll be turning into deuced pagans and dancing stark naked round a maypole.'

'Lord Cottesmore,' Grace continued hesitantly, 'please forgive me if I am being presumptuous, but since the consequences of this whole sordid episode are unlikely to disappear overnight, would you consider allowing Mercedes to accompany us back to Blackmore? She would be most welcome to stay with us until the wedding.' The Duchess paused before finishing in a rush, 'It will give her some company I think...whilst you are otherwise occupied.' She glanced over at her husband, wondering if she'd overstepped the mark. His raised eyebrows did not provide any reassurance.

There was a short silence. Chastity didn't know whether to applaud her sister or gag her. She certainly agreed with Grace's comment that Mercy would benefit from being around other children. She looked anxiously over at Christian who had so far been silent.

'Well, I cannot argue with your reasoning,' the Earl answered at length, his voice wry. 'And in truth, even without the added concern of Witherspoon, I had hoped to make a start on the renovations to Cottesmore before the wedding.' He looked over at Chastity and gave a faint smile. 'Naturally, I would be grateful to know that my daughter's being well taken care of, but I think that's a decision that Mercy herself will need to make.'

'Yes, please,' came three muffled voices from outside the door. Frowning, Grace jumped to her feet and threw open the door to reveal three pyjama-clad figures sitting in a line on the floor.

'What on earth...?' the Duchess began.

'Oh, please Papa,' Mercy interrupted, jumping to her feet and running to her father. 'Miss Sharpham said this morning that she despairs of ever making me into a lady, but when I told Prudence, she said *poof*, who wants to be a lady. If I go to

Blackmore, I can learn to be more like Prudence.'

'God help us all,' the Reverend commented with a shudder.

The Earl grinned, and shook his head before giving his daughter a swift kiss on the cheek. 'Very well, Blackmore and lessons in *how not to be a lady* it is,' he murmured. 'But for now, bed.'

While the Duchess escorted the children back to the nursery wing with Prudence, Nicholas offered an apologetic smile to the Earl. 'Forgive my wife,' he said ruefully. 'When she gets a bee in her bonnet about something... Well, I'm afraid she takes after her father...'

'Steady on...' interrupted the father in question. 'I'm entirely sure you wouldn't have said that if she'd been in the room...'

'With your permission, I should like to stay until she is settled in,' Christian added.

'Of course,' Nicholas responded easily. 'You may stay as long as you wish. I believe Cottesmore is only a day's journey from Blackmore. It may behove you to make your plans from Devonshire. I can certainly put you in touch with the necessary tradesmen.'

He stopped as Grace came back into the room. 'Don't ask,' she muttered helping herself to a glass of Madeira. Grinning, Nicholas, returned back to the subject of their journey. 'The snow is already showing signs of thawing,' he observed, 'so I think if we give it another week, most of the roads will be passable. I suggest we travel in three carriages to ensure Felicity gets as much room as she needs. As there's no urgency, I believe we would do well to take the full four days. I'll have Malcolm make arrangements for our overnight stops.' He looked round the room, pointedly drawing attention to the absence of his valet and gave a small chuckle. 'That's if I can tear him away from his patient for long enough.'

'Have you sent a note to everyone informing them what has happened?' Grace asked, suddenly concerned that her sisters might be thinking them dead or worse.

'I tasked Augustus with it before dinner,' Nicholas answered. He glanced enquiringly towards his father-in-law who gave him an enthusiastic thumbs-up.

There was a small incredulous silence, then...

'What on earth were you thinking, Nicholas?'

'Oh, tell me you didn't.'

'Well that's done it.'

'I'm entirely certain that you should be intimately acquainted with my father's legendary lack of tact after all this time.'

'Now hang on a deuced minute.'

The Duke raised his eyebrows at the sudden onslaught. 'I...' he muttered before trailing off with a wince.

The first carriage arrived five minutes later...

Chastity could honestly say that the following seven days were the most enjoyable she'd spent in London. Indeed, she attended a rout, two dinner parties, a Venetian breakfast, a concert at Vauxhall Gardens, a ball and an opera. She even received a voucher for Almack's.

But the reason she relished each and every occasion, she conceded, was not for the entertainments in themselves but for the company she kept. Lord Cottesmore escorted her everywhere, and each time she looked at his face or listened

BEVERLEY WATTS

to him speak, she became more smitten. His brusque attitude of their earlier meetings had been replaced by an easy good-humoured manner that captivated not only her, but every other young lady who was fortunate enough to spend time in his company.

Indeed, such was his popularity that, despite her enjoyment, Chastity was nonetheless very glad to be going home. Not that the Earl had shown any kind of interest in any of the other unmarried females that flocked around him, but Chastity began to fear that should they stay much longer in London, she wouldn't be the only one who had the temerity to wait in the Earl's bed.

The tingling Chastity had felt during the initial stages of their acquaintance had developed into an embarrassing heat that seemed to envelop her whole body whenever he was near. Yet despite everything, they had yet to indulge in so much as a kiss. She began to wonder if he felt the same desperate need to tug off all his clothes whenever they were in close proximity. If he did, he was doing a very good job of hiding it.

The day before they were due to leave, Chastity decided it was time to take matters into her own hands. She could not leave the Earl in London at the mercy of so many unattached ladies without clearly staking her claim.

She and Christian were spending the evening with the rest of the family currently resident in Town, which meant everyone with the exception of Charity and her husband Jago.

Temperance had laughingly declared the Colbourne dining room the largest so it was agreed that the gathering would take place in the Earl of Ravenstone's sumptuous townhouse, after which the family would go their separate ways until the wedding.

As she dressed for the evening, Chastity found herself missing her twin fiercely. She imagined Charity's expression on hearing her sister's latest idea. Totty-headed would be the least of her comments. But surely a kiss would not put her too beyond the pale? After all, they were betrothed. It wasn't like she was planning to invade the Earl's bed again. At least not this night. Chastity grinned to herself, her happiness suddenly bubbling over.

Dinner was a predictably lively affair with whoever spoke the loudest getting the rest of the table's attention. As soon as dinner was finished, Nicholas stood up to propose a toast to the happy couple and looking round at the smiling, cheering faces, Christian had the most peculiar sense that he'd finally come home.

On this occasion, the men remained at the dining table with their port whilst their wives retired into the drawing room. As Viscount Northwood commented wryly, it gave the sisters time to discuss how best to run their husbands' affairs.

As much as she enjoyed catching up with her siblings, Chastity had been keeping one eye on the door, and as soon as it opened to admit the men, she wasted no time climbing to her feet. 'I think Freddy needs to do his business, Father,' she declared though the foxhound's snores indicated no such thing. Then, before the Reverend had the chance to answer, she turned to Christian and with a wicked smile murmured, 'Perhaps you would like to accompany Freddy and me into the garden, my lord?'

Chapter Twenty

It had to be said that Christian's first reaction on being asked to escort his betrothed outside was to inform her bluntly that it was invitations like that, that had got her in the suds in the first place. The second was purely physical, and he almost groaned as his cock abruptly hardened at the thought of being alone with her for the first time.

As she looked coquettishly over at him, he could swear her eyes sparkled, and the Earl had to resist the urge to laugh. He knew exactly what she was about. Dear God, how he loved her... The voice in his head stilled. Indeed everything stopped. Even his breathing.

When the devil had that happened?

Heart slamming against his ribs, Christian looked over at her father, waiting for his comment. But the Reverend didn't appear to think anything was remiss, and merely warned Chastity not to lose the dog like Patience did.

Abruptly impatient to explore the sudden storm of feelings that had overwhelmed him, the Earl waited for Chastity to put on Freddy's lead, then held out his arm. She smiled up at him as they left the room.

As soon as they were in the hall, however, Chastity found herself unaccountably nervous. It was one thing to plan a seduction, but as she'd already discovered from her brief spell in the Earl's bedchamber, it was quite another actually executing it. Stalling for time, she went to fetch her cloak, but as Christian took it from her, placing it gently over her shoulders, she shivered in a way that had nothing to do with the cold–or her nerves.

The morning room had large French doors leading to the Earl and Countess of Ravenstone's back garden, and Freddy, having been here many times before, excitedly led the way. The candles in the room shed a soft glow over a delightful arbour with a small bench just big enough for two. Her heart now galloping, Chastity bent down to unclip Freddy's lead before allowing the Earl to take her hand.

Once they were seated, both were gripped by an unaccustomed silence. Chastity's stomach was roiling, and her cheeks were flushed. What was she to do now? She laid her hands across her knees, and kept her head down, purportedly admiring her gloves.

'They are very fine,' Christian murmured, a hint of laughter in his voice. Her head snapped up. 'Your gloves,' he continued. 'Indeed, I'm uncertain I've ever had occasion to observe that particular shade of lilac.'

She glanced up at him for a second, then grinned. 'Wretch,' she whispered.

'Indeed, Madam.' He lifted a languid finger and traced a stray curl along her cheek. 'But then I am *your* wretch.' Her eyes met his, and she felt the little hairs on the back of her neck stand to attention, just before he slid his fingers down to brush them along her nape.

'Will you kiss me?' she whispered. In answer, he gave a slow, teasing smile. Was he making fun of her? Suddenly, she didn't care. The tingling had centred itself directly between her legs, and she had to resist the urge to squirm. Either that or throw herself into his arms.

His hand had continued to caress the back of her neck, but at her request, his fingers stilled for a second, then pressed into her nape, leisurely drawing her head towards him. She did not resist, her breath coming quickly through parted lips. Their gazes fused as he eased her head back and slowly, oh so slowly brought his mouth down onto hers in a featherlight touch. She had time to note that he tasted of Cognac, before he gave a low groan, and covered her lips with his again, this time in an all-consuming melding of mouths that both demanded and gave in equal measure. His tongue dipped in between her teeth to tangle with hers.

With a small sound, her hands slid inside his jacket, revelling in the feel of his hard chest. She could feel the heat through his fine linen shirt and fought the urge to rip the fabric apart. Whatever it took to gain access to his hot skin. Suddenly, shockingly, his mouth left hers only to burn a trail down to her neck. Helplessly, she tipped her head back as his lips traced down to her collarbone.

Inside her dress, her breasts ached, nipples hard and straining against the flimsy fabric. Lost in a sea of sensation, she did not protest when he bent her backwards over his arm, using his other hand to part her cloak. His mouth continued its relentless assault down to her shadowy cleavage, even as his hand pulled at the bodice until the milky globes were bare to his gaze. Before the shock of the cold air could register, his warm hand had covered her left breast, cupping it, his thumb brushing the hard tip. She gasped, but it was nothing to the exquisite pleasure that rocked her whole body as his lips closed over her other nipple. Dear God, she was going to die from the sensations coursing round her body.

Christian knew he had to stop, but never had he felt such

desperate need, such a loss of control. His cock was hard, throbbing, and he realised he was close to spilling in his breeches. What would happen if she touched him?

Abruptly, he lifted his head, closing his eyes in an effort to regain some control. When he opened them again, she was staring up at him, eyes glazed, her delectable breasts heaving. Gently, he pulled up her bodice, covering them from his gaze as she gradually became aware of their surroundings. Lifting her close to him, Christian wrapped her back up in the cloak before enfolding her in his arms.

For a few seconds, she didn't speak, content to rest her head against his broad chest. 'Am I deflowered now?' she murmured at length. He chuckled against her hair. 'Sweetheart, not even close.' He felt her stir and looked down as she lifted her head. 'Were you…did you…did it feel as wonderful for you?' she asked shakily. He was still for a moment, then he took her hand and placed it on his still rigid cock. Her eyes widened, and she looked down at the hard shape of him inside his breeches. 'It was amazing–*you* are amazing,' he growled. 'If it had felt any better, I'd have likely been meeting at least one of my brothers-in-law to be in a duel tomorrow morning.' His hand clamped down on her fingers as they sought to trace the shape of him. 'Please my love, for my continued good health, not to mention my sanity, could we wait until after the wedding before we indulge in round two…?'

∞∞∞

It had been decided that Grace would travel to Blackmore with Nicholas and their two children, together with Prudence and Mercy, while the children's maid Briony followed on in the second carriage with Felicity in case the matron needed any additional assistance. Malcolm too insisted on accompanying her, an offer to which she blushingly acquiesced.

Anthony and Jimmy professed themselves more than content to share the box with the coach driver.

The third carriage would be occupied by Chastity, her father, Percy, Lizzy and Christian. The journey to Blackmore apparently took them very close to the Earl's family seat and though much of the building was in ruins, Lord Cottesmore was keen to take the opportunity to finally show his bride to be her future home. To that end, it was decided that the third carriage would take a short detour after Ringwood, spending the afternoon at Cottesmore, before re-joining the other two carriages at their second overnight stop.

By the time they set off on the second leg of their journey, the weather had warmed up significantly. There was a definite air of excitement in the last carriage, broken only by Lizzy's slightly subdued manner. Thinking her in low spirits after everything that had happened, Percy endeavoured to cheer her up by making light conversation while Christian spoke to Chastity and her father of his plans for his country seat.

However, by the time they reached the turnoff to Cottesmore, Lizzy's demeanour was such that Chastity began to fear her unwell. As the carriage slowed down to navigate the narrow roads, she leaned forward and lightly touched the widow's knee. 'Is something wrong, Mrs Fletcher?' she asked in concern. The woman jumped at the touch and for a second looked wildly around.

'Is something troubling you madam?' questioned Christian.

Lizzy shook her head and squeezed her eyes shut. Then she took a deep breath before muttering, 'There was another one.'

Raising his eyebrows, the Earl looked over at Reverend Shackleford, a question in his eyes. The clergyman frowned and shrugged.

'Another one what, Lizzy?' Percy asked gently. He might as well have shouted. She shrank back before suddenly leaning forward and blurting, 'e wos talkin' to someone. I 'eard 'im. But my Charlie were dead by then.' She looked around the carriage before lowering her voice and adding in a whisper, 'Charlie told me. I should 'ave remembered. 'e *told* me right afore 'e went... He said they din't need 'is bloody fancy ideas, but John wouldn't listen.' She shook her head and leaned forward.

'So who 'ad the fancy ideas? Who was it who cut the wheedle wi' my idiot of a brother? It sure as 'ell weren't my Charlie.' She leaned back and gave a chuckle that turned into a low sob.

'You think there was someone else involved,' Christian finished flatly.

Lizzy nodded tearfully. 'I'm sorry,' she whispered. 'I...I just forgot.'

'Please don't trouble yourself, Mrs. Fletcher,' Chastity hurriedly intervened. 'This is not your fault. It is due to your courage that the attempt on the Earl's life did not succeed.'

'So if Charlie Fletcher's cocked up his toes, who and where's the third man?' questioned Reverend Shackleford grimly.'

The Earl leaned back against the seat, thinking quickly.

'Whoever the third man is, I assume he'd be more than happy to let Witherspoon rot in gaol or better still, at the end of a rope. Except he must know the bastard won't go quietly and I assume he does not wish his identity known.' The Earl paused, thinking. 'So, his best option is to make sure Witherspoon walks free. And to do that, he needs to be rid of me.

'But how will that help?' Chastity questioned.

'Because if I die while Witherspoon's locked up, then there's no case to answer and he'll almost certainly be released,' Christian bit out.

'But what about the man who tried to shoot you?' Chastity protested. 'Surely he will be willing to point the finger away from himself?'

The Earl shook his head. 'Unlikely if he's in the pay of the Upright Man.

'Thunder an' turf,' the Reverend muttered. 'What are we going to do?'

'What am *I* going to do,' Christian countered. 'You and the whole of your family have gone above and beyond anything I dared hope, Augustus, but this is for me to finish.'

'We're your family now too,' Chastity interjected tearfully.

Christian quirked a mocking brow and gave a boyish grin. 'Naturally, I'm not yet quite sure whether that's a good thing.'

'It's not,' retorted the Reverend emphatically.

Chastity gave a watery smile as the Earl had obviously intended. 'What will you do?' she asked.

'For now, nothing. But I've survived solely on my wits for a good number of years and am not a complete numbskull.' He shook his head. 'I'm just grateful that Mercy will be safe and sound in Blackmore.'

'Mayhap from murdering deuced sailors,' the Reverend muttered, 'but don't be surprised if she comes back with more than a few bad habits.'

'Those I can deal with,' Christian smiled.

'He says that now,' snorted the clergyman.

The carriage began to slow down as they approached the gates to Cottesmore, effectively bringing the conversation to an end. As they approached the overgrown drive, Christian leaned forward to take Chastity's hand. 'Please don't worry about me,' he murmured. 'I will deal with the matter. For now, I simply want to show you our home to be.'

Chastity stared at him for a second, then nodded. With a small sniff, she determinedly looked out of the window for signs of the house. 'Did you ever visit the house before you unexpectedly inherited it?' she asked at length.

'You mean before it became a smouldering ruin,' Christian answered drily. She glanced back at him sympathetically as he shook his head. 'The poorest of poor relations,' he explained. 'The connection was through my mother's side. Apparently, she was the old Earl's cousin. I can't even remember how many times removed.'

The drive bent to the right, and all of a sudden, the ivy-clad building came into view. From this angle, it looked to be undamaged, but as they came closer, the windows yawned black and empty, the ivy charred and curling around the edges.

Chastity stared without speaking as the carriage came to a halt. Clearly, the fire had started upstairs. She tried to envision what it must have been like to have been trapped with no way out. Silently, Christian helped her down.

'This side is the worst,' he explained. 'It's thought the fire started in the Earl's bedchamber.' Chastity allowed her eyes to follow the direction of his pointed finger. She took his arm and squeezed it in silent acknowledgement of the tragedy.

Slowly, they walked towards the front door, which was still intact. 'Did anybody escape?' she breathed.

'Most of the servants,' Christian answered. 'The stairs up to their quarters in the attic ran along the back. Come, let me show you.'

They picked their way carefully round the side of the house. Slowly evidence of the fire became less and less until they turned the corner to the back. Chastity stopped and gasped. The view from the overgrown terrace was incredible. The New Forest in all its skeletal glory spread out in front of them, the promise of spring still a vague dream. On the exposed areas of moorland, she could see the wild ponies grazing, their coats still rough and thick from the winter. On the higher ground, patches of snow showed beneath the trees, glistening as the early afternoon sun caught them.

It was ethereal, almost otherworldly and quite, quite beautiful.

Face flushed in sudden excitement, Chastity gripped Christian's arm and looked up at him, eyes shining. 'It's...' she stopped and shook her head, unable to put the scene into words. The Earl grinned down at her. 'This is why I wanted to bring you,' he murmured, turning her to face the house. 'From here, you can see what it was and what it can become again.'

The warm red brick poked through the ivy, here green and lush. The windows were mullioned and though thick with the detritus of abandonment, they gave the house a cosy, welcoming air. Pulling her arm, Christian led her to a small wooden door directly in between two windows. There were no fancy French doors opening onto the terrace, but the Earl told her where he proposed to put them. Unlocking the door, he finally led her inside.

The rooms on either side of the narrow hallway were dirty but undamaged. A few items of furniture lay covered in dust sheets. 'The main stairs and front hallway were damaged beyond repair,' he told her, leading the way to a small staircase that had obviously been used by the staff, 'but we can reach the first floor this way.'

Chastity was quiet as she followed him up into the shadows. In truth, her mind was awhirl with possibilities. It had never dawned on her before that she would actually be mistress of her own house. She felt humbled and elated all at once.

Warning her to be careful, Christian stepped out from a small landing, into the main body of the house. Where the main staircase had once been was now a gaping hole, blackened and charred. 'I thought to replace the stairway with oak,' he explained, leading her along the galleried landing, taking care to stay well away from the absent balustrade.

'I can see your reasoning,' came an amused voice behind them. 'But I'd go for cherry myself. Much more warmth in my opinion.' Christian whirled round, instinctively pushing Chastity behind him.

The stranger looked to be dressed in the clothes of an extremely well-to do gentleman. His cravat was tied expertly in a waterfall, and his hair fell artfully over his forehead in a beautifully coiffured Brutus. His royal blue waistcoat fitted across his slightly paunchy form like it was made for him, which it probably was, and his breeches fitted like a proverbial glove.

But the stranger's impeccable dress sense wasn't what drew the Earl's attention and elicited a small gasp from Chastity at his back.

It was the pistol pointing steadily at them in the gentleman's right hand.

Chapter Twenty-One

The Reverend and Percy remained with Lizzy as the other two alighted from the coach. 'Let's give 'em a few minutes to look round alone,' Augustus Shackleford commented in a rare show of thoughtfulness as he caught Percy's enquiring look. Unfortunately, Freddy had no such consideration and quickly disappeared into the bushes on the trail of who knows what. 'Something disgusting no doubt,' was the Reverend's sour observation.

Lizzy Fletcher remained pre-occupied and subdued, refusing to engage in conversation despite Percy's gallant efforts. Clearly she was still upset over her failure to remember everything Charlie Fletcher had told her.

'There's no sense in having a fit of the blue devils,' the Reverend declared to the widow bluntly. 'It's not your fault you've got a deuced blackguard for a brother. And nobody could be expected to remember word for word what someone has to say when they're about to cock up their toes.'

'Sir!' protested Percy, dismayed at his superior's insensitive comments.

'Well, it's not like old Charlie had been much of a husband to you is it?' the Reverend continued unrepentantly. 'I mean take Percy here. How much more agreeable to be wed to a sensitive, caring fellow like him.' He ignored his curate's frantic hand signals and bright red face. 'Not that he's got much backbone. In fact I'd go so far as to say he's a trifle chuckleheaded. But his heart's the right place and believe me, you could do a lot worse.' He paused slightly before adding, 'which of course you already know.'

With a dark chuckle, Augustus Shackleford climbed to his feet. 'Right then, I'll leave you to it. I reckon I've given the lovebirds enough of a head start. Time to have a bit of a nose.' He pushed open the door before turning back to his speechless curate, muttering, 'Don't make a deuced mull of it, Percy lad,' accompanied by a lewd wink.

Clambering down, the Reverend gave a nod to the coach driver who was stamping about in an effort to keep warm. After a sudden thought, the clergyman rummaged around in his cassock, eventually fishing out his small flask of brandy. 'Here you go lad,' he declared, holding the small bottle out to the coachman. 'This'll chase away the cold.'

Leaving the flask with the grateful coach driver, the Reverend wandered round the side of the house, keeping an eye out for Freddy. Arriving at the back, he stood for a second appreciating the view and thinking to himself that despite the small problem of his daughter's betrothed being wanted by a murderous ex sailor, things had turned out rather well.

Stepping towards the house, he peered in through the first window but there was nothing of interest to see. He wondered where the Earl had taken Chastity. The scoundrel had better not be looking for an undamaged bedchamber. Naturally Reverend Shackleford had completely forgotten that only last evening he'd happily allowed the same daughter to be escorted into a dark secluded garden by said scoundrel.

Hurrying a little now and berating himself for his earlier selflessness, the Reverend went towards a large door, noting as he got closer, that it was slightly ajar. Grunting, he pulled it open the rest of the way and tiptoed inside. Unsure why he was being so quiet, he followed the shadowy hall, peeping into each empty room, until he came to a narrow staircase.

Reasoning that as very little remained of the front of the house, the Earl and Chastity must have gone up this way, he began to climb, his knees protesting with every step. He gave a pained grimace. Truly, it was time he stopped gallivanting round the deuced country.

The stairs turned, and he could see another door open slightly at the top. He was just about to continue up when there was a sudden scuffle behind him. He froze in place, not daring to move, until abruptly a cold nose thrust into his hand. Only just managing to stifle an instinctive yell, he sat down abruptly as Freddy clambered all over him. 'Thunder an' turf, you nearly gave me a deuced apoplexy,' he muttered, pushing the foxhound off. He was just about to get back to his feet when the sound of voices drifted down the stairs.

Freddy gave a low warning growl. 'It's only Chastity, you beef-witted dog,' Augustus Shackleford murmured. The foxhound continued to grumble, and the Reverend frowned, glancing up the stairs. 'Quiet,' he whispered, holding onto the dog's muzzle.

'...Not that you're likely to live long enough to decide between either.'

Reverend Shackleford felt his stomach churn. The voice was arrogant, amused and the clergyman was certain he'd never heard it before. Carefully, he climbed to his feet, frantically searching his pockets for the foxhound's lead before remembering it was round his neck. With a mumbled epithet, he clipped the lead back on. 'Let's go and see who it is,' he whispered in Freddy's ear, receiving a low whine in return.

Carefully, the Reverend crept up the remaining steps, his heart beating a tattoo on the inside of his chest. Hardly daring to breathe, he put his eye to the crack in the door. He could see Christian with Chastity behind him. They were watching someone, and the fear on both their faces told him the owner of the voice wasn't making a social call. Slowly, he eased the door open a little more–enough to give him a view of the other end of the landing.

Sure enough, a man stood facing them. His clothes proclaimed him a gentleman, but the Reverend gave them only a cursory glance before his attention was drawn to the pistol in the stranger's hand.

'You're Witherspoon's partner,' the Earl stated matter-of-factly.

'The Honourable Josiah Winters, at your service,' the man sneered with a parody of a bow.

'How did you know I'd be here?'

Winters laughed. 'Servants are notoriously easy to bribe,' he chuckled. 'And yours easier than most. You're not well regarded by your staff, my lord.' He winked and leaned forward slightly as if imparting a secret. 'I think they believe you an upstart bastard.' His unconscious use of the same words spoken by Mercy told Christian all he needed to know.

'She's a very pretty child, your daughter,' Winters went on, his voice chillingly conversational. 'Her name is Mercy, I'm told. Ironic really as we'd originally intended to steal her from you until things came to a head rather more quickly than we'd anticipated.' He gave a low chuckle. 'To be fair, it was my idea really. Witherspoon was content to see you dead. No deuced imagination.'

'If you so much as touch a hair on my daughter's head, I'll kill you,' Christian commented through gritted teeth.

'Well, the poor darling's hardly going to be able to live without her papa, now is she?' Winters shook his head sadly. 'Such a cruel world for orphans.'

Christian took an involuntary step forward, his face white with fury.

In answer, Winters raised the pistol and extended his arm. 'Anyway, as enriching as this little tête-à-tête has been, I must be getting on. Our biggest fight is merely days away, and I'd like to see my associate released before then. He'd be devastated if he missed it.'

Augustus Shackleford knew he had but seconds to act. As he listened to the intruder's chilling words, he bent down and quietly unclipped Freddy's lead, making sure to keep hold of his collar. The foxhound's hackles were raised, his lips curling away from his teeth. Heart thudding, the Reverend held the dog back, but as soon as the blackguard raised his pistol, he took his hand from Freddy's collar with a whispered, 'Get him, Fred.'

The hound needed no further urging. Bursting through the door with a loud snarl, he took Winters completely by surprise. Eyes wide with horror as the foxhound leapt up at him, teeth bared, the man tried to redirect the pistol towards the attacking dog, but instead, accidently fired it into the air. The deafening sound of the gunshot ricocheted around the empty room as the Earl took advantage of the distraction, immediately jumping forward and launching himself at their attacker.

As the two men grappled, Freddy barked and growled, darting in to snap at the intruder's breeches.

Chastity stood fixated with terror as she watched them get closer to the gaping hole where the balustrade should have been. The pistol skidded across the floor, and Chastity darted forward to pick it up, only to stare down at it in bewilderment. She had no idea how to use it. And anyway, she'd just as likely hit the Earl as their attacker if she tried.

She sent a panicked glance towards her father who was hovering as close to the men as he dared, though quite what he intended to do was unclear. She had no idea how he'd known they were in the suds.

Then everything appeared to happen at once. As Christian threw up his hand to block a punch, he connected with the assailant's shoulder, spinning him to one side. At the same time, Freddy finally succeeded in sinking his teeth through the man's breeches. With a yell, Winters kicked out viciously, but the foxhound had already darted out of the way, and his leg met with fresh air. With a panicked cry, he overbalanced, falling backwards. His hands flailed towards Christian and managed to snag the edge of the Earl's jacket. Frantically, Christian tried to prise the fingers off, but just as he thought he'd succeed in freeing himself, Winters went over the edge, the momentum dragging Lord Cottesmore with him.

Winter's scream stopped abruptly as he hit the floor below with a sickening thud. Christian however, managed to grab hold of a section of charred balustrade as he went over the edge, halting his fall but leaving him swinging in midair, desperately hanging onto the wood with one hand.

'Tare an'hounds,' Reverend Shackleford breathed hurrying towards the edge. Looking down, he tried to help by reaching down and grasping the Earl's free hand, but he was too far away.

'PERCY!' he yelled, though quite what he expected the curate to do was uncertain. Hurriedly, the Reverend lay down on his stomach and stretched out his arm. 'Can you reach my hand?' he grunted. Throwing his arm upwards, Christian managed to touch the tip of the clergyman's fingers but could reach no further. He tried a second, then a third time, the strain making his face almost unrecognisable.

Chastity, crouching wordlessly next to her father, silent tears trickling down her cheeks, saw the moment the Earl gave up. His beautiful eyes travelled to her face, and incredulously, she watched him rasp, 'I love you,' as he prepared to let go.

'No,' she screamed, 'Please.'

Suddenly, two heads appeared above the Reverend. 'Move,' ordered Lizzy, unceremoniously shoving the clergyman out of the way. Then, folding down her skirts, she quickly lay down on the floor. 'Hold my legs,' she commanded, clearly speaking to all three of them.

Without arguing, Percy, the Reverend and Chastity threw themselves on Lizzy's legs, pinning them to the floor as she slid her upper body over the edge. Her arms, much longer than the clergyman's, easily grabbed hold of the Earl's flailing hand. Then with her other hand, she gripped the collar of his jacket and yelled, 'Pull me back.'

Without thought for modesty, all three took hold of whichever part of Lizzy's person they could and dragged her backwards. Slowly, Christian's head appeared above the edge, until he was able to hook his arm around the charred stump of wood. Hurriedly, the Reverend let go of his hold on Lizzy's nether regions, and getting down on his knees, assisted the widow by grabbing the Earl's other arm and dragging him the rest of the way up onto solid ground.

Panting, they all remained motionless for a few stunned seconds, then with a small sob, Chastity crawled over to the Earl's prone body and took hold of his arm. In answer, he rolled over onto his back with a pained grunt and folded his weeping bride-to-be in his arms.

'Thunder an' turf, that was a close one,' the Reverend wheezed after a moment, followed by, 'Down Freddy,' as the foxhound endeavoured to climb into his lap and drench his face in slobber.

There was another short silence punctuated by Chastity's

sniffing, then Lizzy declared in a tone much more like herself, 'I think you can remove your hands from my drawers now, Percy Noon.'

Chapter Twenty-Two

Given that they were now in the unenviable position of being in possession of a dead body, it was decided that the best course of action was for Lord Cottesmore and the Duke of Blackmore to return to London with the cadaver. They would enlist the assistance of Jimmy, while Malcolm, the Reverend and Percy escorted the ladies the rest of the way to Blackmore.

Naturally, their first port of call was Bow Street. After describing the incident in detail, the body was despatched to the morgue, and all three men were permitted to return to Grosvenor Square with the proviso that they did not even think about leaving London until the magistrate had finished looking into the matter.

'Who the devil was Josiah Winters?' Nicholas mused, taking a sip of his brandy. It's not a name I'm familiar with. Had you ever laid eyes on him before?' Christian shook his head.

'He had the bearing of a gentleman, but there was something off about him,' the Earl recollected. 'He was too…'

'Too much the gentleman,' finished Jimmy with a grin. Christian looked over at the younger man and nodded. 'That's exactly it. It was as if he was playing the part in a stage production.'

'Then it's likely he's not a toff at all,' Jimmy declared. 'Could be he's pitching the gammon.'

'He implied he was Witherspoon's partner,' the Earl stated with a frown.

'Well, by the look of his clothes, he was certainly better dressed than Witherspoon,' the Duke retorted. 'So if it was a partnership, it could well have been Winters was the one in control.'

'He said they'd got a *big fight* coming up,' Christian commented thoughtfully. 'If he was talking about a boxing match, we didn't see any ring, and the room with the gaming tables didn't look big enough to actually take one.'

The Duke climbed to his feet to pour them all another brandy. 'Jimmy, first thing tomorrow, get yourself to Gentleman Jack's. Find out if there are any big fights coming up anywhere in the City.' He poured the liquid into both men's glasses. 'The magistrate forbade us to leave London. He didn't say we couldn't leave the house.'

The next morning, Jimmy left straight after breakfast to visit Gentleman Jack's boxing establishment. As he strode along the Embankment, he reflected on the strange path his life had taken.

When he was a lad, he'd rarely thought beyond the next purse to be filched or coin to be earned. Failure to lay his hands on any blunt, whether by legal means or not, would see him and his ma with nothing to eat. But the Duke had taken that worry away and over the years, the man he became gradually left that Jimmy behind. But what did that make him now?

Sighing, he put his thoughts aside as he arrived outside Gentleman Jack's at number thirteen Bond Street. It took less than ten minutes to ascertain that there were no legal boxing matches taking place in the next week or so. Certainly not within the City. But the pugilist had heard rumours of an illicit match. One where the boxers fought to the death. He had no idea where it was to be held and advised Jimmy in no uncertain terms to stay well away.

Elated, his earlier misgivings forgotten, Jimmy hurried back to the Duke's townhouse with the information.

'It has to be what Winters was referring to,' Christian responded, unable to hide his excitement.

'The question is–where were they intending to hold it?' Nicholas questioned. 'Are they likely to have a secret venue somewhere?'

'It would be difficult to find a large enough space in Town,' commented the Earl. 'Could they be holding it outside the City?'

'Gentleman Jack reckoned the rumours put it inside the walls,' Jimmy interjected. He paused before giving a small frown. 'What if the *Flying Horse* does have another room? One that no one can see from the outside?'

The three men looked at each other, before saying in concert, 'A cellar!'

Hurriedly, Nicholas called for a carriage to be brought round, and within fifteen minutes, they were on their way to Whitechapel. Naturally, on receiving the Duke's order not to spare the horses, Joseph was in his element. Indeed, even Jimmy, who was accustomed to uncomfortable carriage rides found himself offering a small prayer of thanks as he finally clambered down.

The gates were locked, and the large building looked deserted, but at the Duke's suggestion, they followed the perimeter until they came upon a section of the wrought iron fence that was considerably lower. Without hesitation, all three climbed over, swiftly making their way towards the shadow of the building.

Unsurprisingly, the main door was locked, but again, they skirted round the edge until they came to a small door whose lock had been recently broken. 'This must have been where Lizzy got in,' Jimmy whispered.

Cautiously, Nicholas pushed open the door, leading them into a dark hall. To their left was a narrow staircase, while directly in front, another door. Reasoning that they wouldn't be looking for a cellar upstairs, the three men stepped through the door and found themselves in the den's foyer.

The windows high in the wall were covered in black fabric cutting out the light. But on one window, the cloth had torn, allowing the weak early afternoon sunlight to shine on items of furniture that had clearly seen better days.

'Well, they certainly weren't making a fortune from gaming,' Christian commented looking round.

'Let's split up,' the Duke suggested, 'we'll cover more ground that way. I think we're looking for a small door, likely well-hidden since the Runners found nothing the last time they were here. The three men started in different corners. A quick search of the foyer revealed no hidden doors, so they went into the main gambling hall.

Tables were set up around the room, but here there was hardly any light at all due to the complete absence of windows. 'Bloody hell, this is a death trap if ever I saw one,' the Duke muttered, pushing the double doors wide open to let in a modicum of light.

Quickly now, they began working their way around the outside, pulling aside false drapes and occasional tables. It took them half an hour, but they found nothing.

'Mayhap we were wrong,' Christian growled. 'There's no secret entrance hidden within these walls.'

'It has to be here,' reasoned Nicholas. 'They would be expecting a packed house and would need a large space to get the spectators inside as quickly as possible.'

Abruptly, Jimmy went over to the first table and began pushing it. 'Try the others,' he grunted, pulling aside the threadbare carpet underneath. Without further ado, they each began shifting the tables and lifting up the rugs underneath. Within ten minutes they'd found it. Two large trap doors with room enough for four people to descend the steps at the same time.

'We need some light,' Nicholas murmured peering into the stygian depths below. The smell coming up stank of mould, damp and something else. Hurrying to one of the side tables decorating the walls, Jimmy picked up a half-used candle in its holder and lit it with the flint in his pocket. Back at the entrance to the cellar, he handed the candle holder to the Duke. Glancing round at the tense faces of the other two men, Nicholas murmured, 'Stay close to me,' before descending into the darkness.

The flickering candlelight barely penetrated a quarter of the cellar. The roped-off area where the fight would take place was in the middle, and round it were rows of benches, the furthest ones swallowed by the darkness.

'They could squeeze more than five hundred in here,' breathed Christian as he looked round. 'God forbid they should have a fire.' He shuddered and shook his head. 'What the bloody hell is that smell?'

Slowly the three men made their way between the benches towards the very back of the cavernous room until they came to another door, this one securely locked. 'Where the devil is Patience when you need her,' muttered the Duke. Lord Cottesmore frowned in confusion at the strange comment.

Jimmy didn't speak, but bent down to eye the keyhole, then rummaged around inside his right pocket, at length pulling out a small pin.

'I forgot we had someone with us every bit as industrious as my sister-in-law,' Nicholas commented drily as he held the candle closer to the lock. Jimmy glanced over his shoulder and gave a quick grin. 'We were both taught by the best,' he quipped.

Nicholas held up his hand, trying to stifle a smile. 'I'm entirely sure I don't want to know,' was all he said. Christian frowned, vowing to get to the bottom of the Duke's strange comments as soon as this damn business was finished.

With a soft chuckle, Jimmy expertly inserted the pin in the lock, and seconds later there was a soft click. With a last look at the two men flanking him, the youth, turned the handle and pushed open the door.

The stench that hit them had all three stumbling back. 'What the bloody hell?' muttered Christian, covering his nose and mouth with his arm. Eyes watering, the Duke held a kerchief over his nose and stepped towards the open doorway, lifting the candle high. At first all they could make out was a large sack, but reluctantly stepping closer, Nicholas saw something sticking out the bottom. Glancing at each of his companions, he moved closer and crouched down, holding the candle towards the object.

Which even in the meagre candlelight they could tell was a foot.

It turned out the Right Honourable Josiah Winters's real name was Archie Phelps. A Captain Sharp through and through with a particular flair for cutting a wheedle, he'd been on the run from an unfortunate incident with a wealthy widow in Nottingham when he first met John Witherspoon five years earlier. The two had hit it off straight away, and the former Fourth Lieutenant had been keen to show his new friend the gambling den he owned.

Unfortunately, such establishments were ten a penny in London, and at the time of meeting Phelps, he and Fletcher were making a meagre living at best. But Archie was a man with grand ideas, even though he was entirely lacking in funds to bring any of them to fruition.

And the building Witherspoon owned had an added bonus. A huge cellar which ran under the entirety of the building.

The perfect space to stage a fight.

Whilst frowned upon, boxing matches were not actually *illegal* under normal circumstances. But the fights in the cellar of the *Flying Horse* would have one big difference.

Only one of the contestants would leave the ring alive.

They held them roughly every six weeks or so, varying the times and the days to keep the magistrates off their trail. Neither man could have imagined in their wildest dreams how successful they would be.

The only fly in the ointment at the beginning had been the unexpected arrival of John Witherspoon's sister Lizzy after the death of their mother. But even that turned out to be fortuitous as around the same time, Nicholas Sinclair had been forced to resign his commission and return home to Blackmore to assume the mantle of Duke on the death of his father.

Meanwhile, Charlie Fletcher had become somewhat of a liability due to his penchant for drowning his sorrows in the bottom of a bottle. It was therefore decided that Fletcher would make an honest woman of Lizzy and take her to live in Blackmore to keep an eye on Sinclair. Not that they thought the new Duke would give them any trouble, but at the end of the day, a body couldn't be too careful.

So Charlie was dispatched to Devonshire with the promise of regular money providing he kept Lizzy sweet. Everything would have worked perfectly except they forgot the part about sending the blunt. Which resulted in Fletcher turning up out of the blue like a bad penny...

Of course there was another slight problem. What to do with the poor unfortunates who lost their fights. Despite being on the edge of the Rookeries, it wasn't that easy to dispose of a body without attracting unwanted attention.

At that point, the enterprising Mr. Phelps came up with the idea of donating the corpses for medical science. Or rather handing them over to the Resurrectionists, since medical science had a disturbing tendency to ask where the corpse had come from.

So, all in all, despite the few hiccoughs, they had a very profitable business. Until Stanhope had the bloody gall to come back...

Chapter Twenty-Three

The sudden demise of John Witherspoon in Newgate prison was noted by hardly anyone, except perhaps the gallows bird in the cell next door, who actually reported it.

According to the account given by one John Smith who was serving a life sentence for pilfering a lady's undergarments, he couldn't rightly say how it had happened, though the word carved out on the unfortunate Witherspoon's posterior in big bloody letters was a good indication that the Upright Man did not like leaving loose ends.

Chastity and Christian's wedding was scheduled to take place at the end of May. The Earl had been a guest at Blackmore for a little over a month while he began the repairs on Cottesmore Hall, though it would take nigh on a year before the house was again liveable. Until then, as soon as the wedding was over, the Earl and Countess would reside in their townhouse in London.

Mercy had flourished in the weeks she'd been staying with the Duke and Duchess. She got on with Peter and Jennifer famously, and when he arrived, Christian could not believe the difference in his lonely daughter. Indeed, he finally began to see signs of the confident, captivating woman she might become. He would be forever grateful to Grace and Nicholas for taking her into their home and their hearts.

Naturally, it wasn't all roses. Prudence too had imprinted her mark on Mercy, and if his daughter's confidence was a little on the *determined* side, well, her father reasoned that would be another man's problem to deal with.

By the middle of May, her grace was increasing nicely. She had finally revealed her condition to Nicholas after he'd returned from London. As predicted, he was equally delighted and fearful by turn, leading Grace to demand on more than one occasion that he stop hanging around her like a deuced mother hen.

Felicity too remained a guest at Blackmore, and the Duchess would not hear of the matron returning to Bath until she was certain her dear friend had fully recovered, a stance which was fully endorsed by Malcolm. Indeed, the Duke's valet demonstrated an unexpected enthusiasm to assist with Miss Beaumont's recuperation.

To Reverend Shackleford's relief, his parishioners had not entirely given themselves over to less Godly pursuits, and he was actually quite gratified to discover how much he'd been missed. Well, in the Red Lion anyway.

As for Percy. Well, he was no longer quite so convinced that curtain lectures were not for him, and he and Lizzy went back to enjoying their twice weekly glass of milk. Though to be fair, things had progressed a little further, and Lizzy now came to the vicarage for supper once a fortnight. In truth, the widow had become quite a catch, since she inherited the gambling den on her brother's unfortunate demise. Unsurprisingly not enamoured with the idea of becoming a Madam, Lizzy had quickly put the building up for sale, and the proceeds had been enough to purchase her a large cottage on the edge of the village.

Naturally, this turn of events prompted the Reverend to offer Percy some sage advice, the gist of which was that the curate should remove his head from his posterior and propose to the widow before she had her head turned by someone with charm, charisma and considerably more hair.

∞∞∞

It was two weeks before the wedding, and Chastity was sitting in Blackmore's orchard along with Grace, Nicholas, Felicity and the children. Despite it being warm enough for shirt sleeves, the Duchess was bundled up in her bath chair as though it was the middle of winter. Fanning herself with her straw hat, Chastity eyed her sister in sympathy, wondering if she would show the same admirable restraint if Christian thought to mollycoddle her so.

Unbidden, the thought brought on a sudden flood of anxiety. She and Christian had still not yet discussed the possibility of more children. Oh, she was no longer concerned that the marriage bed would remain idle. Indeed, she could hardly wait for the Earl to incite more of the astonishing sensations she'd experienced in his arms that night in Tempy's garden, though she was not yet entirely sure what exactly that would entail. In truth, she was hoping Charity could be persuaded to offer some clarification when she arrived in the next few days.

But even more importantly, he had not repeated the endearment he'd mouthed when he thought he was about to fall, and Chastity was beginning to fear she had imagined it.

But in all fairness, when had he had the time? Indeed, actually indulging in any kind of in-depth conversation with her betrothed had been almost impossible since they arrived back in Devonshire. If the Earl wasn't at Cottesmore, he was out with

Nicholas, or she was attending fittings for her wedding dress, or the bridesmaid dresses or deciding which flowers she'd prefer, or... Truly she'd had no idea that a wedding entailed so much *preparation*. Indeed, she was a little miffed at Charity for not warning her. But then if her twin had divulged the full extent, Chastity might well have suggested eloping.

Still, Lord Cottesmore was returning to Blackmore this very day and had promised not to leave again until after they were wed, after which, she fully intended to be with him.

As though her thoughts had conjured him up, Chastity suddenly spied a tall figure walking towards them. It was Christian. She would know him anywhere. Her heart began beating faster as it always did whenever the Earl was near, and she had to resist the urge to jump up and run to greet him. But then...

She looked over at her companions, fully occupied with watching the children. Abruptly making up her mind, she jumped to her feet, picked up her skirts and ran towards her intended.

Christian stopped as he caught sight of the diminutive figure sprinting headlong towards him. He knew immediately it was Chastity, and his heart soared at the sight of her. Laughing, without a care for who was watching, he held out his arms and unhesitatingly, she threw herself into them, squealing as he spun her around.

'God I've missed you,' he breathed as he finally put her back onto the ground.

'Have you, my lord?' she whispered, her hand tracing a pattern on his linen shirt. Christian glanced over towards the others who had obligingly turned their backs. With a small smile, he lifted his hand and cupped her cheek. 'Have I told you I love you, Chastity Shackleford,' he murmured hoarsely.

Chastity felt her heart begin to gallop. 'Once,' she whispered, 'but since you were a little emotional at the time...' She let her sentence trail off as she stared up at him, finally allowing the love in her heart to show in her eyes. With a low groan, Christian bent his head and covered her lips with his...

Until a loud cough had them springing apart guiltily.

'This is precisely the kind of wanton behaviour that as a man of the cloth, I am duty bound to discourage,' Reverend Shackleford announced, not a foot away from them.

Hurriedly, Chastity smoothed down her skirt, but just as the Earl began his apologies, the Reverend gave a pained sigh. 'In truth of late, I've been wondering whether it has been my lenience or the admittedly carnal nature of mine and Agnes's relationship that has been instrumental in leading all of you astray these many years.'

Lord Cottesmore blinked at the admission whilst Chastity simply stared at her father, entirely nonplussed. To her knowledge, the only animal element of his relationship with her stepmother was the roast beef lunch they both enjoyed on a Sunday. Indeed, even the thought of ... no, she dared not even contemplate it.

'But then,' Augustus Shackleford went on obliviously, 'I've always maintained that the Almighty works in mysterious ways, and I can't help but have a sneaking suspicion that this was his plan all along. I mean, why else would he have saddled me with eight deuced daughters in the first place?'

Epilogue

There was no doubt that Chastity's wedding to the Earl of Cottesmore was enjoyed by everyone. Indeed, the residents of Blackmore pronounced the festivities second only to those of Hope's wedding, which in all fairness could never be improved upon given that it contained the duck pond incident involving Queen Charlotte.

Jimmy Fowler had watched most of the entertainments from the edge of Blackmore's green. While he'd enthusiastically taken part in previous Shackleford weddings, this time was different. Since the business in London, it felt as though something had changed forever.

Not only had he worked alongside the Duke of Blackmore, but he'd drunk his grace's brandy and ate at the same table. And even more disconcerting, spoken to him as an equal.

The youth sensed that the Duke was beginning to regard him as a friend and companion. But, while Jimmy would lay down his life for Nicholas Sinclair in an instant, he wasn't the Duke's friend. Nor could he ever be.

Indeed, he dared not even contemplate the possibility. That way lay disaster.

He glanced down at the letter in his hand, reflecting that reading and writing were the two most important skills the Duke had ever given him. He couldn't help the wry smile as he thought back to the fight the young Jimmy had put up when forced to learn his letters. But without them...

The adult Jimmy shook his head to clear it. Looking back would not help him now.

He'd left the proceedings early and now stood in the doorway of the Duke of Blackmore's study. Without allowing himself any more time to brood, he quickly strode to his grace's desk and propped the letter up against the inkwell.

Once done, he stood for a few moments looking out at the landscape he'd so long considered home, then he hefted his back pack onto his shoulders and walked out.

He didn't look back.

THE END

The Reverend and the rest of the Shackleford family return in *Prudence:* Book Eight of The Shackleford Sisters, now available from Amazon.

Author's Notes

The minor naval engagement described in Chastity really did take place on 27th June 1798 between British and France frigates at the start of the Napoleonic campaign in Egypt. However, in reality the name of the Royal Navy frigate involved was HMS *Seahorse*, not HMS *Phoenix*.

Those of you who read *Hope* may remember that I named the ship on which Gabriel Atwood travelled to Cadiz HMS *Seahorse*. At the time, I happened to pick the name because I liked it, not thinking it might give me a headache three books down the line!

Rather than change the name of the ship in *Hope* and possibly confuse everyone who had already read it, I felt the easiest option was simply to change the name of the British frigate involved in the above conflict to HMS *Phoenix* and include my fictional crew - hoping you would forgive the liberties I'd taken.

In actual fact the French frigate *Sensible* really was carrying treasure from Malta, looted from the Knights of the Order of St. John of Jersusalem during the French invasion of the island. Whether the hoard contained any rubies however – who knows.

You can read about the battle by pasting the following link into your browser:

https://en.wikipedia.org/wiki/Action_of_27_June_1798

If you are interested in reading more about Admiral Nelson's campaign in Egypt, culminating in the Battle of the Nile, visiting the following website:

https://www.britishbattles.com/napoleonic-wars/battle-of-the-nile/

I have also used a few naval colloquialisms throughout Chastity which I thought might warrant a little more discussion. I've included them in the order they appear in the book:

Frigate: A frigate was a fast and manoeuvrable sailing ship with a single gun deck, used primarily on scouting missions. During the Napoleonic wars, they were the eyes and ears of the Royal Navy.

Sixth rate: A sixth rate was the smallest class of frigate. It typically carried between 22 and 28 guns together with a crew of approximately 150 men.

Six bells and eight bells: Before the introduction of a reliable timepiece, the passage of time was marked by the striking of a bell every time the half-hour-glass was turned. The sea day was divided into watches each of 4 hours duration and the bell was struck once after half an hour, twice after an hour, three times after an hour and a half, etc up to eight bells when the watch was changed. Thus 1030 was 5 bells in the forenoon and 1530 was 7 bells in the afternoon watch.

As used in this book, six bells (of the middle watch) would be 0300 and eight bells would be 0400 in the morning.

Nowadays, the bell is traditionally struck 16 times at midnight on New Year's Eve by the youngest of the ship's company; hence ring out the old, ring in the new.

Information taken from 'Jackspeak' by Rick Jolly.

Grog: Rum diluted with water

Monkey's fist: A small elaborate knot at the end of a heaving line to give it weight to carry to the shore against the wind. Originally it had an additional metal weight inside it which could be lethal to anyone standing in the way...

The Andrew: the widespread nickname for the Royal Navy used by all ranks.

Keeping in Touch

Thank you so much for reading *Chastity*, I really hope you enjoyed it.

For any of you who'd like to connect, I'd really love to hear from you. Feel free to contact me via my facebook page: https://www.facebook.com/beverleywattsromanticcomedyauthor or my website: http://www.beverleywatts.com

If you'd like me to let you know as soon as the next book in the series is available, copy the link below into your browser to sign up to my newsletter and I'll keep you updated about that and all my latest releases.

https://motivated-teacher-3299.ck.page/143a008c18

And lastly, thanks a million for taking the time to read this story. If you'd like a sneak peek at *Prudence - Book 8 of The Shackleford Sisters*, turn the page...

Prudence

Chapter One

The day of Percy and Lizzy's wedding dawned bright and clear, the first rays of sunlight casting a rosy hue across the morning sky, promising that the summer solstice of 1821 would be either pleasantly warm or more likely unbearably sweltering.

As Prudence slipped through the kitchen door, she gave only the briefest of glances to the blaze of orange and gold decorating the horizon as she attempted to juggle a pilfered, but unexpectedly hot scone in one hand and tie the laces to her dress with the other. It was only six a.m., but already, the vicarage cook, Mrs. Tomlinson, had produced an eye-watering profusion of pastries, cooked meats and a multitude of other luxuries for the wedding. It was also very likely that many of the tempting treats on display would contain traces of tears and possibly even a smidgeon of snot since Mrs Tomlinson had been crying almost nonstop for the last three days. Indeed, so impressive were the cook's waterworks, one could be forgiven for thinking that Blackmore's curate was moving to another country rather than two hundred yards down the road.

Prudence's reason for being out of her bed at such an ungodly hour, was predictably to avoid all the tumult that such a momentous occasion was even now provoking. Of course, when she sweetly requested that she be the one to pick the flowers for

Lizzy's bouquet, there were more than a few raised eyebrows, not to mention sniggers from the rest of the family, given that her knowledge of wildflowers had hitherto been confined to being able to spot the difference between a dandelion and a daisy.

To be fair on Prudence, she'd spent at least twenty minutes the night before looking at pictures of wildflowers she'd found inside her father's copy of Gilbert White's *Natural History of Selborne*. She wasn't quite sure where Selborne was but reasoned it couldn't be that different to Blackmore, and as the first three illustrations she'd studied were wild cowslips, cornflowers and poppies, she'd decided that the bride's bouquet would contain wild cowslips, cornflowers and poppies. All she had to do was find them.

And, as she popped the last piece of scone in her mouth, she determined to make her errand last at least three hours, returning just in time to tie a ribbon around the bouquet and hand it to the bride. Allowing another twenty minutes to get back to the vicarage and change her attire, she would be ready just before the ceremony was due to begin. With luck, everyone else would be in church.

Perfect.

Well, it *was* until she found herself on the other side of the village with a grand total of three bedraggled poppies with only an hour and a half to go. Surely Gilbert White hadn't found it this bloody difficult to find a few cowslips and cornflowers. 'Damn and blast', she muttered, secure in the knowledge that she was well out of her father's hearing.

With an irritated sigh, she sat down at the side of the rutted track and stared into the distance. The only noise was the soft cooing of a wood pigeon. The early morning chill had lifted, and she felt the warmth on her back with the promise of more to come. Wincing, she thought of the church, filled to bursting with the whole of Blackmore. It would undoubtedly be more than a little ripe by the end of the ceremony since there was no way any of the villagers would miss the wedding of their only curate – especially given the scandal that accompanied the bride and groom's initial courtship. It was whispered that Lizzy's first husband had actually still been alive at the time...

Prudence chuckled. If only they knew the half of it. Idly picking the stray grass from her skirt, she glanced around her. Just over the hill, she could see the roof of her eldest sister Grace's mansion. She narrowed her eyes thinking about the overabundance of elaborate flower arrangements that usually decorated the large house. With a sudden thought, she climbed to her feet. Cowslips, cornflowers and poppies be damned. At this rate she'd be returning with dandelions. Drastic action was required. Picking up her skirts, she climbed over the dry-stone wall and hurried across the field towards the Duke of Blackmore's Country Seat.

'Tare an' hounds, Percy, anyone would think you a green boy by the way you're fidgeting. You'll wear a hole in Agnes's chaise longue if you don't stop squirming, and I wouldn't want to be in your shoes if that happened.'

'I'm just not accustomed to wearing ... inexpressibles, Sir. Especially when it's hot.'

'What the devil are you talking about, Percy? You wear deuced breeches every day...' The Reverend faltered at the dull flush slowly diffusing his curate's face. 'Tare an' hounds, please tell me you don't deliver sermons in just your *drawers*.'

'Well... I ... the thing is...'

'The pulpit's the draughtiest place in the whole deuced building.

I'm surprised you haven't got chilblains. And what if your cassock suddenly got taken by a gust of wind? Thunder an' turf, Percy, you'd likely give Mrs. Dibbert an apoplexy.' The Reverend stared at Percy as though his curate had suddenly developed two heads.

'I only do it when it's hot, Sir,' Percy repeated desperately. 'And it's likely to be *very* hot in the church today.'

Reverend Shackleford opened his mouth to respond, then paused, finally giving an indignant sniff and muttering, 'I sincerely hope you've kept such a disturbing inclination from your bride-to-be. Even Lizzy would likely swoon at the thought of you delivering God's word in your smalls.' He shook his head, wondering whether it was too early for a brandy.

'It's not really something that's come up in conversation,' Percy mumbled. 'But I can assure you, Sir, that I have been fully clothed during all my dealings with my intended.'

'I'm deuced glad to hear it,' Augustus Shackleford declared fervently. 'It's taken you long enough to pop the question, and I doubt very much she'd have waited all that time if she'd got a glimpse of you in your underwear.'

Though he didn't argue, Percy was of the firm opinion that the only thing that might possibly make his intended run for the hills was not anything he had in his drawers – indeed he doubted he was in possession of anything that Lizzy hadn't already been privy to. No, it was sadly the presence of his mother.

He was ashamed to admit that he'd held out the hope that his mother would choose not to attend the wedding. But the weather had been fine for weeks, and the roads from Salcombe were more than passable. Added to that the fact that the Duke of Blackmore had generously offered to collect her in one of his carriages. Percy sighed. Hell would freeze over before Mary Noon would turn down an offer like that.

'Right then,' Reverend Shackleford was saying, 'I think we've got a little time before the ladies descend, so I believe the Almighty would forgive us a little tot. Something to fortify you, Percy lad, before you finally get leg shackled.' He hurried over to the sideboard and poured three large measures of brandy.

Taking an appreciative sip of the first, he handed the second one to Percy, assuring the curate that this was exactly what he needed to outwit any drafts reaching his nether regions. The third measure he poured into a large saucer on the floor. 'Here you go, Freddy lad. This'll give you a bit of a kick to your gallop.'

The elderly foxhound wagged his tail from his bed of blankets in the corner. Freddy had slowed down considerably in the last few months. He could still give the odd rabbit a bit of competition, but on the whole, he now preferred his dinner a lot less active. His favourite was still a dish of Mrs. Tomlinson's bread and butter pudding, but he made short work of the brandy and was a picture of contentment as he ambled back to his basket, curling up and closing his eyes with a satisfied sigh.

'So, let me get this straight,' the Reverend demanded, as he stared at his curate, who was now nervously jiggling his knees up and down. 'Your fidgeting has everything to do with your surplus of undergarments and nothing at all to do with the fact that you've yet to introduce Lizzy to your mother?' As usual, Augustus Shackleford had gone straight to the heart of the matter.

For a few seconds, Percy said nothing, then with a soft groan, abruptly finished the rest of his brandy in one swallow.

'I don't know why you're so vexed,' the Reverend commented, cheerfully pouring them both another generous measure. 'I mean, old Lizzy might be a good catch since she inherited her brother's ill-gotten gains, but it's not like she's high in the instep. Her first husband ran off and deuced well drank himself to death. Anyone's an improvement on that.'

Percy frowned. He couldn't help but feel that the Reverend's notion of emotional support had not improved over the years. Sighing, the curate took a sip of his brandy.

'And anyway,' the Reverend continued, 'Mary's respectable now she's running the Lobster Pot in Salcombe. I'm persuaded she wouldn't dream of embarrassing you with any inappropriate behaviour.'

Both men turned at a sudden clatter on the stairs followed a few seconds later by Mary Noon tottering into the room dressed in a lilac day dress that looked as though she'd last worn it down a tin mine.

'Bloody hell, those stairs'll be the death o' me,' she announced. 'Right then, Percy lad, where's the grog? I'm drier than a dead nob's nutmegs...'

It took Prudence less than ten minutes to reach the Duke's house, and she hurried round to a side door she knew Anthony and Peter used whenever they were looking to get in or out without attracting attention. As quietly as possible she made her way through the boot room into the main house.

The kitchen was deserted, and she wondered where Mrs. Higgins was. She felt like a thief which was ridiculous because she knew Grace would have happily given her some flowers for the bouquet if she asked for them. Indeed the Duchess had already provided the blooms to decorate the church. It had been entirely Prudence's idea to procure wildflowers for the bride's posy.

Grimacing, Prudence pushed open the door into the large formal dining room. The whole deuced charade was simply because she'd wanted to avoid having to indulge in tiresome conversation. If her father had realised what she was about, he'd likely have told her the Almighty was having a good laugh at her expense.

But perhaps not… Directly in the centre of the large table stood a huge arrangement of flowers. Prudence breathed a sigh of relief. Glancing behind her, she climbed onto a chair and seated herself carefully on the table next to the vase.

Looking once more over at the closed door, she began picking out the flowers she thought looked like they might have once upon a time started life in a hedgerow. She had to be quick about it. Being found perched on the Duke of Blackmore's table pulling flowers out of a priceless vase was not something she wanted to have to explain. But then, they'd probably just think her dicked in the nob - which was what most people thought anyway.

Five minutes later, she had enough flowers to form a sizeable posy and hurriedly scooted off her perch, taking care not to leave any unsightly water stains on her brother-in-law's dining table. She paused at the door. Which was the best way go? Straight out of the kitchen door and through the orchard would be the quickest, and while she didn't know the exact time, she knew she was running out of it.

Doing her best to act like it was a perfectly normal occurrence for her to be wandering around her sister's house dripping water on the floor from the gardener's prize blooms, Prudence made her way back to the kitchen. She was about to push open the door when she heard voices on the other side. Damn and blast. It was too much to hope that she would get in and out without anyone the wiser. Truly, she'd never live this down. God help her if Anthony found out about it. She was about to push open the door and brazen it out, when she suddenly heard her name mentioned.

'It makes a body wonder what in 'eaven's name they're goin' to do with 'er. I mean she's a lovely lass, but still wandering round the countryside past twenty – well I ask yer.' Prudence could almost see Mrs. Higgins shaking her head in disapproval. 'I do know it's keepin' 'er grace awake at night. And she could do without it runnin' around as she does after Master Nicholas.' Her voice turned softer. 'Little man's the spittin' of 'is father. No wonder 'e's got everyone wrapped round 'is little finger.'

'I'm certain Miss Prudence will eventually make a good match, just like her sisters.' The butler Huntley's voice radiated disapproval at the gossip.

'Aye, I dare say yer right,' Mrs. Higgins replied. Prudence heard the sound of a chair scraping back. 'But with that gent – wot's 'is name...'

'Lord Melbury,' another voice Prudence didn't recognise piped up. Who the devil was Lord Melbury?

'That's 'im. I mean with 'im sniffin' around. I reckon 'is grace might be tempted to listen to wot 'e 'as to say. It's not like 'e's purse pinched.'

'Pray tell us how exactly it is you are aware of his financial situation,' the housekeeper Mrs. Tenner asked stiffly, 'or his intentions.'

'Well, if 'e ain't comin' down sniffin' after Miss Prudence, then why's 'e keep comin' all the way down 'ere? 'An you 'ave to admit 'e acts like e's flush in the pockets, but even if 'e ain't, it's not like beggars can be choosers, and at nearly twenty-three the lass is running out o' time.'

'But 'e looks like a toad,' the unknown voice interrupted. Prudence swallowed. There was a rich gentleman who looked like a toad interested in her?

'Rather be wed to a jackanapes than be reduced to wasting wot's left of 'er youth running around after Agnes Shackleford, trying to stop the totty-headed baggage from poisoning 'erself. I wouldn't wish that on anybody.'

Prudence could only agree.

'Please refrain from referring to the Duchess's stepmother as a baggage,' Huntley sniffed.

Prudence winced but couldn't help noting that he didn't question the totty-headed bit.

As I recall,' Mrs. Tenner commented coolly, 'her grace was approaching twenty-five when she
married.'

Prudence frowned and nodded her head in what she thought was the housekeeper's direction.

'Aye, and she led 'is grace a merry dance,' Mrs. Higgins chuckled. There was a thump as she plonked something heavy on the table. 'But the Duchess 'ad the wit and the looks to snare a man. Not like Miss Prudence. Most of the time, the lass looks like she's been chewing a wasp an' I ain't sure she's got a witty bone in 'er body. Leastwise, I've never heard her say anythin' amusin'.'

Prudence stiffened indignantly. What poppycock. She could do witty with the best of them. Why, she made Anthony laugh all the time.

Another thump, then, 'You mark my words, she'll be betrothed to Lord Melbury afore the summer's out.'

Prudence is available from Amazon.

Books available on Amazon

The Shackleford Sisters

Book 1 - Grace
Book 2 - Temperance
Book 3 - Faith
Book 4 - Hope
Book 5 - Patience
Book 6 - Charity
Book 7 - Chastity
Book 8 - Prudence
Book 9 - Anthony

The Shackleford Legacies

Book 1 - Jennifer
Book 2 - Mercedes to be released on 19th September 2024

The Dartmouth Diaries:

Book 1 - Claiming Victory
Book 2 - Sweet Victory
Book 3 - All for Victory
Book 4 - Chasing Victory
Book 5 - Lasting Victory
Book 6 - A Shackleford Victory
Book 7 - Final Victory to be released on 13th December 2024

The Admiral Shackleford Mysteries

Book 1 - A Murderous Valentine
Book 2 -A Murderous Marriage
Book 3 - A Murderous Season

Standalone Titles

An Officer and a Gentleman Wanted

About The Author

Beverley Watts

Beverley spent 8 years teaching English as a Foreign Language to International Military Students in Britannia Royal Naval College, the Royal Navy's premier officer training establishment in the UK. She says that in the whole 8 years there was never a dull moment and many of her wonderful experiences at the College were not only memorable but were most definitely 'the stuff of fiction.' Her debut novel An Officer  And A Gentleman Wanted is very loosely based on her adventures at the College.

Beverley particularly enjoys writing books that make people laugh and currently she has two series of Romantic Comedies, both contemporary and historical, as well as a humorous cosy mystery series under her belt.

She lives with her husband in an apartment overlooking the sea on the beautiful English Riviera. Between them they have 3 adult children and two gorgeous grandchildren plus a menagerie of animals including 4 dogs - 3 Romanian rescues of indeterminate breed called Florence, Trixie, and Lizzie, and a 'Chichon" named Dotty who was the inspiration for Dotty in The Dartmouth Diaries.

You can find out more about Beverley's books at www.beverleywatts.com

Made in the USA
Monee, IL
03 August 2024

63209678R00134